12 Days To Christmas

12 DAYS TO CHRISTMAS

REBECCA ALEXANDRU

Dedicated to the women who influenced my story:

Eleanora Nastase, Rodica Alexandru, and Carol Holt.

CONTENTS

CHAPTER ONE

THURSDAY, DECEMBER 13

Snow settled over the small town of Cedar Springs, Colorado. Christmas lights burned bright, twinkling from the gazebo in the park and along the shops lining Mesa Road. The single stop light shone red for a moment as a silver SUV pulled into town before flickering to green. Junipers sagged under the fluffy white snow. Ornaments swung in the soft breeze from wreaths, bedecking every door.

Except one.

Tucked snugly between the mercantile and Betty's Bakery, was a single shop with no Christmas lights hanging from the eaves or paintings of snowflakes on the windows. The sign above the door read *Vintage Treasures* with an antique teapot painted between the words. A gust of snow fluttered past. Still, a golden glow radiated from the windows of the second-level apartment.

Christmas carols floated inside the warm kitchen but didn't calm Mira's heart. In fact, it left her more flustered. She scrambled around the counter, flour smudged on her apron and her chestnut hair askew, mumbling to herself. "Four cups of flour... four cups of flour. Wait, did mom double or triple the recipe?" She rubbed her face with her hands, leaving streaks of white powder across her forehead and cheeks. "I can't remember."

Occasionally she'd glance down at her recipe book, but it was so tattered with age and stain it was a wonder she could read anything. The leather-bound book was filled with scrumptious meals that had been made again and again with her mother and grandmother. Each page was rich in memories.

The chocolate sugar cookie recipe she was currently glancing at was written in her great-grandmother's elegant script, which leaned so far to the right, it was near impossible for anyone to decipher. Why Mira had the book open was a surprise, since she'd baked this same recipe every year with her mother, grandmother, and several times with her great-grandmother before that. It was their tradition and she had every scribble and oil spot memorized.

In the Christmases before this one, she'd always had one of the older women by her side, coaching her through the steps or dancing in the kitchen to the carols. The music was usually accompanied by laughter, stories, and hugs. But today, even with the furnace on and the oven preheated, Mira felt cold. Perhaps it was the loneliness.

She brushed her worries away and let finger-memory take over, blending the dough with a handheld teal mixer and setting the bowl in the fridge to cool. As she was digging through the cabinet and lining out all the Christmas sprinkles, a bell chimed from downstairs. She'd forgotten to close the antique shop so she could focus on her task.

Mira spun quickly, muttering under her breath, and a glass container tipped off the shelf and hit the ground. The tin lid popped off and scattered holly red and pine green sugar crystals all across the hardwood floor. "Darn it!" She stomped through the mess and ran down the stairs two at a time, leaving the untidiness to clean up later.

The one large room downstairs had walnut hardwood floors, divided by antique furniture, piled high with all types of odds and ends.

Mira passed a myriad of hats hung on the wall, from flat caps and fascinators, to fedoras and pillbox hats. Accessories hung on rotating racks below, sparkling with chunky gems in bright colors, ornate and sleek designs in platinum, and strings of pearls with a single white stone in the center. An old typewriter and porcelain doll balanced on top of a hand-carved dresser. A basket beside it held an assortment of doilies, cloth napkins, and embroidered handkerchiefs. Every available space was filled: books so old the ink was fading, posters of movies filmed in black and white, the old logo of a soda pop company, and a wild variety of saucers, dishes, and goblets. A repurposed sorting box displayed miniature figurines and crystal keepsakes.

A pathway wove through all the items, but Mira took a shortcut, stepping over a vintage record case and past the silent turntable. She ignored the serious stares of long-dead musicians and slipped past a mannequin in a beaded flapper gown, stopping only a moment to readjust the feathered headpiece, until she finally arrived at the front of the shop. A Victorian oak desk with a leather top and carved pull handles waited patiently. She tugged the chain on the

Tiffany lamp and a kaleidoscope of colors poured from beneath the domed glass shade.

"Welcome to Vintage Treasures. I'm Mira. How may I help you?" She schooled her face and greeted the new customer. The little shop was struggling, and every sale made a difference. When her eyes finally settled on who entered her shop, sheer experience kept the smile pasted on her lips.

There weren't many strangers in her small town of Cedar Springs, but this was one of the few. And he wasn't alone. Three boys, between the ages of six and ten, dispersed from behind him. They took off in different directions, like a hyperactive litter of puppies.

Mira's heart jumped in her throat. Besides the few furniture "upcycling" enthusiasts she chased out of her shop, young children were the most dangerous. They didn't mean to be, but they had to touch everything, which left things in peril of falling and breaking.

"What are you looking for?" she asked again, hoping to hurry them on their way.

The man cleared his throat, and she turned her attention toward him. He was in his thirties, around her age but with children, like many of her childhood friends, happy and busy with their families during the holiday season. Some scruff darkened his chin but his hair was combed over in a classic way. His business suit and tie, on the other hand, were very modern. He was average height with broad shoulders and a confident stance. She wasn't sure what to make of him.

Before he could answer, the oldest of the boys called out from a hidden spot behind a bookshelf with boxed sets of traditional favorites. "Told you, Dad! The best place to find Gramma a present is in an old lady shop."

Mira raised her eyebrows at the unintended slight and the man reddened.

"I apologize," he stuttered. "I'm looking for something for my mother. She loves these little trinkets from when she was younger. Got anything?"

Mira bit back her retort through pursed lips and gestured behind her. "I have an entire shop of *things*." She turned around to figure out where the other two children had dashed to. "What does she like?"

The man's reflection shrugged in the cheval mirror beside Mira as she cast him a furtive glance. He rapped his fingers on the jangling keys in his hand. Apparently, he was in a hurry too. She'd make quick work of finding him a pricey knickknack.

"We have some beautiful hand-carved nativity sets, like this authentic one from Israel." Mira directed him to the red brick wall layered with shelves of Christmas decorations. "It's solid olive wood, hand-painted, and gilded. I'm sure she hasn't seen anything so fine in the big box stores."

The man shoved his keys in his pocket as he stared at the price tag below baby Jesus instead of the beautiful crèche set. A frown settled across his forehead.

Mira moved on to the Christmas tree in the shop window. "Or a set of these Christopher Radko glass ornaments from the Shiny Brite collection. They will bring back old memories with their 1940s charm." She reached up to pluck one from the tree. *Because memories are triggered from experiences,* her mom used to say. *If a customer holds an item and is carried back to their childhood, our job is successful.* As she placed it in the stranger's hand, a crash sounded behind them.

Mira's heart rate spiked, and she spun around. Two of the boys ran back to their dad. "It was Liam," they tattled.

Mira's Mary Jane heels clicked against the hardwood as she hurried down the narrow pathway between carved oak dressers and brass-buckled leather trunks. She stopped with a gasp when she found the six-year-old sitting in a pile of glass shards. Pink depression plates, green goblets, and gold mercury vases crushed under his feet, squelching her sanity with every crunch.

But more important was the teapot, hand-painted by her great-grandmother in the 1920s, the central inspiration for her shop. How could Mira have forgotten to take her priceless teapot back upstairs after her breakfast cup?

Mira pressed her fist to her mouth, to hold back a desperate sob or colorful language she never uttered and blinked rapidly. She scrambled to pull her emotions together, ignoring the stranger pass her and lift his son from the wreck. She didn't hear him offer his apologies while he hurried toward the door or see the fifty-dollar bill left on the counter as another son grabbed a random ornament from the tree by the window.

She kneeled beside the wreckage. Most of these items were rare and unique collectables, but she wasn't concerned about their financial cost, now a waste. She reached out a finger and brushed the handle of the teapot, white against the rainbow of colors from all the other broken glass. With a sharp intake of breath, she grasped the pieces and set them on a nearby silver tray. Each shard brought back memories.

It was with this teapot great-grandma Margaret first served tea to great-grandpa George. It was balmy water from this teapot grandma Mary warmed baby Michelle's milk bottles when she was too sick to nurse. And it was over this teapot, a grown-up Michelle with a three-year-old daughter cried herself heartbroken after her husband left to start a new family with someone else. This was the teapot credited with starting the shop. Because, once Michelle cried out all her tears and Mary was done blurting curses, great-grandma Margaret offered them a business proposition. She was old, too old to continue living much longer (her words). She couldn't continue traveling the world and collecting beautiful relics to adorn her estate. They should be put to good use, providing for her family.

And this was how Mirabel grew up: dusting shelves to place priceless treasures, curled with a good book on the blue velvet French settee, and listening to stories of the past over freshly steeped cups of tea. When she was little, Mira used her childish charm to sell items to customers and, as she grew up, she refined her technique to share more than rare heirlooms, but historical experiences as well.

Except now, all those moments, and a hundred years of personal history, were shattered.

Mira stomped back upstairs with the broken pieces of her teapot cradled on the silver tray. She slammed the *off* button on the music player but her fingers, now slick with tears, slid across the silver buttons. Burl Ives' voice continued to ring gaily, wishing her a *Holly Jolly Christmas*.

"Hush up!" she yelled at the cheery voice and yanked the cord from the outlet. The sound died, leaving the room eerily quiet. Mira fell into a heap on the beige rug, cradling the broken shards.

No decorations lit up the gloomy apartment. No ornaments or lights, wreaths or a Christmas tree. Even the flowery couch and colorful lamp shades did little to brighten up the sad space. It matched her mood: despondent.

She should have known better than to plan the 12 Days to Christmas Festival this year. It was a tradition her family started. But this would be the first time she led it alone. Although she hoped it would be a distraction from her loss and loneliness, it only heightened her mother's absence.

The first funeral she remembered crying at was for great-grandma Margaret. Mira was only seven and didn't fully understand she'd never see her great-grandma again, aside from the black and white pictures adorning the shop and the more recent ones in the family photo albums. But the loss hung like a dark cloud over her childhood years.

It grew heavier when she was at the state university and received a call about her grandma Mary passing away. Mira left school that day and never returned, never finished her classes, never told her professors, never graduated with her degree in history. The months after were difficult for her and her mom, especially when Michelle was diagnosed with cancer. The fight was long and hard, with a couple years of thinking she was finally well. Until the sickness came back with a vengeance.

Last Christmas, mother and daughter danced to this same song in the kitchen while baking chocolate sugar cookies for the Cedar Springs Cookie Exchange. This year, Mira was alone, staring at the portrait of her mom on the mantle.

Mira looked longingly at the photo, speaking as if someone could hear her. "I don't want to do any of it this year, Mom. There's nothing to celebrate, nothing to be joyful about. And everything reminds me how desperately I miss you."

A timer blared in the kitchen, yanking Mira from her grief. She pushed herself to her feet, setting the silver tray with broken memories on the cluttered kitchen table, and turned off the timer. Pulling out the cookie dough, she dumped it on the floured counter and began rolling it out. Muscle memory took over. Rolling dough, cutting out gingerbread girls and boys, and sliding the cookie sheets into the oven kept her occupied. She didn't resume the music. Maybe ignoring the holiday would keep her tears away.

꧁ ꧂

Seth nearly died of embarrassment and shame. Everywhere he went with his boys, trouble followed. They'd even carried their bad luck a hundred miles away to this dead-end town in the middle of nowhere Colorado.

As the boys climbed back into the SUV, he checked over Liam for any injuries. "You alright, dude?" he asked his youngest son.

Liam pouted his bottom lip out and lifted his hand. A cut across the top of his thumb leaked the tiniest trickle of red. "I think my finger is going to fall off."

The oldest boy, Noah rolled his eyes. "Why are you such a drama queen?"

"I'm not!" Liam cried, this time with a fat tear rolling down his cheek.

Mason patted his little brother on the back. "You'll be fine, Liam. Besides, that's not a finger, it's your thumb. And if you lose it, you'll always have another one." He gave his brother a thumbs-up.

"How can I play video games without both thumbs?" the little boy cried.

Seth covered his face with his hand and sighed as Liam fell into a fit of hysterics. He closed the car door and clambered into the driver's seat. Thankfully, his mom's house wasn't too far from the main street and she could distract them with sugar or whatever grandma's do to spoil their grandkids. All Seth knew was that he needed a break. A long one.

As the SUV pulled away from the antique shop, he glanced back at the dark building. The stop had been strange from beginning to end. He'd hoped to run in and find a gift for his mom, not a portal into a different dimension. It was as if he'd stepped back in time, with the history of the world flashing before his eyes.

The most confusing part of it all was the woman, Mira. Her hair was a strange style of messy bun he'd only seen in history books and her clothes, although flattering her figure, was out of fashion for nearly a hundred years. He felt as if he'd entered one of those productions where all the actors played their parts perfectly and reality was only a far away dream.

He'd been in a World War II reenactment nearly fifteen years ago when he was in college. It'd been a wild learning experience, especially when a fellow student fell deep into character and hit him across the head with his own helmet. It left a gash above his right eyebrow and he'd been declared "wounded on the battlefield," then sent to the first aid tent.

He'd been embarrassed when his friends laughed at him but later he bragged about his scar from his time fighting the Germans.

If only reality was as simple as a reenactment, without the arguing boys in the back of the car and the constant noise. It had been a distraction the past year but he knew everything was catching up to him and eventually he'd snap, like a tree branch carrying a too-heavy load of snow falling to the earth to be buried under the weight. He let out another long sigh and pulled into his mom's front driveway.

As the boys cheered for finally arriving and grabbed their backpacks, Seth took a moment alone at the back of the SUV. He saw the suitcases waiting for him to carry inside, the boys' favorite pillows and action figures, tablets and chargers, all the things *he* had to do and his shoulders slumped.

Instead, he turned his attention to his mom's new house. It was a cute little blue building with a tiny front porch. Empty flower pots held buckets of snow and a Christmas tree glittered through the large window. A trickle of smoke rose from the chimney and the smell of fresh baked sourdough bread wafted toward him. The wreath bounced on the red door as it swung open and his mom snatched all three boys inside.

When she announced to him several years ago she was selling his childhood home and moving hundreds of miles away to a small town he'd never heard of, he didn't believe her. But she'd proven him wrong and settled into a new life. She called him frequently to share what she was up to and checkup on him but this was the first time he finally visited. He was glad she was happy here but didn't think a quiet, small town suited him.

Before he had too long to himself to face emotions he'd pushed away the past year, he yanked up the suitcases and entered the chaos.

His mom was still hugging all three boys and kissing their cheeks. Noah pulled away first but handed her the gift they'd just bought, one that cost Seth way more than what it was worth, in his opinion.

"How beautiful!" she said and hugged Noah again. "You must have stopped at Mira's shop on the way in."

Seth let out a *humph* as he set down the suitcases. "Merry Christmas, Mom." He wrapped her in a hug and held her several seconds longer than needed.

"About time you came and visited me." She squeezed him back. "How was the drive?"

Before Seth could answer how long and obnoxious the entire trip was, the boys stole her attention and rattled off all the things they'd seen.

"We almost hit a deer!"

"Did you know if I blinked, we would have passed through your town and I wouldn't even know it was here?"

"Boring."

Seth collapsed on the couch and closed his eyes. He wasn't sure what was worse: working long hours in the city in a stale office or a noisy vacation with his rambunctious boys. Either way, this would be a long two weeks.

※※※※ ※※※※

The park in the center of Cedar Springs was filled with people gathered under the twinkling Christmas lights. They laughed and caught up on holiday plans. Tables beneath the glowing pavilion were filled with trays of sugar cookies, gingerbread, peanut butter blossoms, and chocolate crinkle cookies. The scent of sweets permeated the cold air, drawing the crowd closer. Children ran around the outskirts playing tag or nibbling a stolen treat.

Mira would have preferred to hide behind the bronze horse statue with the twin toddlers, Caleb and Teddy, as they gobbled down a powdered sugar cookie rather than be trapped in the pavilion with the town gossip and self-proclaimed matchmaker, Luella. But here she was, being an adult.

"He isn't *that* young and imagine how charming your children would be!" Luella elbowed Mira in the ribs and waggled her eyebrows. The fifty-year-old woman's hair was short and blonde, bobbing as she pointed to her nephew. It didn't matter that he was ten years younger and enrolled in an out-of-state university, Luella was determined in changing Mira's relationship status. Beverly, an older woman who'd been friends with her grandma Mary, caught Mira's eye roll and offered a sympathetic smile.

Mira preferred spending her time with her mother and grandmother's friends, even though they were at least twice her age. She'd never connected well with anyone in her generation. Most thirty-year-olds didn't know how to dance the Wah Watusi, make a fluffernutter, or use a rotary phone on a shared line. But here, she felt like she belonged.

"I'll make sure the tables are stocked with cookies and decorating supplies." Mira ducked away from Luella's newest barrage of advice and darted from the pavilion.

She walked along the perimeter, greeting people she'd known all her life but rarely spoke to. They waved back. Her family had been a pillar of the small community for generations and, although she was the only one left, she aimed to continue that tradition if possible. Except sometimes it meant interacting with people. This wasn't something she felt competent at, especially with those residents who never entered her antique shop. What would she talk to them about? Current events? She didn't know or care much about all the new technology her peers surrounded themselves with. They were always staring at one screen or another.

Mira wanted a calm life surrounded by things she knew well and held value for decades, like solid wood furniture instead of compressed cardboard. When listening to music, she'd rather play a vinyl than any other recording. Even her clothes reflected this. She was wearing a pleated wool skirt with low heels and navy stockings. She kept warm with a fitted trench coat and a knitted scarf. A simple sailor hat pinned over her low bun completed the look. Although those her age and younger sometimes questioned her interest in history or disdain of electronics with a quirk of an eyebrow, they all complimented her fashion style.

She looked over the gathering as people waited eagerly for Mayor Chavez to start the festivities. Without her mother's help this year, she had enlisted several people from the community and was nervous how everything would play out. Most people didn't understand why she'd connect the holiday to historical events. But to her, it was a way of bringing everyone together, learning about the past, and building encouragement within the small town. Maybe it would even lead more people to her shop, she hoped.

Mayor Chavez finally stepped on the concrete stage in front of the pavilion and people gathered around. The stage was decorated in all the Christmas finery by the owner of the mercantile, Danielle Chen, and her three generations of family who lived in the area. The back wall was draped in a deep green garland, frosted with snowflakes and hung with red and gold ornaments. Christmas lights twinkled along the frame, brightening up the stage and the red sleigh waiting behind Mayor Chavez.

As he spoke, Mira studied the crowd. Elizabeth, the leader of their high school Christian club and now the town librarian, leaned over to giggle with her husband Jesse; Carly, the local 4th grade teacher, was surrounded by students even on her day off; and Cody, the town electrician, played a game on the smart watch wrapped around his wrist. Mira was thankful to see so many familiar faces and hoped this year's Christmas festival would be another success. She had invested so much time and worry.

Her glance snagged on a face she didn't grow up knowing. The stranger from earlier stood near the back of the crowd. He looked much the same as earlier, frustrated and annoyed with the world around him. Two of his three boys tugged at his winter coat but he brushed them off. Mira turned away, thinking about her broken teapot and blinked back tears. The next two weeks would be difficult enough without the memory of her family shattered by the new stranger and his sons.

Mayor Chavez' voice redirected her gloomy thoughts. "...and before we begin the Twelve Days to Christmas Festival, let's learn about the history we're celebrating today from Mirabel Turner."

All eyes turned toward Mira and she froze. She'd prepared for this speech, had it written down since the summer, but her brain took a moment to catch up, to tear away from her anger at a certain stranger.

Mayor Chavez stepped away from the microphone and Mira took his place. This part had been her mother's forte. Mira wasn't very good with people or entertaining crowds. She swallowed a nervous breath. What if her daydreams stole her away back in time again? Who would pull her back to reality?

"Merry Christmas," she stumbled. "Joyeux Noël, Fröhliche Weihnachten, and Mutlu Noeller." Her focus narrowed in on the memorized words and she closed her eyes, imagining she stood in the trenches of World War I. History became alive in her mind.

The dark sky hung heavy overhead with peaceful stars instead of the crackle of rifles. She leaned against a mud wall and stared at her freezing fingers, showing through the unraveling of her gloves. She pulled her hands close to her face and breathed warm air over them but it did little to help. Her blue uniform was stained with mud, matching the brown leather straps of her belt. Mira readjusted it and hung her head. Spending Christmas in a military trench during the Great War was the last place she wished to be. She pulled deeper within herself and tried to relax during the temporary ceasefire.

Mira's voice carried over the Cedar Springs crowd. "It all began with the words of Stille Nacht, Heilige Nacht, or as we know it: Silent Night, Holy Night. This was how war, and hate, crumbled for a day. It was Christmas Eve in 1914 and German troops on the front lines began singing this favorite Christmas hymn when British soldiers joined in with their English version, maybe to drown them out or befriend their enemies."

Mira lifted her head at the sound of singing. It echoed across the treacherous No Man's Land, past barbed wire and over muddy pits. Although she didn't recognize the words, she knew the tune. It was familiar and released some of the tension in her heart.

With a shaky voice, she sang "Noapte Sfântă" in her language. It wasn't long before others in the trench beside her joined in.

"It broke down barriers and soon both sides climbed out from the cold muddy holes for an unofficial armistice."

One of the younger men was the first to look over the edge of the trench, a movement that would've killed him on any other day. But today was Christmas. A moment later he climbed out and Mira followed, shocked at what she saw. Hours ago this gap between armies, filled with hate and weapons, smoke and rubble, now stood with soldiers singing softly and walking across the divide. Rifles had been set aside and barbed wire pushed away.

"Both sides crossed 'No Man's Land' trading gifts: scarves for buttons, cigarettes for cognac..."

Mira watched in confusion at men who shot to kill each other the day before, now smiling and shaking hands. She blinked several times, imagining it was a moving picture instead of reality. But the sounds around her proved she was not in a dream. Especially as one of those soldiers reached across the divide and tapped her arm.

Mira turned to face the enemy soldier and was startled when she recognized him. He had short, scruffy facial hair but soft brown eyes. With a hesitant smile, he held out a clean pair of gloves and pointed to her tattered ones. Mira reached in her pocket to the only item she received for Christmas, a half-eaten chocolate bar, and traded with him.

"And chocolate for gloves. Some games of soccer started, kicking the ball over frozen snow and around shell holes, made even more amusing when a Highlander's kilt caught the wind."

As she tore off her old gloves and replaced them, she watched the enemy soldier from the corner of her eye as he stared across the No Man's Land. A group of soldiers played a game of fútbol, laughing while they had to dodge shell holes and leap over mounds of dirt. A Scottish soldier she knew from her trench jumped into the game until a gust of wind tugged his uniform kilt. The enemy behind her chuckled at the sight and turned back to her.

The audience in the town park laughed, yanking Mira from her daydream in history. Her gaze had settled on the face of the soldier, standing in the center of Cedar Springs. Except he wasn't Austro-Hungarian infantry. And he wasn't smiling. Seth's brown eyes stared back at her, unamused.

Mira swallowed the knot in her throat and focused back on her notes. She scrambled to finish reading before her imagination whisked her away again. "The most important lesson that Christmas was the knowledge: this season is about peace and hope, forgiveness and love, trusting and giving."

She held up a bright red and green flyer listing the events planned for the next two weeks.

"As the first day of our Twelve Days to Christmas Festival, we will begin in the same manner. You are invited to invest in the lives of those who are celebrating with us, helping children decorate cookies or play a game of soccer with your neighbors; forget past mistakes; open yourselves for new opportunities and change; and provide canned food and personal items for our local food pantry and homeless shelter in the giant cardboard gift boxes behind me. Let this be a season of joy! Merry Christmas!"

When Mira finished, the middle school choir sang *Silent Night, Holy Night* in gentle, although out of pitch, tones. The audience, spurred by her speech, began to mingle. She watched in surprise at the owners of the two bakery shops clasp hands and swap recipes, the captain of the football team kneeled down to help a four-year old boy tie his shoe, and squabbling neighbors shared cookies and kicked a soccer ball back and forth.

Mira joined the children at the tables under the pavilion. Royal icing, sprinkles, and smiles covered every face. A grin tugged at the corners of Mira's lips as toddlers gobbled down the desserts, covering their cheeks with more frosting than was on the cookie. A little girl in pigtails tied with giant red bows showed Mira her creation proudly. It didn't matter that the gingerbread man was decorated upside down or that her fluffy tulle skirt was smeared with white buttercream, she was beaming. This was one of the reasons Mira loved Christmas. She kneeled down beside the girl and listened to her rattle off a story about a gingerbread man escaping the tricky fox by doing cartwheels.

Similarly, she was trying to escape her own thoughts. Her daydream earlier hadn't been the first time her imagination carried her back in time where she could live through the events she only read about in history books. It's what she loved the most about hearing and learning the old stories. The more she knew, the more vivid her visions were. But this was the first time someone from reality broke into her reverie. She tried to shake it off but it clung to her like the frosting staining the edge of her scarf.

Mira hid away from the merriment, sneaking to the back of the stage where a canopy tent had been set up, storing the totes of extra cookies. To her relief, Luella had moved on, coaxing Harriet's granddaughter, Brandi, to talk with her grandson. The poor teenage girl's face was as red as her hair, in embarrassment.

Several of the older women volunteers were cleaning the used supplies and cookie trays already. Evelyn, nearly sixty and newest to their group since she moved to town two years ago, glanced at Harriet. "You might need to intervene." But the old woman shrugged at the matchmaking of her granddaughter and bit into another cookie. No one was brave enough to cross Luella.

Mira looked on from her spot in the corner. "I don't think there's anything we could say to dissuade her meddling. I've learned the best thing to do is let her talk until she's out of breath..."

Beverly chuckled. "That doesn't happen often."

"...Or out of men to throw at me."

Evelyn shook her head, red curls bouncing across her colorful coat. "Eventually someone will have to stand up to her. I don't want to disturb the peace, but if she dare approach my son while he's visiting, it might have to be me." She readjusted her black rimmed glasses.

"Oh, your son is here?" Beverly tactfully changed the conversation. "What a wonderful way to spend Christmas!" She had a smile that was contagious and wise eyes that crinkled at the dark corners every time she laughed, which was often. With her seventy-two years of life experience, she understood more about people than they did themselves. Lately, Mira had taken to spending her few moments of free time with the older woman. She felt like home.

The ladies continued chatting about their families, how many grandchildren and great-grandchildren they each had, what they were doing, and how rare they visited. They bragged about accomplishments, all possible because of their contribution: getting married and having children. Some grew up to be doctors, teachers, or lawyers.

Mira wilted toward the corner of the tent beside Harriet and munched on extra cookies in silence. She didn't have anyone to brag about but that didn't bother her as much as the fact there was no one bragging about her anymore. In past years, when the women shared their stories, her mom would hold her head up high and pronounce, *"But they all married and left you. My Mira has stayed by my side all these years."*

That night, after the pavilion was cleaned of sticky sugar spots and all the cookie crumbles were swept away, Mira and Beverly walked the silent main street toward their homes. Under the glow of the moon, the chill clung to their coats and snow glistened in patches beside the sidewalk. The scent of fresh pine trees and wreaths mixed with wood-smoke from warm fireplaces drifted through the air.

Beverly's house was one of Mira's favorites, with engraved wooden trim in craftsman style and a wide porch, perfect for long conversations. Mira loved visiting with the older woman. Not only did she appreciate antiques as Mira's best customer, they were also friends, forged when grandma Mary was still alive. Sometimes Mira wondered if Beverly viewed her as a granddaughter or friend.

As they walked, they laughed about the many cookie decorations they saw, especially the "painting" by the pastor's two-year old son. He'd taken globs of frosting, in every color, and smudged a mural on the wall of the pavilion. He was so proud of his art that he ran around the festival taking the hand of anyone who'd let him and show them his picture. His mom froze in panic until Walter, the park supervisor, laughed it off and said he had just the thing to clean it. Then pictures were taken with the two-year old beaming with joy in his parents' arms.

Beverly laughed. "Ah, I miss my own children when they were young. They say the days are long but the years are short. How true that is. I suppose it's been so long ago, I don't remember the days I wanted to ship them off to the zoo or invest in a spaceship to take me to the moon." She glanced down at her phone screen. The faces of her two grown children, their spouses, and teenage grandchildren smiled back.

"Will they visit for Christmas this year?" Mira asked. While she enjoyed Beverly's family and shared her happiness when they visited, it meant Beverly was occupied with them. This year, of all Christmases, Mira didn't want to be alone. Even though every moment reminded her she would be.

Beverly grinned, the wrinkles on her face highlighting her dimples. "They will arrive in time for Christmas and stay for several days. I have so much to do until then."

"I'm happy for you." Mira's voice didn't echo her words.

"Oh, sweetheart." Beverly stopped and took Mira's hand in her own. "You are invited to spend Christmas with us. Don't stay locked up in your house all alone. Promise me?"

She fought to tug on a smile, but she'd held herself together all day and didn't have any energy left. A tear stole its way down her cheek. "I don't want to be alone," she cried, and the walls broke loose. Beverly pulled her close.

It was a minute before Mira gathered enough breath to form words again. "Like in the tent today, everyone was talking about their families and how they have someone. I don't. I am utterly and completely alone." She hiccupped. "I'm sure Luella means well, but...it just makes me feel worse. I don't have a husband. Or children. Or even my mom. I miss her...so desperately."

Beverly wiped Mira's tears with her own handkerchief. "Now, don't let anything Luella says bother you. She's an old curmudgeon with nothing else to do but match up the lives of everyone around her. I admire how you haven't given in to any of her ridiculous demands."

Mira frowned. "But isn't she your friend?"

"Of course she is! That's why I can say that with certainty," Beverly giggled. "We stay friends through all of our wild and weird ways. That's what makes our group so...dynamic!"

With the tears wiped away, Mira finally offered a smile. "And which one am I?"

They continued walking as Beverly pursed her lips in thought. "You, my dear, are the youthful gal. The one who keeps us all together when we get cranky and impatient; you are the reason we still feel worthwhile."

Mira sighed and hooked her elbow with Beverly's. "It's kind of you to say so."

"I'm serious. You make the things we are familiar with seem popular again and you bring it back to life for the younger generations. You, Mira, transcend the decades!"

They stopped at the mahogany front door of Beverly's house and the older woman took Mira's hand again. "Sweetheart, you are living a good life and making a beautiful difference in the world around you. Your mother and grandmother would be proud, as am I. Be sure to appreciate what you have instead of what you don't."

The door swung open, revealing Beverly's husband Charles in slippers and a night robe. He waved to Mira and took the basket of cookies from his wife's hand.

Before she slipped inside and closed the door, Beverly turned back with a wink and whispered to Mira, "But it wouldn't hurt to have a man around."

Chapter Two

Friday, December 14

Seth wasn't a morning person, at least not before he had children. Now, the early morning hours were rare moments he had to himself, and he maximized every minute. He tugged on his boots and stepped outside.

The sun hadn't risen yet, leaving the small town looking cold and gray. It matched his mood. Pulling the scarf tighter around his neck, he started his jog down Mesa Road. The path led him through the park, and he slowed by the pavilion where he leaned his hands on his knees and took a moment to catch his breath. He also wasn't a runner. It became a new habit to give him time alone.

He wasn't sure what to make of Cedar Springs or its residents. His mom enjoyed living here but he knew he could never settle for the small town atmosphere. At last night's gathering, he could feel the judgmental stares, confused glances, and gossiping whispers. There was an older woman with short blonde hair who kept watching him, like a prowling "Karen", as if he'd turn into a wild beast and attack. He'd almost been tempted to snarl back but he knew how quick rumors spread through close-knit communities. He didn't want to make any drama his mom would have to deal with once he left.

The strangest person who caught his attention was the woman from the shop. He'd seen her wandering around the festivities instead of partaking in the fun. He came to the assumption that she was a stand-offish recluse. It was strange the mayor credited her with putting together the entire event.

Once again, the woman had been wearing strange clothes and the weirdest hat. Even Noah had remarked on it, making jokes. Seth had cut off his son and changed the subject, sending the boys to get cookies.

When he had glanced back up, she was sharing about the Christmas Truce during World War I. He'd visited a memorial during his travels through Belgium and had seen part of the trenches Mira spoke of. They were rich with history and deep in loss and pain. It'd been a terrible time for the world. He'd imagined himself as one of the soldiers when he stood at the ridge of a trench. Since he was college-age at the time of his visit, he was old enough to have been drafted, if he lived through that time.

By the look on the woman's face, she was imagining herself there as well. It wasn't until her gaze settled on him with a puzzled expression, that Seth began listening to her words. It was all garbage. Who was she to tell others to enjoy the peace and hope of Christmas? Obviously, she didn't have children.

He huffed and began jogging again. His steps took him past the mercantile, still closed at this hour, but his feet slowed in front of the antique shop. It was dark and the front sign stated it was closed. He'd have to come by another time to pay for the damage Liam caused. He didn't want to think about the interaction, not that the financial cost was an issue, but trying to maintain a serious conversation with a woman who lived in the wrong century would be awkward. Especially, one who overreacted to a small child's accident.

Instead, he stepped into the bakery and was comforted by the smell of fresh bread and donuts. Betty's was the only shop open at this time of the morning and the scattered tables and chairs were already occupied by older couples sipping coffee. Seth placed his order and leaned against the far wall, waiting. His glance caught newspaper snippets and local photography wallpapered above a fireplace. He sauntered over to examine them.

The space was dedicated to the local history and current events of the small town. One newspaper boasted about a high school graduate entering a prestigious university while another displayed a local art show put together by the senior center. The oldest item pasted to the wall showed a black and white photograph of a mansion and credited it as the heart of Cedar Springs. It brought culture to the small town hidden in a mountain valley. Three women stood in front of the big house and held the hand of a toddler in pigtails.

"Seth!" the barista called. He took his hot drink with a nod.

He left the shop with an old-fashioned donut in hand and continued his walk. Going out for a "jog" was always a better experience with proper motivation. Hot chocolate and a donut were the best reasons he could imagine.

Around him, the town was waking up and people hurried to work. A school bus passed with a rowdy group of children spending their last day in class before the Christmas break. Two women walked past while whispering furiously. He recognized the "Karen" from her staring yesterday but ignored her. Instead, he shoved the rest of the donut in his mouth and downed the hot drink. It scalded his throat but he didn't care. He turned his focus back to exercise and used jogging as an excuse to put more space between himself and the two women.

In his travels, he'd been in many small towns. They were relaxing enough to spend a couple days, but no more than a week. Once the residents recognized his name, it meant it was time to move on. Being known meant responsibility, and he was already juggling enough. He was hoping to thin his daily workload, not add more. He'd promised his mom to stay two weeks – already breaking his own rules – but he planned to leave before she came up with ideas or anyone got to know him.

The lap around town was less than a mile but running after eating cramped his side. Seth hobbled back to his mom's house. He took a deep breath and returned to his chaos.

꙳꙳꙳꙳ ꙳꙳꙳꙳

The school gym was sparsely decorated and smelled of sweat. But Mira wasn't daunted in the least. She turned around to face her crew of high school student volunteers.

"Ready to transform this place?"

Within two hours, they had wreaths hanging on the walls, an electric fireplace crackling by the door, and tables lined with holly and berries. Candles smelling of cinnamon and apples flickered on tables donned in burgundy tablecloths. Chairs tucked around them.

This year Mira had helped with Christmas decorating at the school, town park and pavilion, and in the senior center but she still hadn't put any ornaments or lights in her apartment. Sure, she'd placed a wooden Christmas tree display in her shop and took out the annual nativity sets she sold, but that was it. Usually, her mother would go all out on garlands, lights, and ornaments even before Thanksgiving. They kept a special box of ornaments alive with memories. In the past, they'd place them on the tree and share its story. But this year she hadn't pulled out any of it. It would be too painful to hold all those precious reminders and think of what she'd lost. Of memories that no longer lived but were all buried away. She didn't have the heart for it.

She turned her attention to the last items rolling into the gym. The library carts were laden with game boxes and stacks of cards.

"What's this one?" a teenager lifted Mira's personal copy of *Facts in Five*.

"Tonight's community game night will feature games from the 1960's." Mira glanced at the double doors where the first guests arrived. "This one is all about trivia."

The boy returned the game to the cart, choosing *Strat-O-Matic Pro Football* instead. "This is more my style. And I feel sorry for any dummy who goes up against you in historic trivia."

Mira laughed, "I'm not surprised no one plays with me. The only people I might convince will probably be over seventy years old."

"Good luck with that."

Mira remained by the carts of games, handing out boxes to families who entered. To the pastor's family with the artistic two-year-old, she gave *The Last Straw* knowing their children would love watching the straws tip and spill over when too much weight dropped the plastic camel. A group of college students, home for the holidays, received *Rivers, Roads, and Rails* with excitement, commenting on the similarity of a popular modern game. For Luella and Harriet she handed them *Scrabble*.

"You know us too well, Mira darling," Luella laughed.

Soon the gym was bustling with laughter. Mira walked around watching games and listening to stories. A group of elementary age kids played *The Game of Life* and high school girls giggled over *Mystery Date*.

It wasn't until Beverly found her that she finally grabbed some refreshments.

"I know you want to play *Facts,* but we don't have enough people to make it fair. Can't let you win so easily this time," the older woman teased Mira. Beverly pointed her to a table and walked off to find her husband.

Mira took a deep breath and sank in the chair. This was her mother's game, and they played it every year, sometimes staying up late New Year's Eve seeing how quickly they could go through five rounds. When she creaked open the lid, she was hit with the smell of age and old ink. Memories floated on the dust motes and stung her eyes.

"Are you alright?" Evelyn took a chair at the corner of the table.

Mira quickly blinked back tears and made a feeble excuse. "Allergies."

"Oh dear," Evelyn handed her a tissue. "Getting sick for Christmas is absolutely dreadful."

Beverly rejoined them with Charles. "Especially with all the activities you're orchestrating for the Festival." Then she turned and pulled out the chair in front of Mira, looking up to a fifth player. "We'd love for you to join us."

Mira glanced up, wondering who would dare play trivia against her. Her hazel eyes settled on the stranger from yesterday. The cards she was shuffling nearly dropped from her hands as he took the seat across from her with a shy smile.

"...and this is Mira, our resident historical expert." Beverly finished making introductions, but Mira had missed his name.

Evelyn chuckled. "She knows more about history than those of us who lived it."

"We met," he offered to the other two women before his eyes met Mira's again. "I apologize for the broken items. I'd like to come by your shop and pay for the damages."

Mira opened her mouth to appraise the teapot as priceless and nothing he had could ever replace the memories of four generations. Instead came a less-sharp retort. "We're closed for the season."

Silence engulfed the table while the older women assessed the tension between them.

Mira turned back to shuffling cards and Evelyn organized the letter tiles. Beverly passed out the playgrid sheets while Charles asked the stranger, "Have you played before?"

He fidgeted. "No, but I'm good with trivia, especially history."

Evelyn reached across the table and patted his hand. "We'll see." Then she turned and winked at Mira. "Care for a challenge?"

Mira's heart rate still hadn't settled from the surprise of sitting across from the man who destroyed something so valuable, but she wouldn't let him ruin her reputation in this game. She felt as if she was standing on the battlefield of World War I again but this time it wasn't the Christmas Day Truce. Her eyes narrowed and she responded by handing out five class cards.

"It's really simple actually," Evelyn explained. "We'll all share our card category, then everyone writes it at the top of the columns on your playgrid. You'll have five minutes to write something for each category. The trick is…" she paused for effect and slid the box of letter tiles toward him. "…your words can only start with these five letters."

When Mira picked her five letters, she groaned inwardly. Y and Q were the worst letters to have, and she lucked out with both. She glanced across the table at the stranger's playgrid, but she could barely read his messy handwriting. They took turns sharing the category cards and Mira stretched her fingers. This was her game, and she'd prove it.

When the timer clicked on, she bent over her paper and recorded her answers. It was difficult recalling the U.S. state flowers but she was sure *yucca* made the list. She scrambled to find something for Q but after several seconds skipped it for later. *Fictional characters from books* was a breeze since she spent so much time reading. Not even Ancient Military Figures caused her to blink twice. She scribbled the names quickly. But her hand slowed when she reached units of currency. *Yen* was simple enough to remember but once again the Q stumped her. What countries started with Q? Oh, yes. Qatar. But what did they use for money? A glance up revealed she was nearly out of time. She still had one more row: Famous historical structures. She scribbled her answers as quickly as she could, her hand trying to keep up with her mind.

"Times up!" Evelyn called with a grin.

Mira stared at her paper and wondered how the woman could be pleased. Then her eyes stole across the table at the stranger's page. Each of the twenty-five boxes were filled. Mira had missed two. She shriveled lower in her seat.

When they shared their answers, Beverly thought it was uproariously funny that Evelyn listed Colonel Sanders for an ancient military figure. "He sold fried chicken, not war."

"But didn't he fight in something?"

Mira shook her head, trying to suppress her own giggle. "No, he never fought in any war. He was given the title of Colonel by the Kentucky Governor because of his delicious food."

"Aw, shucks." Evelyn scribbled his name off her page. "What about you? Is that two blank spots I see?"

Mira flushed. "There aren't any state flowers or currencies starting with Q."

"Actually, there is," the stranger interrupted.

Everyone at the table turned to look at him. His eyes met Mira's unflinchingly. "There's a currency. Two I can remember."

Mira seethed inwardly. "Well?"

"The Guatemalan Quetzal and the Qatari riyal."

Charles cleared his throat and added, "Also, the Iranian Qi-ran. But I don't think they use it anymore."

Evelyn patted Mira's shoulder. "It's okay. We can't always know everything."

"Yes," Beverly added. "As long as we have each other we can fill in the rest."

"And Google." Charles held up his smart phone, the screen winking between searches. His smile was hidden under his white mustache, but his whiskers turned up mischievously. Beverly turned toward him and smacked the phone from his hand.

"Were you using that the whole time? No wonder your score is much higher than usual."

He lifted his hands in surrender as the others laughed. "I'm only using my resources wisely. And I'm getting so old I've forgotten most of these things. The phone helps remind me." He tapped the bald spot at the top of his head.

"Oh, Charles," Beverly laughed.

"They call them smart phones because in a couple genera-tions we won't need to use our brains at all, the phone will do it for us!" Evelyn joined in.

The stranger's eyes met Mira's, and he shrugged. "Some days my boys prove her right."

Mira set her lips in a straight line and passed out another playgrid. "The game is five rounds. Are you up for four more?" She pointed at Charles. "But the rules are the same for everyone: no phones, no Google, only your brain. Got it?"

Charles agreed and dropped his phone back into his pocket. "It's not like I could keep up with you even if I used a little help."

"Except for Seth." Evelyn smiled at the stranger. "Apparently Mira's met her match."

Other games continued around them but Mira didn't notice. Her hand scribbled answers as if on fire, hurrying to make up for the two she missed on the first round. The stranger, who she now knew was named Seth, kept up with her score and made her fight until she finally claimed the victory. Barely. By only two points.

She hadn't played a tough game in at least two years, when her mother was well enough and offered friendly competition. But it wasn't the same with Seth. He understood a variety of subjects from traveling overseas in his college years, answering how he knew about foreign currency. Charles was fascinated by the younger man's stories and slowed the game down with conversation. Mira learned more about Seth than she cared to. Yet she remained polite and avoided rolling her eyes every time he scored the highest points in anything pertaining to military history.

Eventually the game ended and Charles pulled Seth over to share his stories about Vietnam. Normally Mira loved to listen in but she'd already heard them all and wanted to avoid Seth's prying eyes. Because every time she'd glance up, she noticed how he watched her with slight confusion, trying to figure her out or pinpoint what he'd done to gain her irritation. As if destroying her shop wasn't enough to be detestable.

Mira was still trying not to glance back at him when Beverly tugged at her arm. "Mira, aren't you supposed to share with everyone *why* this game night is themed after the groovy sixties?"

She gasped and hurried for the microphone. Her mother was usually the one to remind Mira they needed to go on stage and Michelle would encourage the crowd with some playful banter and connections before Mira would share her history bit. But now she stood alone.

She held up the mic with a nervous grip before welcoming everyone. "Thank you for joining us for another awesome community game night. You may have noticed a certain theme. Can anyone guess?"

A couple rowdy teenagers shouted out the wrong answers to make their friends laugh and a six-year old asked if it was special because it was her birthday. After a pitching rendition of *Happy Birthday*, Mira finally answered her own question. The distraction had sent her mind spinning and she tried to reground herself.

"December 24, 1968 was a historic moment for our world as three men rocketed into space and orbited the moon." Mira's eyes fluttered closed.

When she opened them again, she wasn't in the high school gym but the cramped spaceship, Apollo 8, instead. She peered out a small round window and gasped at the view. The white craters of the moon gleamed beneath her. A dark expanse spread out in every direction and, there, straight in front of her was a miniature version of earth. Except it wasn't a small globe, but the world as seen from the other side of the moon.

"For the first time ever, humankind witnessed Earth rise from the vastness of space while astronauts Borman, Lovell, and Anders read the first ten verses from the book of Genesis."

She reached out and touched the window, feeling small and insignificant. Moments like these reminded her how little control she had, even of her own life. Behind her, she heard the echo of another astronaut read the passage into the speaker transmitting their words back to Earth. His words rang clear, "And God saw that it was good."

Mira spun around, recognizing his voice. Seth, ensconced in a spacesuit, sat less than a foot away from her and met her gaze. There was a seriousness in that stare, one that questioned who she was and why she was there.

Mira knew women weren't visible in certain times of history but it didn't stop her. She allowed her daydreams to carry her on a rocket to space. But more confusing was why Seth appeared in her imagination again. It was enough of a shock to pull her back to reality though. She shook his image from her mind and continued speaking to the audience in the Cedar Springs High School gym.

Mira's voice shook as she fought to regain focus. "As John F. Kennedy said in his momentous speech, 'We choose to go to the Moon in this decade and do the other things, not because they are easy, but because they are hard.'"

Charles interrupted by shouting, "I was there!"

Everyone laughed.

"What? On the moon?" Beverly teased.

Mira continued, pushing past the multiple distractions. "Christmas is a time of joy and wonder, a time when we must choose what our goals are, as this year ends and another begins. Celebrate the miracles of the season but also begin asking yourself: What difficult task will you tackle in the coming year?" She couldn't help flicking a glance toward the table she had been sitting at, catching Seth raise an eyebrow at her words. He was becoming an annoying distraction. Mira looked away and forced a smile. "Thank you all! And Merry Christmas!"

Those in the gym politely applauded but Mira knew it wasn't her best speech. She felt rattled and not herself, probably since her mother's funeral. It was as if half of who Mira had been was buried as well.

It would only make her feel worse if she joined the others again, especially with Luella and Harriet chatting at the table. She ducked her head to hurry out for a breath of fresh air but a small hand stopped her. A glance down showed the six-year-old birthday girl, Abby.

"Has anyone been on the moon since then? Can we build houses and live there?"

Mira chuckled. "Yes, two astronauts stepped on the moon less than a year later. Have you heard of Neil Armstrong and Edwin Buzz Aldrin?"

"Nope! But I want to be like them when I grow up!"

"Maybe you can be the first person to build a house on the moon," Mira smiled.

Abby beamed with a lopsided grin and Mira stopped herself from asking her if all she wanted for Christmas was her two front teeth. "I think after I grow up, I should go."

Mira was pulled from the cute conversation by the sound of Evelyn's voice. She stared across the room to see an distracting sight.

Evelyn was red in the face, glaring back at Luella. The other woman only shrugged and held up a board game. From this distance, Mira couldn't tell what it was, but she knew she'd need to intervene before the two women disrupted the event.

Mira turned back to the little girl. "I hope you do. We need more girls in space." She patted Abby on the shoulder and hurried away.

As she neared the arguing pair, Mira understood. Luella set the game *Mystery Date* on the table and pointed to Seth. His face was flushed in embarrassment.

"All I'm saying," explained Luella. "Is that we should play one round and see how it goes."

"No one is playing that infernal game with you," Evelyn snapped. Her red curls moved like a fire set ablaze on her head.

Mira stepped between the two ladies. "Can we talk in the hall, please?"

Evelyn huffed and pushed past them. "Maybe if Luella didn't stick her nose into other people's business, we could enjoy the evening."

Luella sighed, exasperated. "I'm only trying to help."

They stepped out of the gym. The school hall was empty, benches lined the space between lockers and closed classroom doors. Evelyn and Luella faced each other with crossed arms and rolling eyes.

"What happened?" Mira asked.

Luella threw her hands up. "I just tried to set up a game of *Mystery Date*."

"Nobody likes that game," Evelyn spat.

"That's why I was going to make it more fun," Luella exaggerated. "With real people, instead of pretend boyfriends."

"Not with my son."

Mira glanced between the women. "Seth is your son?" she asked Evelyn.

"Yes—" she began but Luella cut her off.

"—He would've enjoyed playing since he's single and his boys need a mom."

"His boys *had* a mom!" Evelyn pushed past Mira and yelled in the other woman's face. "But she died. This is their first Christmas without her and you're making it worse, Luella! Don't you shut up sometimes?"

Mira stepped back in shock. Christmas was a time of jolly laughter and happy families. She intimately understood the loss of that. The empty house, the dark loneliness, the gloomy songs highlighting her ache. Apparently, others held the same pain and loss. This had been a terrible year for Seth and his sons, as well.

Luella rolled her eyes. "I was only trying to help. Maybe they need a new mom for Christmas—"

Mira jumped between the women before Evelyn did more than growl, "Get out."

She tugged Luella back into the gym and passed her off to Harriet. "I think *Rummikub* would be a fun game for you two to play."

The room had settled back into jovial games and laughter, so Mira slipped back into the hallway to be with Evelyn. She was sitting on one of the benches across from a classroom door decked out in Hannukah-themed wrapping paper. Evelyn wiped her tears with a sleeve.

"I'm sorry about that." Mira offered a hug.

The older woman sniffled. "I didn't mean to get so angry but…"

"No," Mira patted her arm. "It was wrong what Luella tried to do, even though she was ignorant. Sometimes she tries to help but makes things worse."

"I hope I didn't do that."

"How? You were defending your son." Mira blinked back her frustration against Seth. He was struggling through the holiday just as she was. Losing a loved one was painful. She reached out her hand to Evelyn.

"I hope I didn't embarrass him," the older lady whispered.

She accepted Mira's comfort and shared her loss.

"Her name was Ana, and those boys were her pride and joy. But a drunk driver hit her when she was coming home from work. It wasn't until Seth arrived home to find Noah, Mason, and Liam hadn't been picked up from their after-school program that he knew something was wrong. It was heart-breaking and they still haven't healed. I don't know how they can."

⟫⟫⟫⟫ ⟪⟪⟪⟪

Seth stared down at his hands while he listened to Charles talk about his boot camp experience over five decades ago. "They don't build 'em the way they used to," the old man chuckled and adjusted his large glasses. It helped having him talk about something completely unrelated to the drama that just unfolded.

He knew he didn't like the blonde woman Luella from the moment she stared at him. Now, she was interfering in his life and riling up his mom, it made her detestable.

He didn't want to be rude to Charles, but he knew he needed to find his mom. She'd been emotional lately and this confrontation didn't help. He slipped out the side door and took the first hallway. His steps faltered when he saw his mom talking with Mira. Tears rolled down his mom's cheeks and Seth knew she was spilling his entire tragic story. He clenched his fists and turned the other direction, walking until he was outside.

The cold air felt comforting on his face, burning from the embarrassment of it all. It whisked away the heat of his anger. He wasn't upset with his mom. She was grieving too but it wasn't fair he was left alone. Seth sucked in a tight breath and steeled himself against a barrage of emotions. He wasn't allowed to fall apart or break down. Three boys depended on him to keep it all together and balance everything.

He juggled their everyday needs, kept up with his work responsibilities, and made it appear he'd figured out his new normal. But the truth was the exact opposite. He floundered and failed more times than not. He fed his boys fast food, missed teacher's conferences, and focused on his career because it was the only part of his life that followed any sort of routine. But when he'd settled down for the night, laid in his bed alone and stared into the darkness, he felt loss like a gaping hole, ready to swallow him up at any misstep.

Even now, as he walked around the school with his hands in his pockets, trying to regain his composure, the worries weighed down his shoulders. The cold wind nipped at his face and tugged away some of his thoughts. They swirled in the frosty air and spun around him.

At least his boys seemed to be enjoying this trip and loved being spoiled by their grandma the past two days. They were excited about tonight's games, or he wouldn't have come. Yesterday's event was annoying enough.

Surprisingly though, he'd enjoyed tonight, at least before he was picked out by that woman Luella. The game he'd been playing with Charles and the women had tested his skills and made him drag up information he forgot he knew. It reminded him of the young man he'd been after college, traveling the world excited for the adventure. The emotions revived a wanderlust he forgot about while he had focused on the grind of daily life. He also appreciated the challenge Mira had presented. She was a strong opponent, although he should have expected it, seeing how she lived in the past.

Seth chuckled at the thought. Tonight, her outfit was inspired by the groovy sixties, except it wasn't the best style for her. She barely pulled off the big frizzy hair, bowler cap, floral dress shirt and bright purple stockings. But her makeup made her brown eyes look bigger and drew him in, especially when she gave her speech about the moon orbit. She'd stared right at him as if he was an intruder to her thoughts. It should have pushed him away but instead he wondered what those thoughts were. During Mira's talks about history, her eyes glazed over with a dreamy far-off look. What was she imagining about the world around her? At least, until reality snapped back.

A gust of loose snow blew into his face and yanked him out of his observations. Those amber brown eyes would look at him with pity, now that his mom was spilling his past to her. She would know about Ana and the car accident, how his entire life fell apart in an instant, and how he hadn't been able to put any of it back together since that terrible day in January. Neither had his sons.

The creak of a swing caught his attention and he glanced up. One boy sat alone on the playset between the high school and elementary classrooms. The movement was sluggish but familiar to Seth.

He crossed the sidewalk hidden under a thin layer of snow and sat in the swing next to Noah. "Hey, too noisy for you too?"

Noah huffed.

"Yeah, it's crowded. Much better out here."

"Why are we even here?" Noah demanded.

Seth sighed, frustrated with his oldest son's attitude but recognizing his own grief reflected in it. "Because your grandma and brothers wanted to come. Did you play any games?"

"With strangers? No."

They sat in silence with snow settling around them. Since his mom passed, Noah had closed off to everyone, even Seth. He was at the end of his rope with knowing how to deal with his son. They'd gone through the grieving process together, had their fights, went to counseling, and talked with teachers, but each day Noah grew angrier and pushed everyone farther away. Seth finally agreed to his mom's pleas to visit, hoping the trip and seeing his grandma would help Noah. But in the past two days, the boy's attitude worsened. He was blatantly rude and offensive to everyone, including his grandma when he asked why her hair was such a weird color. Thankfully she had a sense of humor and laughed it off, but Seth had been mortified and apologized for him. Maybe, he thought with a smirk, he should introduce Noah to Luella. He wouldn't retract his son's insults then.

Or maybe they could hide out here in silence until the event was over. Some people needed distractions to pull them away from the emotions weighing down their soul, but – right now for Seth and Noah – the quiet snow and peaceful darkness was the only calm in their lives.

Chapter Three

SATURDAY, DECEMBER 15

Snow mounds lined the edges of the parking lot and empty flower baskets in front of the Cedar Springs Recreation Center and boot prints marked a path toward the wide stairs. The sun peeked over the edges of the mountain, bathing the early morning in bright light.

"Good morning and thank you for joining us!" Mira looked out over the audience, where they waited with hands tucked in pockets and bouncing from foot to foot to keep warm. A puff of white cloud rose over their heads, from warm breath reacting to the winter air.

Mira was surprised so many people actually showed up. The cold usually dampened her spirit to the point she just wanted to hide under a handmade quilt in her toasty warm apartment. It was very begrudgingly that she dragged herself out of bed this morning, only spurred on by the fact that she had to lead the event. She bit down her own nervousness and tried to imitate what her mother had done in past years. "We only have ten days until Christmas!"

A cheer erupted and Mira smiled. She needed the extra enthusiasm today. "So, for the next several days we'll be sharing our joy of the holidays by *giving*. Today, we are giving our time and work." She turned around and pointed to the double doors of the old recreation center. It was a decrepit building, the outside wood fading from age and weather but it still remained a popular spot among the locals, especially during the winter months. "We'll need teams to work with our contractors in fixing up anything that's broken, like doors, knobs, drywall, and trim. Another team will follow behind them and add a fresh coat of paint, generously donated by our local painter, Bill." Applause filled the cold morning air. Mira shuffled from one foot to the other and glanced down at her list. "Children are asked to remain in the gym where several teachers have organized activities, including making gingerbread houses. And for lunch, our local senior center is setting up a delicious feast of chicken chili, cornbread, and cookies."

Now that she had gotten the basics out of the way, she could dive into her story. "Can anyone guess what historical Christmas we're celebrating today?"

Several voices murmured but no one volunteered an answer. Mira wasn't surprised though. Most people came to her 12 Days to Christmas events for the food and fun, not a history lesson. But she would give them one anyway.

"In the year 800 A.D., on December 25, an emperor was crowned." She let herself fall into the story. "Tension between politics and the church was strong even then. So the pope combined them under King Charlemagne's leadership, as the first Holy Roman Emperor."

Mira knelt down in prayer, barefoot and wearing a plain white gown. Behind her, a red robe draped over the marble stairs. She took in a deep breath as a crown was set upon her head. It was heavy but the impact this moment carried through history was weightier. The hopes of how she would make the world a better place for all filled her mind with ideas and lit a fire in her heart.

"We remember his contribution today because of what he did for the European continent in literacy and culture, but mostly through architecture."

Mira lifted her eyes to stare at the beauty of St. Peter's Basilica in Rome but her eyes snagged on the man who set the crown on her head. Seth looked down on her with a mixture of confusion and interest. Her heart hesitated when he stepped back and she faced the crowd.

"Today, we'll breathe new life into this building that is used by every age and group in our community."

A smattering of half-hearted claps pulled her back to reality and she blinked away Seth's image. She wouldn't let herself search the audience for him. Instead, she turned her attention to the double doors the rec staff just pushed open for the crowd to file in.

People sorted into teams listening to Bill direct them from the entrance. Mira stood beside him and greeted those walking in. Their voices bubbled together, a mix of blending sounds and indiscernible words. Until Seth passed, speaking to his sons.

"Are we painting our own Palatine Chapel?"

The oldest responded with an eye roll. "That doesn't make sense, Dad."

Only someone who studied that particular line in history would know the chapel was made from a section of Charlemagne's original palace in Germany. She glanced away before he caught her looking or admitting his comment was clever.

Another of his boys chimed in. "Is that where Emperor Palpatine lives?"

Seth laughed but Mira didn't understand the reference until the youngest boy asked, "Does that mean Star Wars is real?"

They entered the building before Mira could hear Seth's response.

Instead of following the crowd, Mira snuck through the back entrance into the warm kitchen where Beverly and several older women mixed cornmeal dough and a couple men prepared the chili in the army of crock pots lining the counter. The scents enveloped her like a comfort blanket and sparked hunger. She snatched a gingerbread cookie from an unsupervised tray.

"How's it going?"

Beverly took Mira's hand. "Smoothly. You, take a breath and relax." Mira tried to listen to her friend's instructions but glanced at the busy kitchen for something to do until Beverly pushed her out the door. "Go paint a wall or play with the kids. There's no need to stress about anything since you've planned and delegated."

"But this is the first big workday I've organized on my own— "

"—And your mother would be proud. Now, go have some fun. Make friends your own age." She winked and shut the door in Mira's face.

Mira found herself listening to painting instructions beside a boy who appeared to be in fifth grade. "Shouldn't you be in the gym?" she leaned over and whispered.

"Shouldn't you be with the old ladies?" he retorted.

Mira's eyebrows shot up and she turned to get a better look at the ornery imp. His parents would definitely hear about his disrespect. But she swallowed back her threat when she noticed he was Seth's eldest son, the one who'd made comments about her shop. "I suppose I can keep your secret if you keep mine."

He shrugged. "Whatever."

Mira bit down on her lip to keep herself from saying something she'd regret and focused on Bill's explanation about painting duties. Some volunteers would go ahead using the rollers and those with steadier hands could follow behind with a paint brush for the edges and corners.

Mira found herself with a paintbrush, covering the old beige walls in fresh white paint in one of the game rooms.

The smell of the paint hinted to newness, erasing the old and covering it with modernity. She cringed at the scent.

She had played games here when she was younger. Her mother used to be the queen of Bridge with a group of older ladies. Mira always joined in, even though she was two decades younger than everyone else. Her favorite part was listening to the women gab about their lives, share stories from their past, and swap recipes of Jello meals – although the last one entertained her more than made her hungry. But that was before the sickness and treatments sapped all of her mother's energy.

As she focused on moving her paintbrush up and down, she fought back tears. They threatened to make her vision blurry. If she couldn't keep her mood in check, she'd have to hide in the bathroom until she wasn't emotional. She inhaled deeply but it hitched at the end, a swallow of paint fumes choking her breath. This time she wouldn't be able to hold back the sob. What would the other people working in the room think?

The sound of a guitar strumming distracted her thoughts, and she spun around. Elvis Presley's voice echoed in the room, singing *Blue Christmas*. Seth set his phone down at the top of a step ladder, the speakers at full volume. "I thought we could use some music." He nodded to the others in the room but before he could make eye contact with her, Mira turned back around.

With its upbeat swing and high background vocals, the music pulled her attention away from her memories. Her hand settled into rhythm, moving the paintbrush along with the tempo. It was a short song, but long enough to pull her back to reality and out of her memories. More songs poured from Seth's phone, filling the room with Christmas cheer as the other painters sang along. Eventually Mira joined in.

The work went quickly and, after a while, most of the helpers moved to another room but the music continued playing. Mira was engrossed in her work, carefully tracing along the top edge of the wall and cautious not to touch the ten-foot ceiling with wet paint, despite the bright blue masking tape lining the corner. Mira completely invested herself into everything she did. Mistakes were a sign of distraction or inattention.

This was why she didn't notice those around her while she stretched out toward the last corner. She reached on tiptoes and leaned as far as she could. Beneath her, the metal ladder slid on the slick floor and tipped. It clattered with a screech of scraping metal. The nearly empty paint cup toppled over and bounced, streaking the white paint and dripping on the collapsed rungs.

Mira tumbled. She scrambled at the empty air. A squeak escaped her lungs. Her mind mapped out possible injuries in a split second. Broken leg, fractured arm, and a fancy goose egg. Before she even hit the ground, worries filled her head. How would she ice skate at the next event if she was wearing a cast and hobbling on crutches?

But her fall was softened by a warm arm. She glanced up to meet dark brown eyes, wrinkled in concern. She blinked back at Seth. The closed hostility he displayed in reality vanished. His gaze reflected openness she'd only seen in her historic imaginations: the soft smile of a soldier, the encouraging grin of an astronaut, the hope of a pope crowning the king. She wasn't sure which one was the true Seth anymore. But his arm around her waist, warm and strong, was undeniable and not a figment of a daydream. Her breath hitched and she quickly pulled away.

"Thank you," she mumbled and readjusted her Christmas sweater, searching for a distraction. Something to hide the wild pulse echoing in her chest. She focused on the streak of bright white paint slashed across the front of her clothes. The others must have finished their painting and left earlier. Leaving only the two of them.

"Are you okay?" Seth asked. He held his arm out. He seemed unsure if he should steady her but also uncomfortable about touching her again. Mira avoided his gaze.

Instead, her eyes caught on the splatter of paint from her brush and Seth's roller, both abandoned on the wooden floor. "I'm fine."

Even though they'd stepped apart, she could still feel the grip of Seth's arm around her waist. Her mind was still reeling, trying to catch up with the shift of emotions. He caught her from sure disaster. Concerns for possible injuries brushed aside to make room for a different thought. One she didn't want to explore and was glad no one else was witness to.

She busied herself with cleaning and wiping the wet paint on the floor before it dried.

Seth kneeled beside her. He unrolled a handful of paper towels. "Don't worry about this mess. You can...um..."

Mira glanced at him to see he pointed at her face. "What?" she reached up and felt her cheekbone. Her hand came away slick with paint. "Oh."

"I'll take care of this." He crumpled the paint-soaked towels and tossed them in the trash can, grabbing more from the roll.

Embarrassed, Mira hurried away to wash her face in the bathroom. The streak of paint covered the side of her face and even coated strands of her hair. It took several minutes of scrubbing her skin raw before she got it all off. But instead of rejoining the event, she hid in the restroom a little longer.

She leaned against the sink and stared at her reflection. Her beige skin was red from the washing, but she was sure it wasn't all from rubbing the paint off. Some of the color shift was from mortification. Her heart was still racing, and she cursed the strange emotion coursing through her. He was a stranger she barely knew; one she disliked and pitied.

Determined to push the interaction from her thoughts, she emerged from hiding. By then, most of the interior of the building was bright in the fresh new paint. Mira walked the entire rec center before checking the room she had been working in. Thankfully Seth was no longer there, and the floor had been cleaned from the splattered paint.

After turning on fans to help the paint dry, she joined everyone in the gym. Long tables stretched the length with one large buffet table near the kitchen doors. It was filled with stacks of steaming cornbread, pots of bubbling chili, and trays of leftover cookies.

Mira hurried to the back to help, but Beverly shooed her away again. "You've been working so hard already. Get something to eat and rest a bit." It frustrated Mira since she needed an excuse to block unwanted conversations, with a stranger or people she grew up knowing. Both left her blundering incoherently.

But Mira complied with Beverly's demands and stepped in line. Her arms ached and she must have scraped her knee somehow during her fall. If Seth hadn't been there to catch her, she could've had worse injuries. She tried not to think about how quickly he jumped to help her or how the moment replayed in her mind again and again.

Instead, she forcibly turned her attention to the food. In her hurry to prepare for today's event, she skipped breakfast, and now her stomach was demanding sustenance.

A little hand tapped her arm, and she looked down. The boy standing in front of her in line passed her a paper bowl. Mira smiled and took the offered dish with a thank you.

He grinned back. "My dad says I can have two cookies for lunch!"

"Oh, you're so lucky! I'm only allowed to have one."

"Why? Can't grownups do whatever they want?"

She surprised herself by giggling. "I wish!"

"Do your dad and mom not let you have more?" he asked innocently.

Mira bit her lip. "Well...they're not here."

The little boy looked sad. "My mom isn't here either. She's in Heaven."

Mira blinked, finally recognizing the boy as Evelyn's grandson, Liam – the boy who broke her teapot. Tears gathered in the corner of her vision. Her eyes trailed to Seth several spaces ahead of her in line. He was busy talking with his oldest son in a low voice. It seemed like a serious conversation.

Others were struggling with Christmas, just as she was. Her heart hitched at the thought of this six-year-old having so little time with his mom before her accident. Mira was thankful she'd been blessed by thirty years and thousands of memories with her mother. She turned back to Liam and knelt to his level.

"My mother is in Heaven, too. Maybe they're both watching and hoping we get two cookies each."

The little boy nodded with excitement. "That would make them happy, I think."

Mira smiled. "I think so, too."

As they went through the line and held their bowls out for food, Mira caught herself reaching out to help Liam. Somewhere, between the cornbread and the cookies, she forgave him for his mistake in her shop. Her smiles came easier. They both placed two cookies on their plates, ignoring the judgmental gaze of Luella as she supervised the buffet table.

But when Liam asked her to sit with him, she glanced up to see Seth and his other two sons settling down in the chairs. Mira was ready to befriend this boy who felt alone in the world like her, but she hesitated. Something about Seth rattled her. She wasn't sure what it was and it wasn't something she wanted to pursue. Instead, she wished the boy a delicious lunch and joined a table with people her age, Elizabeth and Jesse. It was a rare occurrence for her, but easier to face than a man she didn't like and who'd saved her from injury.

Jesse was talking about a new book series he was reading with his high school students, but Mira hadn't heard of it. Her favorite books were the classics. Something about rereading was comforting and familiar.

"You need to branch out to something new," Jesse said after Mira mentioned reading *Pride and Prejudice* for the sixth time. "I can guarantee you will find something to love."

Elizabeth chimed in. "I can give you some recommendations!"

Mira hesitated. Too much had changed in her life this past year. Couldn't she burrow herself in the security of stories she knew would end well? She needed something she could count on; something she knew the ending of, a happily ever after.

"I know what kind of books you like," Elizabeth gave her a side eye. "Trust me."

Mira didn't have the energy to argue so she submitted with a shrug. "Fine, but make sure it's wholesome and uplifting."

Her friend smiled. "I know the exact thing for you." Mira didn't doubt that Elizabeth, the town librarian, knew enough books to recommend and perked up at the thought of a fresh story. Everything needed a new beginning every now and then, she thought while she glanced at the freshly painted walls of the gym around her. As long as it didn't erase the history that breathed life into it in the first place.

***

The gym was filled with people. The hum of conversation floated through the air like the scent of comfort food in crockpots, but it only gave Seth a headache. He sat at the nearest table with his two older boys. Beside him Mason was chattering away about the games he played while Seth had been working. Other than a scuffle with Liam, they had listened to the teacher and didn't get a bad report. Thankfully Noah wasn't adding to the noise. He leaned over his plate grumpily and glared whenever Seth asked where he'd gone off to during the work hour. So, not exactly an improvement.

Earlier in the food line, Seth had glanced back to see how Liam was doing and if he needed any help when he saw Mira kneel beside his youngest son. The two of them were focused on a conversation. He recognized the sad pout Liam used when he was talking about missing his mom and it added tension to the pain in his chest. Mourning his wife, while comforting his boys had become too much for him to juggle alone. His heart softened at Mira's smile to Liam before she took the little boy's hand. He glanced at them collecting their food, when he knew she wouldn't see him and a little warmth returned at the smile on his son's face.

When he had started painting earlier, the quiet was deafening. In a room of complete strangers, working together, he needed a distraction. Before the awkward silence could bury him in emotions, he pulled out his phone and set his Spotify to play Christmas music. Elvis' *Blue Christmas* seemed fitting for the occasion. He had noticed the shift in the other volunteers as well. Everyone worked in tandem, and conversations sprouted easier.

He had a conversation with the painter Bill about the sports people played in the rec center and, for a moment, was tempted to join in some of the activities. Keeping busy had been his therapy the past year and it'd been working so far.

But, when music filled the room, he'd seen the change in Mira the most. Her shoulders had been slumped where she hid herself in a corner to work but the old Christmas song sparked a change. It wasn't something he could identify, since he didn't know her well enough but he could feel the transformation. She had leaned back on her heels and swayed in time with the music.

Now he was watching her interaction as Liam pulled her to the table where Seth was sitting. He shifted in his seat wondering what conversation he could engage without drawing attention to the awkward moment they faced earlier. He shook away the feeling that bloomed when she tripped from the ladder and landed in his arms. Or the way her amber brown eyes had stared up at him after he didn't let go immediately. He swallowed.

But when Liam sat down across from him alone and Mira walked in a different direction, he frowned. "What did you talk about with her?" he asked Liam.

Innocent and goofy as only a youngest child can be, he grinned and answered, "Cookies!"

Seth raised his eyebrows.

"She's nice! She likes cookies too." Liam bit into a chocolate chip cookie.

"Hey," Seth said. "You know you need to eat your food before dessert."

Liam pouted. "But the nice lady said it'd make mommy happy if I got to eat two cookies."

"She did?"

"Yup!" Liam nodded and shoved the rest of the cookie in his mouth.

Seth's gaze stole back to where Mira sat with her friends and narrowed thoughtfully. He'd been surprised to see her talking to Liam in the first place, since he was responsible for the mishap in her shop. Mira hadn't hesitated to show her displeasure with Seth at the game night, holding it over his head. He'd thought she was overreacting to a simple accident but maybe it was because she didn't like him.

"Dad!" Mason ran up with a welcome distraction. "Did you hear we get to make our own gingerbread house?"

Liam's eyes lit up in excitement. "Do we get to eat it?"

Mason and Liam turned pleading eyes toward their dad, and he grinned. It was Christmas break, and they could be grandma's responsibility afterwards. "Sure," he laughed. "Why not? Just don't have too much."

They cheered and finished the rest of their food quickly.

⁕⁕⁕⁕⁕ ⁕⁕⁕⁕⁕

Mira knew the day would be long and exhausting, but it was a welcome relief rather than sitting at home alone. She flitted between those painting and those cleaning up the meal, among groups of friends and gathered families helping serve. It was mostly a pleasant time. She even enjoyed a conversation with Luella about her secret cookie recipe, although the older woman didn't share what made her treats so fluffy and sweet. She snagged another cookie as she walked toward the children making gingerbread houses.

She helped Liam hold up the walls of his house while the royal icing hardened. When his middle brother came and sat next to them carrying a bowl filled to the brim with candies and goodies to decorate his gingerbread with, Mira's eyes grew wide.

"I don't think your house is big enough for that much candy."

The boy grinned, "That's okay. Most of it is for me to eat!"

"Mason, dad won't let you have *that* much." Liam shook his head.

His brother glanced between them and lowered his voice. "Dad doesn't need to know." Before his younger brother could tattle, Mason leaned in closer. "And if you tell him, I'll let him know *your* secret."

Liam turned red as holly berries. "No! Don't!"

Mira wasn't sure what was going on between them, especially since she'd never had siblings to keep secrets with or tattle on, but she knew enough to distract them. "Mason, you're such a nice brother to bring enough candy for the two of you to share."

The middle brother's mouth dropped open. "Is she on your side, Liam?"

"Yes!" The youngest brother stuck out his tongue.

"Now, now, none of that, Liam. You want Mason to share, right?" When he nodded, Mira continued, "Then you need to be kind to your brother. After all, brothers are important. You will always need your family, so keep them close and encourage them."

"Especially now," Mason frowned.

He didn't need to explain himself since she could see the sadness drooping his features. It was similar to the one reflected back at her every time she looked in a mirror. She set a hand on his shoulder. "It's good you have each other. Don't lose that."

Liam kept prattling like it was normal to talk about loss. "Her mommy is in Heaven, too."

Mason met her gaze and, before she could say anything, he wrapped his arms around her. She went stiff with surprise. This past year, she'd received an occasional hug from Beverly or her other friends, but she had forgotten how it felt to be in contact with other humans. It made her miss her mother even more. She returned Mason's hug. When he finally let go, the loneliness returned but not as heavy as before.

"Thank you," she whispered, not trusting her voice.

Mason grinned back. "You hug like my mommy used to."

"I'm sure your mom gave the best hugs."

Liam nodded, candy filling his cheeks and staining his lips. "She did! She gave the best snuggles. Sometimes she'd tickle me too!"

"I miss that," Mason added.

"My mom would squeeze me tight," Mira said. She didn't know why she was opening up to the six and eight-year-old boys, but it was nice remembering her in this moment. It was her mother who recommended updating the rec center last year even though she wasn't in physical condition to help. "She used to hide chocolate kisses around the house." Mira unwrapped one of the candies and placed it on Liam's gingerbread chimney. "When I would find one, she'd chase after me until I gave her a kiss." The memory brought a smile to Mira's face.

"I wish we could hide candy around the house!" Liam laughed.

Mira pulled away the nearly empty bowl from him. "That's too much candy for you! You'll get a stomachache!"

Mason took the bowl and popped some candy in his mouth. "The rest is for me. Grandma said I'm the sweetest!"

Mira laughed.

But Liam frowned. She followed his gaze to see Seth walking beside Noah. The oldest brother looked grumpy, and their dad was tense. They stepped out the side door and stopped. Seth turned Noah to face him. The boy crossed his arms and stared defiantly at his dad through the lecture, refusing to answer any questions or acknowledge his dad's frustration.

Liam plucked a candy from his gingerbread house and set it to the side. "This is for Noah. He isn't sweet at all."

⁂

"That's stupid," Noah crossed his arms and glanced at his dad. "I wish I was home instead."

Seth ran a hand through his hair, most likely messing it up but he was too frustrated to care. "People worked hard to make today possible. Grandma was hoping you'd bring her a gingerbread house. But here you are, acting rude."

"I told you I didn't want to come."

"That wasn't your choice. Grandma invited us and we haven't seen her since... I brought us up to be with her."

Noah glared back. "It won't replace mom."

Seth sighed. "I'm not trying to. I want us to have a family Christmas together with Grandma. Can't you be a part of making it a good time for her?"

"You want me to fake it? Pretend everything is okay when it's not?"

"Obviously it's not, Noah! But you're going to have to accept it and continue life. She wouldn't want you to treat the rest of your family like this." Seth stared up at the gray sky above them, the clouds heavy with more snow and echoing the weight he carried on his shoulders. "I loved your mom, and I love you too but we have to keep living."

Noah crossed his arms and sat down against the wall. "Then go live your life and leave me alone."

Seth turned around and slammed the door behind him. Noah was too much to deal with right now. His mom had already remarked about his attitude and expressed her concern on his mental health. Everyone was worried about the boys and doing everything they could to help them through their grief, even bending over backwards.

But did anyone care about Seth's?

CHAPTER FOUR

SUNDAY, DECEMBER 16

A chilly wind blew across the ice invigorating Mira. She tucked her hands in the warm muff and wished she had worn a beanie over her ears, even if it clashed with her bodice. It was flowery pink with white ruffles from the neck down to her hips and usually matched better with the rest of her colonial gown. But, for practicality's sake, she chose to wear thick leggings. Her red cloak draped over most of her body but still left enough room for movement, which she needed stepping out now.

The skate slid beneath her as she glided onto the frozen lake. The grind of the metal cutting into the ice and the scrape when she swung around to skate backwards filled her with adrenaline. People were arriving and she would need that energy for her speech and to keep up with conversations, but she used some of it now to slide to a stop and spin in place. Mira didn't have formal training, but she enjoyed being on the ice and floating across weightlessly. It gave her a freedom, unburdened by the worries descending on her shoulders the past year: losing her mom, her passion, and soon her shop. Money became tight after the funeral, and she wasn't sure how much longer she'd be able to hang on after the holidays. But that was a problem for next year.

Mira chewed her bottom lip and tried not to grow overwhelmed when she saw the amount of people showing up for today's ice skating and sledding day. Behind them, the small creek meandered under the foot bridge from Main Street to the New Hope Church a quarter of a mile away. People gathered in small groups under the patch of cedar trees, ready to pull on their skates and join her, while others walked up Evergreen Hill planning to sled down. Their laughter and chatter carried across the fresh dusting of snow and pulled her from her own worries. This was why she planned these events, to bring people together. It was the only thing keeping her going this Christmas season.

She took a deep breath and turned back to the Apple Shed, a wooden ranch house built alongside the creek and one of the oldest structures in town. The original buildings were all of the remains of Old Town until a generous donor brought new life to the dilapidated structure and restored it into one large hall for community gatherings. It was now a museum, art gallery, and events center. When she was in elementary school, her class came and learned how to make apple cider, shuck corn, and dip candles here. That day became one of Mira's favorite memories. She relived it every year by volunteering for the third-grade field trip.

Mira took off her skates and walked up the wooden steps into the Apple Shed where Evelyn and Beverly were setting out serving spoons. Today's potluck filled the room with warm smells of beef stew, mashed potatoes, and fresh bread. She paused to take in all the scents.

Luella rushed in with a huff, shattering the moment. "Everything that could go wrong today did. I'm glad you haven't started the meal without me."

Mira reached out and helped Luella find a place for her casserole as the older woman filled the silence.

"This is my tried-and-true Christmas casserole. I've received so many compliments on it. I'm sure it's the best you've ever tasted."

Beverly chuckled behind them. "I'm sure it is, but this isn't a food competition."

"Oh," Luella sighed. "It should be. I know this would be a top contender. I'm only sorry I didn't make more. Those who don't get any will be so disappointed."

Charles entered at that moment, patting his stomach. "They'll survive. But me, I'll be the first in line and ready to try everything." He breathed in deep and grinned.

Mira laughed. "Would you like to do the honors?"

She hadn't even finished her question before Charles hurried back to the wooden porch outside and rang a large dinner bell. It echoed across the creek, loud and clear. The women chuckled and joined him.

"You never have to ask Charles twice when it comes to food," Beverly said.

People gathered around the Apple Shed and waited for Mira to speak. She stood on the highest step and took a deep breath. This is why she needed the moment of quiet to herself earlier. Once she spoke, the chaos would begin. She placed a finger to her lips and waited until everyone hushed.

When she finally spoke, her voice was barely a whisper. "It was a frigid winter, and supplies were running low."

Mira shivered as a cold wind tore at her coat. She pulled it tighter, but it did little to protect her from the snow and sleet stinging her face. The frost bit into her bones and made all her muscles ache.

"The soldiers were beginning to despair since the patriots were outnumbered but General George Washington had a secret plan."

Despite the freezing weather, hope hummed in her heart. She knew this event would rally her troops and encourage more soldiers to fight on her side if it succeeded. It had to.

"On Christmas Day in 1776, at 11 pm, he led 2,400 soldiers across the half-frozen Delaware River and reached the other side just before dawn."

Her gloved hands gripped the sides of the cargo boat while it lurched across the river, its hull bumping through chunks of ice, but she didn't whisper her orders yet. Secrecy was the most important part of this mission; one she'd planned with several councils. Every detail was accounted for. But if the Loyalists knew what she was about to do, she'd be targeted by their allies and her men would suffer.

Although her preparations were delayed, crossing the ice-choked river took three extra hours, and her reinforcements weren't waiting on the riverbank, she went through with the strategy. There was no other choice.

Her soldiers leapt from the boat and hit the ground with confidence. It was another ten miles of marching before they would reach Trenton and those supporting her enemies, but she wouldn't give up this close to success.

Beside her, a soldier tripped on the slick ice, and she reached down to help him back to his feet. When she glanced at him, her eyebrows lifted in concern. Seth, in the blue coat of the Continental Army, stood and saluted to her. Mira returned the motion, and a silent understanding passed between them. Side by side, they marched toward Trenton.

"In a surprise attack, they surrounded the hired Hessian warriors and won a remarkable victory."

With her ivory-hilted cuttoe extended and the troops kneeling with rifles beside her, Mira called the attack. Victory or Death. She pointed her pistol and fired.

Instead of the crack from ignited black powder, the sound of clapping hands brought Mira back to the Apple Shed with a crowd of eager and hungry people watching. A set of brown eyes stared from the back. This time, instead of annoyance, Seth met Mira's eyes with interest. She pulled away from his look, casting around for a distraction. She snatched a ladle from a nearby food table and swung it forward like a sword. "The Battle of Trenton raised the spirits of the colonists and led them forward to continue fighting for their freedom, eventually leading to the creation of our beautiful country."

She passed the ladle to Charles who snuck back into the Apple Shed while she continued speaking. "This Christmas we are all fighting something: exhaustion, emotions, or overwhelming ourselves with everything we think we need to accomplish. Instead, surprise yourself and your loved ones with triumph. Maybe it can be something as simple as allowing someone else to go before you in line or it can be giving up a bad habit and becoming a stronger person. Whatever your 'battle' is, face it like a general, and win your victory!"

Mira stepped back and the crowd surged forward, plates in hand and silverware ready to dig into the meal. She wondered if anyone listened to her historical speeches or if she was pandering to her own interests. Either way, she was grateful for the turnout.

⁂

Seth watched from the back of the audience. He'd arrived late with his boys because Noah was in one of his moods again and didn't want to come. But his worries dispersed from his mind when he listened to the fervor in Mira's voice. He wasn't sure where his boys were now, if they'd run ahead in the food line or hopefully found their grandma. Instead, he was caught up in the retelling.

American history, especially its Independence, was a favorite subject of his. Seeing the gleam in Mira's eye when she spoke and hearing the inflections in her voice transported him to that moment in time. She might not connect well with people in the modern world, but she had a gift and passion for the past. He almost wished he could talk with her about it or maybe challenge her to another game of trivia.

Except it was obvious she was avoiding him. Yesterday she spent time with his boys but left the moment he approached, and today she glanced over the audience and averted her eyes from meeting his. It was better than a pitying glance, though.

His mom told him about their conversation after the game night drama and how considerate Mira had been. It encouraged him to see how comfortable his mom was in her new home and how welcoming the small town had been to her. He'd lived in the city for over five years but still didn't have a good circle of friends he could confide in. It shouldn't have bothered him as much as it did.

Except, right now, standing along the edge of the frozen lake and looking at the Apple Shed filled with talking and laughing people, he didn't feel so alone. He wouldn't sit on the fringes anymore but join in the merriment. At the other events, he escaped when his emotions dragged him down. He recognized the same response in Noah. They pulled away and avoided making relationships. Perhaps he needed to breach his own worries and fears to help his son. He needed to start by example. Pushing himself from his comfort zone, he grabbed a plate and stepped into line.

Several other latecomers picked through the buffet of food but most of the best dishes were already scraped clean. Seth reached out to a mostly full casserole and took hold of the spoon.

"I wouldn't do that." The guy ahead of him cautioned.

Seth looked up with a question in his eyes but didn't let go of the serving utensil. "Why? It looks like regular meatloaf."

"It's not. It was supposed to be a tater tot casserole."

Seth let go of the spoon and moved on to the next dish, but the other guy continued talking.

"My wife made it. She forgot it in the oven."

"Thanks for the warning." He reached out. "Seth. I'm visiting family for the holidays."

"Jesse." They shook hands. "My wife is great at everything else but sometimes I wish she'd check out some cookbooks from the library she works at."

They finished filling their plates and looked out over the crowded tables.

"You mentioned family. Who are you related to?" Jesse asked.

"My mom, Evelyn Reiner. She's been begging for time with the grandkids."

Jesse found two empty seats and motioned for Seth to join him. Before long they talked about their jobs, compared the ages of their children, and discussed the scores of their favorite sports teams.

It made for a decent lunch while Seth connected with someone other than his mom in Cedar Springs. Just like his trips around the world, places needed to be explored. This included the people. Getting to know them and understand the pulse of Cedar Springs would help him understand his mom's choice better, why she moved here. Maybe this small town wasn't so bad.

Mira leaned back in her seat, stuffed with delicious comfort food. She was a decent cook but tired of eating from her own recipes at home. Potlucks were a wonderful time to scour for new ideas and discover new flavors. She only wished people would attach their recipes to her favorite dishes.

Charles sat across from her, now on his third plate, this one filled with a variety of desserts, most of them chocolate. "Luella wasn't joking when she said her casserole is delicious. You should get the recipe." He nudged Beverly.

His wife rolled her eyes. "If you like her cooking so much, why don't you move into her house?" She smirked playfully. "Although, once she sees how much you eat and how costly your groceries are, she'll send you right back." The old couple laughed together, and Charles scooped a bite of lemon cake on his fork.

"I don't know who made this, but it's the best cake I've ever tasted." He lifted the fork to Beverly's lips and shared it with her.

Beverly pretended to savor the flavor and tapped her chin like a judge on a cooking show. "You know Charles, this might be the first time you've ever been right."

He chuckled. When he noticed Mira watching them with a smile, he winked. "It's Beverly's."

Beverly laughed. "After forty-eight years of marriage, we have to find new ways to entertain each other."

"Only forty-eight? I thought it's been longer." Beverly swatted Charles' arm but when it tipped the chocolate brownie off his fork and onto his lap, the couple laughed harder. She leaned in and kissed him, using the distraction to slide the dessert plate away.

"If you want to make it to our golden anniversary, that should be enough sweets for you."

Charles snatched the plate back. "No, not yet." When Beverly turned back to counter, he caught her hand and placed another kiss on her wrist. "You're sweeter than all the chocolate brownies and lemon cakes in the world."

Beverly chuckled and rolled her eyes, despite the blush blooming on her face. "Oh, you're something else."

Mira loved watching their exchange but knew she had to leave the Apple Shed and check on the rest of the event. She left them to their flirting and wrapped her cloak tight around her as she stepped down the creaking stairs.

Their camaraderie and banter were more than entertaining. They gave Mira an expectation to hope for, should she ever find her significant other. At many of these events, Beverly and Charles would still be together, making each other laugh. Many mornings, they would stop by her shop and regale her with stories of growing up, meeting each other, and starting a family. Every decade came with interesting challenges and diverse learning experiences, yet they supported each other through it all. After impressing Mira with their memoirs, they'd leave the shop hand in hand.

It was their example Mira looked to when she considered her future. If she couldn't connect with someone intellectually and emotionally, she didn't see it worth continuing. She felt very much like Elizabeth Bennet, rational and resolved in her own way of life. If someone didn't fit into it, they didn't belong. That might be why she was alone now, but she refused to let it bother her. Maybe if she ignored the loneliness clawing inside her chest, she could distract herself with stories in history, great romances passed down through time, tales that weren't hers.

The lake was already busy with people ice skating and a line formed at the top of Evergreen Hill where others were sledding down. A pre-teen whooped as he flipped his sled and landed face first in the snow. His friends gathered around him and laughed. Before Mira could check no one was injured, he'd already leaped to his feet and was running back to the line.

On the ice, children showed off hockey and skating tricks, couples skimmed past holding hands, and others tripped and fell with amused giggles. Even standing alone, Mira felt a part of it. She'd worked hard the past several months setting up these events. Seeing people enjoy it was an acknowledgment to her invested time. With the infectious joy around her, the loneliness faded, at least temporarily. She couldn't help smiling while she put her ice skates back on and joined in. When the blades hit the ice, they carried her forward. She glided away from all her worries, letting them slip away so she could appreciate the moment and company. People waved skating past, and she smiled back.

Mira came to an abrupt stop at seeing a little boy sitting in a heap at the center of the lake.

"Liam?" She skated to him and kneeled down. "What's wrong?"

He looked at her with pouting lips. "I keep falling."

She took his hand. "So did I when I first went skating. Would you like some help?"

Liam nodded and pulled himself up next to her. Except, the moment he stood, his feet slid out from under him again. Only his hold on Mira kept him from scraping his knee.

"It can be tricky at first." She pulled him back to his feet. "But it is so much fun once you get the hang of it."

She taught him how to balance on the skates and soon they slowly shuffled along.

Liam looked up with bright eyes. "This is kind of fun."

Mira chuckled. "Once you're comfortable and can start racing, I know you'll love it!"

"Maybe," he shrugged. "If I can beat Mason or Noah."

"Sometimes it's more fun not to beat your brothers, but to play with them. Wouldn't you enjoy a hockey game better?"

"I suppose."

As they spoke, Mira guided them around obstacles, slowly transforming their shuffle into skating. Liam gripped her hand tightly but kept up without falling again.

"Sometimes they are fun. Except when they win. I never beat them at anything."

"What do you mean?"

"Like at wrestling. Noah is the best cause he's too strong. And when Mason plays video games with me, he wins every time."

"Is it because they have more practice?" Mira asked.

"Probably."

"So, maybe *you* need more practice?"

"How are you so smart?" Liam caught Mira off guard, and she almost lost her balance.

"Smart?"

"Yeah, you know everything!" Liam said. "You know how to skate, how to make gingerbread houses, and all about George Washington!"

Mira chuckled and tapped Liam's red nose. "I listened in school. You should too and then you can know lots and lots of things."

"You are smart like my dad. He knows lots of things too. He's the boss at a big company." As Liam bragged, he skated faster. Mira glanced over at him to make sure she wasn't pushing him too quickly and her eyes met Seth's. He pulled up and took hold of Liam's other hand.

"What are you talking about, Liam?" Seth asked.

Mira focused on her balance so she wouldn't trip on the skates. Clammy warmth spread across her ribs as she tried to fight away the memory of his arms around her. Nothing romantic. He had only been helping her avoid a broken leg, she told herself.

Her eyes flicked up, but Seth was focused on Liam. It would be too awkward for Mira to sneak away now. Maybe she could hold a light conversation and make her escape soon. She forced a smile.

Seth explained, "Liam's at that stage where he tends to exaggerate. I'm an account executive."

"But you have your own office!" Liam added.

"Yes," Seth nodded. "But I have three bosses I work for too."

Mira wasn't very familiar with the outside world and what modern people did to make a living. She was better at talking about all the jobs women stepped into during World War II or the change transportation played in living conditions and career choices, so she changed the subject. "Liam is doing so well skating."

"Now I won't fall!" the little boy giggled.

Mira took this opportunity to make her escape, but Liam wouldn't let go of her hand. She tried to pull away, but his grip tightened.

"You're doing great!" Seth looked over Liam's head at Mira. "Thank you."

Mira shifted uncomfortably. "He's a fast learner."

"I hope he's learning all the history lessons you've been teaching."

"Yes!" Liam bounced up and down, almost losing his balance. Mira and Seth pulled him back up on his feet. "I learned all about the awesome soldiers today! George Washington was a hero!"

"He was," Seth agreed. "But did you know that battle didn't go as planned?"

Liam stared up at his dad with big brown eyes and then turned to Mira. "What happened?"

She chuckled. "It's more about what didn't happen. There were two more forces of Continental soldiers led by Colonel Cadwalader and General James Ewing that were supposed to meet with General Washington on the opposite side of the river...but they never arrived!"

"What did General Washington do?"

"He attacked the enemy without them...and still won!"

"Woohoo!" Liam cheered.

"I've really enjoyed these history lessons connected with the events you've planned," Seth said.

Mira smiled. "Thank you."

"I take it you're a history buff?"

"I run an antique shop, so I should know something about the items I sell. People connect when there's a story involved."

His brown eyes warmed. "And history has some of the best stories."

Mira agreed with his statement. She wasn't sure of the glint in his eye, though. Even when it made her forget why she disliked him.

They skated in silence for several more moments. Mira kept trying to extradite herself from Liam's grip, but he refused to let go. The little boy appeared to be having the best time ever. He glanced between Mira and his dad more than once.

She focused on the repetition of sliding one foot in front of the other, skating in a wide arch around the perimeter of the lake. Her gaze stared downwards where she studied each scrape on the ice and avoided them as her blades cut through the divots.

"What's the next lesson?" Seth broke the awkward silence.

Mira was thankful for the distraction. "Not so much history for us, but the younger generations will enjoy it."

"That has me intrigued. Are we already the 'older generation'?"

She chuckled. "We're always older than someone else."

"Even me?" Liam piped up.

"Yes, even you," Mira said. "Tomorrow we remember the Internet's first test run."

Seth threw his head back and laughed. "Oh, boy. Have we really aged that quickly?"

"I like to consider what our parents and grandparents think about the world we live in. How much has changed! Especially in the last several decades. We're a cross-generation, growing up with and without technology." Mira added, "At least some of us."

A quirky expression filled Seth's face as his eyes brightened and he grew animated. "I remember going outside after school, playing until dark, and reading books under my blanket with a flashlight. I miss those old games, like Super Mario World and the original SIMS. We learned how to use computers by playing the Oregon Trail."

"What's the Oregon Trail?" Liam asked.

"A game of hunting and dysentery," Seth answered. Both adults laughed.

As Seth explained the game and history to his son, Mira studied him. The scruff on his chin had grown out a bit the past two days, more a close-cropped beard, and the tension in his eyes softened when he smiled at his son. Perhaps she had judged him too harshly at their first meeting. So far, from what she'd noticed, he was an attentive father to his boys and a supportive son to Evelyn. Knowing his wife had passed this year, Mira couldn't believe how difficult it must have been for him. She was heartbroken over her loss, but she didn't have to take care of anyone else in her grief.

She blinked when Seth looked back and caught her staring. With a nervous chuckle, she shared her own memories of playing the game at the school library. Her grandmother never accepted new technology and Mira barely knew how to use it. Now she saw others with smartphones, tablets, and touch screens and felt so far behind, she couldn't catch up. The only times she used a computer was at the local library searching for information she couldn't find in books.

"Is that where your interest in history began?" Seth asked.

"Oregon Trail? No. I've always enjoyed studying the past, the way they lived, and embracing their fashions." She glanced down at the frilled bodice she was wearing and adjusted her burgundy cloak. Her style was part of who she was, so why did she suddenly feel self-conscious about it? "In fact, I was going to be a history teacher."

"Really? What changed that?"

Mira bit her lip, uneasy about getting into all the things she lost and the dreams she discarded along the way. "Life." She gestured noncommittally.

"Ah, I understand," Seth answered, although he had no idea what her life had been like. "It's never too late to pursue it. I think you'd have a bright future in education." Mira wanted to brush off the compliment, but Seth pointed to the sledding hill. "Look at the difference a five-minute speech made."

At the bottom of the hill, a group of boys and girls built a fort out of snow. Mason hid behind the wall and formed a snowball. When two sledders raced down the hill, he shouted, and the group threw their frozen ammunition. The kids chanted, their voices reaching across the frozen lake: "Victory or Death!"

Seth chuckled. "I think they learned a little something today, don't you?"

"I suppose so." Mira bit her lip, hoping parents wouldn't find her later to complain. Children were like sponges, absorbing anything of interest. She felt proud her speech ignited their minds toward history and all the treasures they could uncover from the past.

"I learned a lot!" Liam bounced between them. Mira had forgotten he was still there.

Seth smiled down at his son and then back up at Mira. "I think we all did."

When Liam was done skating and Mira skittered off with some excuse about cleaning the food tables, Seth joined Mason and helped him add to his snow fort. Most of the parents stood along the outskirts, talking and laughing with each other. A group of boys ran around together, undoubtedly friends since the womb. That's how it worked in small towns. His boys bounced in and out of the gang, not quite part of it.

Normally, Seth left his boys to figure things out like that for themselves, but it grated on him. Especially when he saw Liam making snowballs by himself, far from the other kids. He dropped in the snow next to his youngest and helped. It wasn't long before Mason copied.

Together, they started a snowball fight. The boy gang jumped in and everyone was covered in white powder and giggling. Soon, Mason and Liam were racing down the sledding hill with the others and Seth was calling out the winners. He even pelted snowballs at the racers. The boys loved trying to dodge them and broke into hysterical laughs when they couldn't.

Seth's life was normally too busy to allow time for fun moments like this so he made the most of it. While other dads stood on the sidelines or went back to the Apple Shed for extra desserts, he rolled down the side of the hill after his boys. Liam and Mason thought it was uproariously funny, especially when he stood up, covered in snow.

"You're a snowman!" Liam giggled.

Mason smirked. "No, he's a *snowdad!*"

"Let's go again!" Both boys ran up the hill.

Seth stayed back, needing to sit for a minute because his head continued to spin. His thirties were no joke. He used to have enough energy for the bull runs in Spain but now a little hill winded him. "I'll watch you this time!" he cheered the others on.

While he regained his energy, he watched Noah shuffle around the perimeter of the lake. A path had been cleared and several older folks also walked along but Noah never acknowledged them. Even when Charles and Beverly waved to him, he slouched his shoulders and ducked his head, ignoring their greeting.

Seth frowned, unsure what more he could do to help Noah. He knew from his own experience that grief took a long time to process but he couldn't imagine how tough it was for his ten-year-old son. Noah's world revolved around his mom before her accident in January. He fell apart at the news and became a husk of his former self at her funeral. It wasn't a thing a young boy should ever go through. Now, he was still floundering, and it seemed that everything Seth did made him feel worse. Perhaps giving him space to work through his complicated emotions would lead to healing and a rift in their broken relationship.

When his mom joined Noah on the path, Seth's heart lightened a little. Although the boy barely glanced at his grandma, they walked side by side, neither of them speaking. The tension in the boy's shoulders lessened. Maybe this was the comfort Noah needed.

Chapter Five

MONDAY, DECEMBER 17

Seth had to admit, his mom's house was a nice place. It was too small for all of them, with only two bedrooms and a living room, but it was perfect for her. He wondered if she felt crowded by their visit. Probably the opposite was true. She grinned from ear to ear each time she looked at the boys.

The house was covered in Christmas and Hannukah decorations, the red and green mixed with the blue and white. It was a blast of primary colors but it worked. Evelyn had taken two polar opposite holidays and mixed them together in her own way, just like she celebrated most things in life. Seth loved that about his mom. Last night, after watching *The Grinch* with the boys, she pulled out a bowl of chocolate coins and taught them how to play dreidel. Liam loved spinning it as fast as he could. Mason's favorite part was the chocolate, hiding it in his fist until it melted out of the wrapper and no one else wanted it. He licked it off his fingers while Noah scowled. This morning, she had more planned for them, from crafts, games, and a surprise advent calendar.

Seth looked over Liam's shoulder at a sun catcher he was painting while Charlie Brown Christmas played on the TV.

"Aren't suncatchers a bit ironic for winter?" he laughed. "Not to mention seeing bright red light coming through Santa's suit. Awkward."

Evelyn grinned. "They're entertained! Besides, it gives them little souvenirs from their time at Grandma's."

Seth followed the wave of her hand pointing at Mason and Liam, occupied with their art projects. They were focused and content. Except Noah, who slumped in his seat, staring at his phone. A frown descended on Seth's face when he saw Noah's finished sun catcher painted in all black. The reindeer design wasn't visible, and no light would shine through the thick paint.

"I don't know what to do with him anymore," Seth confessed to his mom. "He's been in counseling and spoken with a grief therapist. I've given him the things he asked for, like his own phone, but it seems to make things worse. I'm at a loss."

"Everyone heals at their own rate, son."

"I know, but..." Seth ran a hand through his hair. "It's almost been a year. Look at Liam and Mason. They still have moments of grief, but they can join in with other kids and have fun."

"They have different personalities and ways to cope."

"I suppose. But what am I supposed to do with Noah in the meantime? He can't continue this belligerent attitude with everyone. He's burning every bridge."

"Hmm..." Evelyn raised an eyebrow. "Sounds like another young man I knew."

"That was different."

"Remember how long it took you to heal after your father died?"

Seth's shoulders drooped. "I get it. That's why I've been trying to give Noah that space to grow and figure things out."

"But he isn't taking his inheritance and traipsing across the world, is he?"

Seth sunk on the couch beside her. "I was going through stuff."

"Yes, and so is he. Give him time. Be there for him and support him in any way he needs. Sometimes he'll need space and other times he will need a hug." Evelyn pulled Seth into a hug of his own and held him longer than he was comfortable. "Someday your boys will grow too old for cuddles, so catch as many as you can now."

He chuckled. "I know that feeling."

When Evelyn let him go, she studied him with narrowed eyes. "What about you? You're worried about Noah, which you should, but I worry about my son too. How are you coping?"

The muscles in Seth's jaw tensed. "Surviving. Some days are better than others."

"You need a support system."

"I wish. But there's no time. With work and the boys' school and sports, we're constantly busy."

She laid a gentle hand on his restless leg. "It sounds to me like you're avoiding something yourself."

"Who else is going to take care of everything?" He refused to make a mental checklist of all the responsibilities he'd have to take back once they left his mom's house. At least here, he didn't have to think about what to eat for every meal, following bedtime routines, or keeping up with work. Maybe if the boys enjoyed grandma's house so much, he could leave them a little longer.

"Those can all wait. Your health is more important than all that."

He rolled his eyes. "I'm fine."

"Ha! You do realize I've known you for thirty-five years, right? You can't lie to your own mom."

"I mean, of course I'm going through the stages of grief. I've done all my research and know about it—"

"You might know all the answers up here..." Evelyn tapped the side of Seth's forehead. "...But what about here?" Her hand stopped above his heart, resting it on his chest.

His frown deepened. "That part...takes a lot longer."

The fire crackled and popped. The warmth radiated all around her. Mira was thankful for friends who helped. This evening's event was at Mayor Chavez' house and his wife, Tina, had already set up a booth with all the marshmallows, graham crackers, and chocolate anyone could want. Several crock pots of hot chocolate and cider steamed on a table on the patio.

Snow dusted the edges of the area but most of it had been cleared away so everyone could gather around the fire pit. Mira helped herself to another s'more before guests arrived. The fluffy marshmallow was melted to perfection but left her fingers sticky.

Beverly and Charles were the first, soon followed by Luella. The four of them talked pleasantly with Mayor Chavez and Tina about a problem at the senior center. Apparently, several of the bunnies in their petting zoo had escaped the barn. The elders who lived there enjoyed snuggling the sweet fluffers, helping with emotional needs as well. But the three bunnies were now running amok...not outside where the cold and occasional hawk could pick them off, but *inside* the senior center and through the retirement apartments connected to the main building. No one knew how the bunnies were finding their way around so quickly, but snacks were missing and little *not-chocolate* balls were left behind.

Charles found the entire situation uproariously funny. "What's the matter? They're living life to the fullest!"

Luella huffed. "They're getting into everything. My friend Doris said she was working on a quilt for months and when she finally completed it and laid it out on her bed...she found holes and chew marks all over it!"

Beverly, an avid quilter, gasped but Charles shrugged. "Sounds like it's a breathable fabric now."

Mira had to hide her laugh. She'd visited the senior center several times and knew exactly which bunnies they were talking about. One was speckled in browns and blacks across its white coat, another was honey brown with long, perky ears, but the most sassy bunny was all black with lop ears and had a notorious sweet tooth. She had loved petting their silky fur and wished she could take one home with her.

Mayor Chavez promised to find a solution that was beneficial to everyone and safe for the bunnies as more people arrived. Mira walked around, trying to make time to speak to everyone but got caught reminiscing with two of the women she'd grown up going to school with, Elizabeth and Carly.

Elizabeth pushed back her dark brown hair and adjusted her glasses, showing off her ugly Christmas sweater. It was bright red and neon green, resonating with the clash of colors in the 90s. The knit pattern displayed an open book with the words *"What about second breakfast?"* inked across. "I'm so glad we've moved past this style. I feel like a gleaming billboard."

Carly laughed, "Maybe that's better than the grunge look. Remember that?" Her sweater was all-black with red and green cat silhouettes chasing each other around the hem. She showed them the back where her students demanded she add a jingle bell tail.

Mira glanced down at her own sweater. It'd been difficult to find something that was an ugly Christmas sweater *and* from the 1990s. Her mother had been like her, preferring to dress in fashions that were decades old. She finally settled on a gold and silver striped turtleneck with high waist jeans and a denim jacket. Iron-on patches of reindeer decorated the shoulders and sleeves of the jacket, complete with bedazzled sparkles and puffy paint words "Watch out for the rain, dear."

Tina giggled when she saw it. "Cute and punny."

They helped themselves to hot chocolate and stood around the fire. "What were your favorite things from our childhood?" Mira asked the others. She felt like she'd missed out in a lot of generational connections since she'd always been focused on history instead of the present. But it only really mattered when she tried to converse with people her own age. Usually, it felt stilted and awkward with Mira's mind playing catch up to what everyone else viewed as normal.

Elizabeth shared about the pop music she listened to on repeat from her Walkman and even included a quick running man dance she performed in a school talent show. Carly talked about the TV shows she watched with her mother. Their favorites were Magic School Bus, Full House, and Xena.

Jesse and Seth joined them, the former adding a hysterical but painful story of the game Red Rover. "And that's how I broke my arm," Jesse finished.

The others weren't sure if they should laugh at his comedic telling or wince at the melodramatic ending. "Must've been *rad*!" Seth chuckled, "Kids had to be tougher back then."

Carly shook her head. "I think we know more now about the effects games like that had on growing children's physical and emotional well-being, and how much damage it can cause."

"Nah," Elizabeth shrugged. "I think there are too many lawyers and helicopter parents now."

"Maybe it's a bit of both," Seth said. "I know my three boys are as different as brothers could be. One would love Red Rover, another would rather play video games, and the youngest would cry or break a bone like Jesse here. As the adults, we should help kids figure out what they need, individually." The others shrugged, finding a compromise they could all agree on.

His glance settled on Mira as she contemplated the insight of his advice. In the rare times she worked as a substitute teacher at the local elementary school, she'd considered this, how everyone learned and achieved things differently. They only needed someone willing and able to present knowledge in the best way they could understand. That's what stood out between a good teacher and a great one.

Tina tapped Mira's shoulder. "Are you ready to share the historical inspiration for tonight's event?"

She nodded and the other woman quieted the crowd with a clap of her hands.

Everyone turned toward Mira. She felt awkward in the center of the circle, stared at from every angle. She wanted to step back into the shadows, especially for today's event. Talking with her peers exposed how little she knew about recent history and how much she'd missed growing up. Regardless, she'd have to speak up anyway. She started with a song, her voice shaky until she settled back into speech.

"All I want for Christmas is...the World Wide Web! Christmas Day in 1990 marks a very special occasion as the first test run of the internet." The snap of the fire transformed to the crackle of a dial-up modem in her imagination.

Mira was sitting in an uncomfortable chair at CERN, watching the computer's black screen where green binary text flickered in lines. It zipped away for a moment and a hesitant worry gnawed in her chest, but her mind remained logical. Every pathway, hypertext, and linked information had been checked multiple times in the past two years. It would connect people automatically, despite distance and regardless of time. She would be able to communicate and share ideas immediately with the other team members on the network, sharing multiple documents and information. It would revolutionize the way they operated.

"It started as quiet research on computers of ones and zeros in dotted-decimal notation to keep track of research through an open network by Tim Berners-Lee and became the first online message board."

The black screen blinked back, and letters fell into place. The green script read: World Wide Web. Behind her, the rest of the team cheered. She leaned back with a sigh of success. The others shook hands and congratulated each other. She finally stood, the stress of the past two years falling from her mind, to join in the celebration. Mira looked up toward the hand on her shoulder and didn't flinch at Seth's smile. He wore a white dress shirt with the top buttons undone like he'd been working late, and his hair was a bit rumpled but a wide smile brightened his face.

The real Seth anchored her back into reality. This time, his expression matched the one in her daydream.

Mira was always confused when she settled back in the real world, her thoughts still grasping for some historical threads instead. But this time she floated back to Mayor Chavez' backyard without a hiccup.

This decade had been the most difficult for her to research. There were a few books about it but she couldn't lose herself in the research like she normally did until she logged in to the library computer. That's where all the facts and fads presented themselves through short videos, pictures, and songs. She'd gone down an endless rabbit hole of research, which she spouted off now. "Many of us can't function without the internet! It helped me find other cultural influences from the 90s: from favorite music like Mariah Carey's *All I Want for Christmas*, financial investments of Beanie Babies, and movie classics like *Home Alone* and *Die Hard.*"

At the last movie, the crowd laughed genuinely. It sparked a strange feeling in Mira. She'd finally said something right, connecting with the group, even though it was over a reference she found online but didn't understand. Her smile came easier, and, for the first time, she didn't feel completely separate from the group.

With each mention, those her age and older in the audience laughed or shared stories. Before she lost their attention, she added the thought-provoking challenge. This was her mother's favorite part of the festival. She would say: *The season is a time of reflecting and correcting any missteps throughout the year so we can start the next one fresh and ready.* Mira drew in a deep breath. "It surprises us when things in our life move from nostalgic to historic, but it offers us the opportunity to share our personal experiences and what we've lived through. We can provide our knowledge and stories with younger generations. So, tonight while we enjoy s'mores and cider, let's unplug from technology and share our history with someone. Open up to what you've faced and conquered, what brings you joy and comfort, but most of all, the lessons you've learned along the way."

Charles shouted out, "Beanie Babies are *not* a financial investment!" Those gathered around him chuckled but Beverly frowned.

"I didn't spend *that* much." More laughter followed. "But if anyone is interested, I have some rare ones I'm willing to auction off." She winked at Mira who was thankful to no longer be the center of attention.

Mira slipped back to the group where Carly, Elizabeth, and Jesse shared their favorite memories from childhood. Seth met her gaze with a raised eyebrow. "I'm glad you consider *Die Hard* a Christmas movie."

Mira shifted nervously. "I have to confess; I've never seen it."

"What?" he asked, shocked. "It's a classic!"

Jesse agreed. "I watch it every year."

"And while he's watching those movies, I sit in bed with popcorn and watch real Christmas movies, like the ones on the Hallmark channel," Elizabeth said.

The others laughed. Mira listened to their exchange although she didn't know half of the titles they rattled off. She didn't offer her traditional favorites because most were filmed in black and white and were around seventy years old. She considered retreating to spend time with friends she was more familiar with and who she could connect to. Beverly would probably enjoy talking about *It's a Wonderful Life* or how dreamy Gregory Peck was.

Before she could step away though, the conversation turned to books and snagged Mira's attention again. Jesse shared how he had his students read a Christmas classic every year during their two-week break from school. This was a familiar subject to Mira.

"Which ones?" she asked.

"I change it up every year to keep them on their toes. I've done *A Christmas Story, The Nutcracker*—"

"The ballet?" Carly asked.

Jesse grinned like an English professor. "The book is better." They all laughed. "Anyone know what book inspired *It's a Wonderful Life?*"

"*The Greatest Gift.*" Mira answered in a heartbeat.

"Yup!"

Elizabeth rolled her eyes. "Of course, Mira would be the first to know that."

"Have you ever assigned Agatha Christie's Christmas mystery?" Seth asked.

"No, I should read that." Jesse looked thoughtful then added, "But one year I assigned *How the Grinch Stole Christmas*. They loved that one...although I still had some students watch the movie instead."

"We were given an assignment tonight," Carly stated, always the teacher. "What is it we're supposed to talk about, Mira?"

"Stories," Elizabeth answered for her. "*Our* stories."

"But we all know each other already. We grew up together," Carly said.

Jesse shook his head. "Except Seth." They all turned to look at him. "What brought you to Cedar Springs?"

Seth shuffled awkwardly under everyone's gaze before he answered. "I brought my boys to have Christmas with my mom. It's nice to get out of the big city once in a while."

"But what's your *story*?" Elizabeth goaded.

"Not much to tell. I went to college, didn't enjoy it so I worked and saved money to travel. One time I got stuck overseas and had to clean toilets to make enough to get back." He chuckled along with them.

"What countries did you visit?" Mira's eyes lit up at the thought of a world outside of Cedar Springs, and all the places she read about in her books.

He met her gaze. "I sprained my leg climbing Machu Picchu in Peru, had my passport stolen while exploring the Colosseum in Italy, and sadly, did not meet Indiana Jones in Petra, Jordan."

Mira's mind spun with the history of each location. She'd read about those places and her mind pinged with different facts: Petra was one of the oldest cities in the world, Emperor Vespasian had the Colosseum built in the heart of the Roman Empire, and Machu Picchu meant "Old Mountain" in Quecha...That's how Seth knew the answer while playing *Facts in Five*!

Mira glanced back at Seth and studied him with more interest. While she recognized these places from books, he'd seen them in person, reached out and touched age-old stones, breathed the air rich with the past. What stories could he share with her?

"Not much to tell," Jesse snorted in sarcasm. "You're full of stories! And which country did you end up cleaning toilets?"

Seth laughed. "That was in England. I explored different places each day between jobs."

Mira blurted, "Did you visit Westminster Abbey?" She could see it as if she'd been there herself. She had countless dreams of exploring the hallways, staring at the paintings, and hearing the stories of those who were laid to rest there.

Seth's grin widened. "Many times. If walls could speak..."

"What was your favorite part?" Her heart yearned with long-forgotten dreams.

"I couldn't pick just one." He described everything in detail and Mira soaked it all up. It reignited the spark inside her.

The others moved on to a new conversation, leaving Seth and Mira to gush over World Heritage Sites and the people who'd walked within those walls. From the ten bells hanging in the north-west tower, the fifteen kings and queens buried within The Lady Chapel, and a nearly one thousand-year-old door in the Chapter House. Then they spoke of the talent that had crossed the threshold or had a memorial at the Abbey, people Mira could never grow tired talking about.

"That sounds like a dream come true." She couldn't help but wish her life would change and she could explore the world.

"A dream?" Another voice interrupted their conversation. Mira turned to find Luella standing beside them, with a tray of chocolates, marshmallows, and s'mores. "I'm passing around some desserts, but I see you two are already having a sweet time."

Mira's mind was still wrapped up in their discussion about the stained glass and oil paintings of Westminster Abbey. She frowned, unsure what Luella meant. But the red filling Seth's face and Luella's suggestively lifting eyebrow dropped Mira back to the present. She blushed and stuttered, at a loss for words.

Seth saved her from more embarrassment by nodding to both women. "I'm sorry, but I need to check on my sons."

Luella clucked her tongue when he left, and she faced Mira. "I hope I didn't interrupt an important conversation." Luella stared unblinking, her expression boring into the younger woman's face. Mira felt as if she was being picked apart, her mind and emotions dissected for juicy gossip later. Her pale blue eyes were like lasers, investigating every blink and fidgeting movement.

Mira wasn't one to argue, especially with her elders, but her tone was snappy. "We were talking about dead people."

Luella's eyes grew wide.

Mira hadn't meant to scare the older woman or even to be rude, but the opportunity presented itself as perfectly as a toasted marshmallow. She rattled off names: "George Eliot, Jenny Lind, Geoffrey Chaucer, John Dryden, Margaret Beaufort, Charles Dickens, Aphra Behn, and Winston Churchill."

Luella's expression grew more confused.

"Ah, history." Beverly noticed the exchange and joined them. "It has so many...interesting stories!"

"That's one way to put it." Luella huffed and stomped away.

Beverly turned to Mira with a question in her eyes. "What was that about?"

Mira shook her head, embarrassed by Luella's teasing and her own reaction. "Nothing."

"It didn't seem like nothing—"

Before Beverly could question Mira more, the young woman ducked away with an excuse. "I should check with Tina to make sure everything is going smoothly." She made her escape and slowed her steps when she neared the open door into the mayor's house. Mira needed a moment alone to collect her thoughts and breathe in the silence.

She stepped through the doorway and into the kitchen where several candles flickered on the island. Christmas lights gleamed from garlands and the tree in the living room while quiet carols played from a hidden speaker. It both relaxed Mira and set her on edge. She loved the decorations, music, and all the holiday cheer. It was her favorite time of year.

But she couldn't bring herself to embrace the season or accept the joy without grief digging its claws deeper into her heart. The dancing lights only lit up the corners she couldn't bear to face, the songs tugged emotions she no longer could draw up, the cheery laughter reminded her of the one person she loved, and had lost.

Each smile made her feel guilty and tonight, for just a moment, she forgot to cling to her mourning. She'd blinked away the grasping grief in a rare moment of hope. She let her mother's memory slip away temporarily and that scared her more than anything. How could she be happy when her mother was gone?

⟫⟫⟫⟶ ⟵⟪⟪⟪

Seth was thankful for an excuse to escape that infernal woman and her rude questions. Who was she to stick her nose into a private conversation he was enjoying with Mira? He paced outside the mayor's yard and paused in front of the school playground. Most of the kids had taken off after finishing up their s'mores and were now playing on the jungle gym and in the field. Because it was dark, it was difficult for him to pick out his children in the mass of dark shadows squealing and running around. He assumed they were having fun with their new friends.

Through the past several events, both Mason and Liam connected with the other children and had already been accepted into a gang of boys. They ran around building snow forts, reenacting battles, and using up all their energy. Seth was thankful for these newfound connections they'd made. He already noticed the difference in his son's attitudes. They smiled and laughed more.

Well, all except Noah. He was still closed off to everyone, including Seth. Maybe tonight he'd play with the others.

Seth kicked at a clod of snow and watched it crumble apart. Instead of letting gloomy thoughts overtake him, though, he surprised himself by smiling. Just like his boys, he was connecting with people in this small town, too. Jesse had some hilarious stories and the two women, Elizabeth and Carly, held interesting conversations. He enjoyed talking with all of them. But it was Mira who drew his attention.

Her amber eyes had sparked with curiosity as he shared his stories. She even bounced on her feet, eager to hop a plane and see the monuments herself. Something about her, the desire to learn more and experience history, drew him closer. He'd been lost in those memories and excited to share them with her. It revived a part of him that had been dormant for too many years. After his travels, he settled down and had to focus on his work, providing for his family, and pushing aside his own life goals.

A yelp and cry snatched his attention back to those needs. Mason ran up to him, tears and blood streaming down his face. Seth caught him and inspected him. "What happened?"

The sobbing boy answered incoherently.

Studying him revealed the blood came from his nose, otherwise he wasn't majorly hurt. Seth put his arm around the boy's shoulder and led him back toward the mayor's house. Hopefully there was a first aid kit inside to help him clean up this mess.

⚜⚜⚜ ⚜⚜⚜

Mira covered her face with her hands and let out a long, ragged breath when she sank into one of the stools beside the kitchen island. It had surprised her how much she enjoyed Seth's company and hearing about his travels. She didn't expect to find camaraderie with the stranger who was responsible for the broken teapot...until Luella ruined it all. It was a welcome relief to dream of far-off places again. She wished to hear more about his adventures, but how could she face him again after Luella's inappropriate suggestions? Romance hadn't even been on Mira's mind.

"Is there anyone inside?" As if he materialized from her thoughts, Seth hurried into the kitchen.

Mira fought back the color rising in her cheeks.

"Oh, Mira! Could you please help us?"

That's when Mira saw Seth was leading Mason toward the sink. A bright streak of red blood smudged across the boy's face. She leapt into action.

"Oh no! What happened?" She soaked some paper towels and placed them in Mason's hand, helping the boy hold them to his nose. He mumbled something but Mira couldn't understand.

Seth shrugged. "All I could figure out was they were playing, and he fell."

"No!" Mason pulled the paper towels from his face. "Noah threw a football, and it hit me in the face!"

Seth kneeled beside his son with a hand around his shoulder. "Well..." His worried expression broke into a teasing grin. "Why didn't you catch it?"

Mason stuck his tongue out with a giggle. "Cause it was dark. Obviously."

Mira stared at the exchange, confused. Seth noticed and explained, "He can cry about it, or I can make him laugh."

"Oh."

She watched Seth lead Mason to the island counter and help him up on a stool. "Let's stay here for several minutes until you're feeling better, okay, buddy?"

Mason nodded.

"Or..." Mira stepped closer. "I can share what people have done throughout history to help stop nosebleeds." Both man and boy quirked their heads, confused or interested. Mira couldn't tell which, but she forged ahead. "We could find some moss and stuff it in your nose."

Mason's eyes grew wide.

Mira laughed, "That's what they did in the Middle Ages. Or we can do what the Victorians did."

"What was that?" Mason grew fascinated, he forgot to worry about his bloody nose. He held the paper towels next to his chin and leaned forward. The bleeding had stopped.

"They inflated a balloon!"

"Up their nose?"

"Yes!" Mira nodded. "There are other ancient Egyptian and Chinese methods, too. Creating a concoction of plants and herbs to put in your nose, making other parts of your body cold, or soaking your feet in warm water."

"How would putting my feet in water stop my nose from bleeding?"

"Not sure, I'm not a scientist." She shrugged. "Maybe it's just a distraction."

Mason reached up and felt his nose and then glanced back at both adults. "Well, I'm glad you didn't blow up a balloon in my nose." He wiped the rest of the blood from his face and ran back out to play.

"How do you do that?" Seth asked.

Mira glanced up in confusion. "What?"

"Pull the most random ancient facts and inject them into a normal conversation." He shook his head. "In just a couple minutes, you calmed a crying boy *and* taught him history."

A thoughtful look crossed her face when they walked outside. The firepit crackled and groups of people laughed around it. The glow lit everything in shades of red, orange, and yellow. Embers danced like fireflies.

"I know you said life got in the way of you becoming a history teacher, but you have a gift. It'd be tragic if you couldn't share it."

"I went to university..." All the nostalgia of the night dug up things she'd buried in her past, and now they were rising to the surface. She wasn't sure why she was sharing these treasured secrets with a stranger. But, she supposed, Seth wasn't a stranger anymore. She smiled past the heartbreak of her personal story. "I left before graduating."

"Why?" At some point in her musings, they'd stopped walking and now she faced Seth. He studied her face intently, making her stomach flop awkwardly. She turned away.

"I was needed back at home," she answered, staring at the fire pit. Smoke rose in thin wisps, the remains of disintegrated dreams. The dulled pain of failure grew sharp again and dredged up memories of funerals and loneliness. She fought the lump in her throat.

"As a wise person said yesterday, *win your victory* and share what you've faced and conquered." Seth met her glance as he quoted from her own speech. "You have an incredible talent for bringing history alive. You should use it. Watching Mason's face when you talked to him was a wonderful moment. He learned something he'll never forget."

Instead of walking toward the fire pit and the other guests, they strolled around the perimeter. The glow didn't quite reach them. They were two faceless shadows unearthing words they thought were already laid to rest. Mira wasn't sure which one of them directed their steps and kept them from engaging with the others, but it was healing in its own way.

Seth continued, "This past year has been difficult on my boys. Their mom was in a fatal accident and passed away. It's been a challenge as a single parent and taking care of every little thing. They miss her and I can't replace what she was. No one can.

"But I notice when they perk up around someone they like, their smiles come easier and their laughs are freer. You've done that for Liam and Mason and that's the best Christmas gift a dad could ever hope for. Thank you."

He met her gaze and held it. A burst of firelight danced across his face and brightened his eyes, catching a gleam rimmed around the edges. Mira found she couldn't turn away from him again. Even if she could, she wasn't sure she wanted to.

CHAPTER SIX

TUESDAY, DECEMBER 18

Seth was out for another morning jog. This time he circled the town several times before stopping at Betty's Bakery for a donut and hot chocolate. He found a seat by a window that overlooked the park, then sat to read a local newspaper.

The high school students published a paper every month and raised support for their activities by selling it to community businesses. This month's page presented Mira's 12 Days to Christmas festival, listing each day and where the event was held, what items were being collected for charity, and how the community could contribute. Everything was decorated in clipart of traditional Christmas favorites and littered with testimonials of business owners.

The 12 Days to Christmas festival is my favorite time of year! It reminds me of the true spirit of the season! —Danielle Chen, Mercantile

We absolutely love the community supporting us through the 12 Days to Christmas! Our senior center is looking forward to the caroling. —Shawna Holt, Senior Center Director

The heart of our small town is in these wonderful events led by Mira Turner. We are so thankful! —Evelyn Reiner, local resident

Seth smiled on seeing his mom's recommendation. The past several days, he'd watched to see how she was connecting and settling in her new life. After his dad passed away, she'd struggled finding a place she fit in. But Cedar Springs seemed perfect for her. She had a group of friends she would spend her days with and quickly plugged herself in with a crafting club. Early retirement looked good on her. He appreciated seeing the joy she had for life again.

As he stared through the window and considered the differences of small town living versus the big city life he'd been trapped in, a hand pulled out the chair across from him. Charles smiled as he sat down.

"How are you doing, Seth?"

He nodded while hurrying to swallow the last bite of the donut he had stuffed into his mouth. "Good," he coughed.

"Evelyn has bragged many times to Beverly about her oldest son. She was especially excited when she heard you were coming down for Christmas."

Seth grinned. He was sure his mom had run everywhere in town and told anyone who would listen. That's how she was, always feeling everything with strong emotions that she had to share with others. Usually, it was a wonderful moment seeing his mom light up with happiness or pride for him or his brother's and sisters' accomplishments but the past year meant she had carried the heavy burden alongside him. "She's a great mom," he acknowledged.

"And your boys have a great dad." Charles smiled when a box of a dozen donuts was set in front of him. He thanked the barista and looked back at Seth. "I'll eat only one of these. The rest are for you to take back to your boys."

Seth balked. "I couldn't—"

"Well, that'd be a shame waste of donuts, wouldn't it?" He pointed to two women talking at the counter. Seth recognized one as the rude woman who interrupted his conversation with Mira yesterday, but the other was Beverly. "My wife wouldn't be too happy if she found out I bought all these for me to eat."

Seth had been worried about small town judgment and gossiping, not their overbearing generosity. He dipped his head. "Thank you. My boys will be thrilled." He didn't add: *Then they will have an outburst of energy and I'll have to come up with something to keep them busy so they don't fight.*

"Ah, you're reading the Cedar Springs Tabloids." Charles chuckled, "Now you'll know all our secrets."

Seth raised an eyebrow. "Oh?"

He leaned back in his chair and sipped his coffee. "Don't you know small towns have So. Many. Secrets."

"Such as?"

"See the other woman talking to my wife? That's Luella. Rumors are that the town matchmaker might secure her own engagement. Maybe a ring by spring." Charles pointed out the window to a young couple walking hand in hand. "They haven't announced anything yet, but they're expecting their first child." His fingers tapped on the pages in front of Seth. "And the best secret of all, is the town is expecting a Christmas surprise for the 12 Days Festival."

Seth glanced up from the event list. "A surprise?"

Charles shrugged. "The rumor is not even Mira knows."

"But you do?"

Charles pointed to his bald forehead with a smirk. "I know everything that happens in Cedar Springs. It's the benefit of living here for so long."

"Okay, so..." Seth leaned in, testing the older man. "Tell me about my mom. What do people think about her?"

"Evelyn? Ah, well, according to my wife, she's a 'peach'."

Seth laughed.

"She's connected well with the ladies in town. We're glad she moved here," Charles continued. "Why? I hope you don't plan on convincing her to move."

"No," Seth shook his head, satisfied. "I wanted to make sure she felt at home."

"Any other questions?"

"About this 12 Days Festival..." Seth folded the newspaper. "Is it some kind of small town tradition?"

"It's become that, I suppose. About five years ago, Mira and her mother, Michelle, offered to help with the town's

Christmas party. In the past, it was just a gathering in the town park for cookies and caroling but they weren't content with that." Charles turned his attention out the window and stared at the cloudy morning sky.

It reminded Seth he'd need to leave soon since his boys would be waking up and demanding breakfast. They'd love the donuts he was bringing back. But he wanted to hear what Charles was sharing.

"Mira actually came up with the idea of having events for twelve days, after the song popularized by Bing Crosby and The Andrews Sisters."

"But why before Christmas instead of after? Like the tradition," Seth asked.

"You mean December 25th to January 6th? Mira wanted it to be a countdown for Christmas. Also, many of the events aren't just about having a grand ol' time. Each one has a purpose and helps provide for others' needs."

"How so?"

"Didn't you notice the sleigh collecting canned food and toys? The entire goal is to draw attention away from ourselves and focus on others. After all, that's the beauty of the season, giving and sharing with our neighbors.

"The first year Mira set up the festival, it was themed after the 12 Days of Christmas song. Every day, the community provided gifts for local non-profits, underprivileged families, and Operation Christmas Child. Each year since, Mira has chosen a new charity to support. That's my favorite part of these gatherings."

Seth nodded. "That sounds wonderful. It really brings together the community in a great way and allows people to get to know each other better."

"That it does. That it does." A small smile reached Charles' lips as he took another sip from his coffee and glanced out the window. The clouds had parted to let the cool rays of sunrise shine over the town. It lifted Seth's spirits. He thanked Charles for the donuts again and walked back to his mom's house.

He was convinced this was the best place for his mom to live. But, he wondered, what would it be like for children?

⋙⋙⋙ ⋘⋘⋘

Mira rushed to answer the knock at her door and Beverly smiled when she opened it. "We thought we'd meet you here and all walk to the town center together."

"Thank you!" Mira hurried to put on her long slim cloak with the white fur trim and tied a ruffled burgundy bonnet beneath her chin. "I was afraid I was going to run late but I finally found the song books!" She held up a stack of old music books. "I'm almost ready..."

As she dug through her shoe closet to find leather ankle boots, Beverly stepped inside. "Oh no!" Her eyes settled on the silver tray, still holding the shattered teapot in the center of Mira's kitchen table. It had split into five big chunks. It was possible to reassemble but it probably wouldn't hold water anymore. "What happened?"

Mira's smile fell. "An accident," she mumbled. Before her eyes could fill with tears again, she turned back to pulling on her boots and winter gloves. "After all this is over, I'll try to fix it."

"Oh, Mira, I'm so sorry. I know how much this teapot meant to you." Beverly hugged the younger woman, and they stepped outside to meet Charles.

"Did you tell her yet?" he asked.

Beverly shook her head as Mira glanced between them confused. "Tell me what?"

The older woman hooked her arms between them and began walking down the sidewalk. A cold gust of wind brushed several snowflakes past them while Beverly answered. "You have so much to do and think about, dear. Charles had the excellent idea of us helping out."

"You can let us do the talking and splitting people into groups for caroling...before your speech of course," Charles said. "Beverly is great at knowing which voices blend best—she was a choir director, you know!"

Mira breathed a sigh of relief. "That would be so helpful! Thank you!"

The town center was already bustling with a small crowd when they arrived. Families gathered in circles and talked about holiday plans, boys and girls whispered what gifts they hoped to receive, and older folks wished their grown children would surprise them with a visit. The low muttering held hopes and dreams with a sparkle of Christmas magic. Some people were dressed in traditional caroling cloaks matching Mira, but most were bundled up in their winter gear.

Beverly quickly got to work, organizing and rearranging. Mira took the moment to read over the note in her hand. She looked over the words several times but felt a slight panic. After Seth's compliment the other night, she felt more pressure to bring history to life, but she wasn't sure how to do that tonight. The words on her paper weren't in English and she didn't know German well enough to sing Silent Night in the original language.

She glanced back at the waiting crowd. Beverly was nearly done gathering them in groups and the swell of conversation hushed. They were expecting her. She walked up the steps in front of the gazebo. Lights twinkled, brightening the falling snow, and giving the night an ethereal quality. It settled calmly over her heart, and she began.

"I was going to start tonight by singing Silent Night in German...but I've done that already."

The crowd chuckled and Mira felt more confident. She sensed the loss of her mother the most during these moments, but she could distract herself with history. Mostly, though, she was connecting with others and that strengthened her.

"So instead, we'll begin our festival this evening in the same way as a young Austrian priest, Joseph Mohr." The snow fell softly around her, and she let it carry her away to a small town on the other side of the world.

Her steps crunched through the snow, but it didn't settle her heart and calm her nerves. It heaped more worries on her mind.

"The past several years had been disastrous, from the Napoleonic Wars to climate change ruining the harvest, and ultimately a flooded church resulting in a damaged organ. The hours before he was required to lead a Christmas Eve service, Joseph Mohr was struggling and took a quiet walk in the soft falling snow."

Mira knew the year had been difficult for more than her. Many of her friends were struggling to survive. Although all these anxious thoughts plagued her mind, she wanted to encourage others and bring them hope for the season. But she had no idea how. Her steps continued leading her around the cold and silent town.

"During that moment of quiet reflection, a song was born."

Mira's voice hummed softly, looking up at the starry sky, cold settling around her without a sound. Silent night. The town would be coming to church to share in God's love. Holy night. Finally, after long years of war, droughts and famine...all is calm. The stars glimmered in the sky above her, bringing hope and faith in the future...all is bright.

"He penned the lyrics to Silent Night and his friend, Franz Gruber, wrote the music to be played on a guitar."

Mira returned to the church and stood in front of people she had suffered alongside with. Although she didn't recognize any of them, she felt the kinship. Opening her heart, she sang these words with them. A guitar from the side accompanied, adding a deeper level to the music that enveloped her. Mira glanced over to see Seth in the robes of a choir director. A smile crossed her face as their voices joined together, entwined and rising above the others.

"The people of Oberndorf were the first to hear this tune before it was carried across the continent and around the world by traveling singers where it has become a yearly tradition." Mira hesitated. White powder drifted softly around them, swallowing the moment with a hush. She'd lost herself in her daydream and had to shake distracted thoughts loose. "With that same mindset, let us follow Mohr's example and listen to the falling snow while we let go of the pain this past year has brought us. Let it slip away so we can enjoy the peace of this night."

A calm settled over the people gathered around the gazebo where everyone, including children, took a moment of silence. Her year had been full of loss and pain. Sometimes it overwhelmed her at the most random moment. Like now, as she stood on the gazebo steps alone, staring at the empty spot her mother had filled in previous years.

Mira slid back into the shadows and waited for the stillness to reach her. She wanted it to take away the worries gnawing at the back of her mind, the uncomfortable feeling of loneliness, and the sorrow that weighed heavier on her heart each day Christmas moved nearer. The heavy silence of her empty apartment, the missing laughs that used to fill her cozy home. Several minutes went by drawing out those beautiful and painful memories in Mira's thoughts. A hushed sky, burdened with the grief of many others, hung over her head.

The stillness broke when Beverly's voice lifted in song, carrying the words over the crowd. "All is calm, all is bright." Others joined in until everyone sang together. Mira didn't feel so alone with the voices of so many enveloping around her. It softened the ache inside.

Slowly groups stepped away, following the paths highlighted on the cover of their music books. Each public area and neighborhood in Cedar Springs would have carolers tonight, sharing in the spirit wherever they were.

As they dispersed, Mira rejoined Charles and Beverly. "Where are we singing tonight?" she asked, fighting back the tremble in her voice. She blinked and tried to discard the gloom that had settled over her. It was easier when she was with Beverly because the older woman understood the burden of grief and responsibility.

"We'll sing at the senior center first, dear." The older woman took her hand as they walked down the sidewalk with an encouraging smile. "Your speech was wonderful."

Charles dabbed at his eye. "Very moving."

"The magic of Christmas must be alive tonight. It even kept Charles quiet for several minutes." Beverly nudged her husband with her elbow and placed a kiss on his cheek.

He smirked back with a glance at both women. "Men are allowed to have feelings."

"Of course they are!" Beverly agreed. "I just find it amusing that an old Christmas story moves you more than beating cancer." She turned to fill in Mira on the story. "After finishing his treatment and meeting with his doctor, do you know what he told me?"

Mira shook her head. She knew the past several years had been difficult for Charles and Beverly, too.

"Instead of sharing the good news, he simply told me I'd be stuck with him for several more years. *How many years?* I asked, fearing the worst. And this old turtle had the nerve to say, *As long as the good Lord wishes.* Did he tell me his cancer was gone? Did he say that the doctor gave him a clean bill of health? Not at all!"

Charles took Beverly's hand in his with a sly smile. "Are you regretting it now?"

"I could never!" She rested her head on his shoulder.

Mira smiled at their exchange until they were all distracted by the slamming doors of a car. Four figures ran toward them from the parking lot. "I'm sorry. Are we late?" Seth asked when he joined.

"That depends," Charles chuckled. "If you're here for the tree lighting, you're several days early. If it's for the caroling, you almost missed it."

Liam hurried beside Mira and took her hand while the other two boys hung behind their dad.

Beverly smiled at the newcomers. "You may join our group."

"We might see some wild bunnies in their natural habitat," Charles joked.

Liam bounced with excitement when they entered through the main doors of the senior center. Christmas trees strained under the weight of too many ornaments and a dazzling amount of tinsel gleamed beside them as they met the administrator, Shawna. She directed them to the main living area where nearly thirty people waited for them.

"What's your favorite song?" Mira asked Liam.

"The one from Charlie Brown Christmas!"

Mira glanced at her music book. Before she could tell him, she didn't have that song, Seth joined them and held out his phone. The lyrics brightened up the screen.

Charles ruffled Liam's hair. "Of course, we know that one! You know I was alive when that came out?"

Liam's eyes grew wide. "You're old!"

"You have no idea," Charles laughed.

Beverly gave them the first chord and they all began singing.

The next song was an old carol Mira had printed in her book. She turned to the right page, thinking of the last time she sang carols and used this book with her mother. They stood in this same place, arms hooked at the elbows, and singing despite her mother's weakness. She'd demanded to join in despite that cold night.

Mira sucked in a tight breath and looked up. Elderly faces, wrinkled with stories and lives well-lived, stared back. Everyone in this room knew about loss on an intimate level. The eyes watching her understood the weight of tears. In this one place, she knew she belonged. She connected deeply.

Mira's voice rang out, "O holy night!"

Seth stood behind her, sharing the book over her shoulder. His voice was a low and rich bass, hitting the notes clearly and following the rhythm. Mira focused on the words, joining in with a matching harmony in her alto voice. Beverly rose over it all with a clear soprano and Charles hung on in a balanced tenor. Their four voices blended perfectly together as they continued singing other carols. The boys joined in occasionally with the songs they knew or for the choruses of familiar lyrics. The residents watched with glee. Some joined in on the singing. One spritely older man, stood up with the help of his walker, and danced a little jig.

After half an hour of singing, they set down the music books and greeted the senior residents in the room. Many had joined in with the music, the familiar tunes lighting up their faces with recognition and reminiscence. A couple even had tears in their eyes.

"It was beautiful," a woman patted Mira's hand. "Thank you for singing and bringing those fine young men along." She pointed to Noah, Mason, and Liam. The youngest was examining the dentures an older man removed from his mouth to startle the boys. Mason and Liam thought it was uproariously funny. Noah kept the same pose he had the past several days, standing back with arms crossed and a sullen look on his face.

Another elderly woman agreed with the first. "It is so nice to see happy families together."

Mira spun back toward them while the two continued speaking.

"So handsome!"

"And such wonderful singing voices."

"You're doing a great job in raising them."

Mira's face burned bright red. "Oh, they're not—"

"And your husband is quite attractive. Reminds me of my George..."

"No, no," Mira stuttered. "I'm not—they're not—We're not married."

"What?" the old woman looked offended. "Well, young lady, why not?"

She wasn't sure how to answer or what to say as her mind reeled. Especially since Seth chose that moment to walk toward them. How would she explain the misunderstanding?

A flutter just beyond Seth snagged her attention. Two velvety ears poked out from under a table and the twitching nose of a bunny wiggled in her direction.

"Bunny!" she yelped and pointed at the fluffy blob darting under a table. The black bunny snatched the crumbs of a cookie that had fallen under a chair. At her shout, it turned toward her and lifted one ear, its nose and whiskers twitching.

Everyone turned to stare. One of the seniors yelled out, "The bunny can't have cookies!" and the chase began. Trying to save the bunny from a sugar high, chaos erupted. People rushed after it. Beverly laughed and Liam jumped on a chair, squealing. Mason slid across the linoleum, passing others who chased the bunny, and Charles took the lead.

As noise broke around the room, two more bunnies popped their heads out from under a tablecloth and wheelchair. The startled floofers sprinted out the door and down the hallway. Half of the crowd followed, some leaning on canes, others panting. The old man with the walker raced after. Mira stayed back with those who couldn't run, or wouldn't chase after a speedy rabbit.

Seth joined her and chuckled. "That was the best entertainment I've had in a long time."

"The singing or the rabbits?" she asked.

"Both."

They stood in awkward silence for several moments as Mira tried to forget what the old women assumed about them.

Seth cleared his throat. "The singing went well."

Mira nodded.

"You sing well."

"Um, thank you. So do you."

"I'm sorry we missed the first part. What history fact did you share?" he asked.

Mira glanced up and back down again. Seth's dark brown eyes were distracting. Especially with the elderly women's conversation still whispering in her mind no matter how hard she tried to push it away. She'd finally accepted him interrupting her dreams of living through history. In fact, she looked forward to finding where he'd be hiding in her imagination. But she wasn't ready to talk about either.

Maybe getting to know Seth better would answer some of the confusion in her mind. She could test him on how well he knew his history, if it was something he'd learned from his travels or if it was a passion of his. He seemed to be well-informed during their trivia game, but those were important facts, tied to wars and world events. Mira wondered how well he knew more obscure details, especially about Christmas. She smiled.

"You know a lot about history." She sat down in an empty chair and asked, "What do you think I would have spoken about before an evening of caroling?"

He grinned at the challenge, sitting beside her. "Well, it could be any number of things. There are so many Christmas carols, even earlier than the 16th century you could have chosen to focus on. The *12 Days of Christmas*, for example, but it refers to the days after Christmas up to January 6. Or it could have been about the oldest carols but those are still debated. Maybe it was about Charlie Brown, Liam's favorite song."

Mira smiled. "I'm impressed by your guesses but none of those are correct. Need a hint?"

"A hint!" Seth raised his eyebrows. "I'm offended you think I need the help. Watch," he pointed his finger between them. "My next guess will be the right one."

"I doubt it," she laughed.

"Fine then. Let's make a bet."

"I don't gamble."

"No, this will be a draw. Winner will buy the other hot chocolate later."

"Not coffee?" Mira asked.

"I don't like the stuff. Chocolate is always better."

"Okay," Mira said with a smile. "If you can guess what moment in all of history I chose for tonight, I'll get you a hot chocolate."

Seth grinned. "It's too easy. Tonight is about singing carols, so it's obviously a Christmas song. And, judging by the style of your cloak and winter bonnet, I'd place it roughly in the 17—no, 18 century."

Mira bit her lip. There was still so much history in those hundred years, so many Christmas songs.

The pause in Seth's musing lasted too long and she looked back at him. His smile grew wider. "With everyone out there, it's nice to enjoy how *silent* it is in here, wouldn't you say?"

She narrowed her eyes.

"Makes for a wonderful *night*." He grew confident as she pursed her lips. "Was it about Oberndorf and the beginning of *Silent Night*?"

"How did you know?" She swung the music book at him and it hit his chest. He pointed behind her. She spun around to see the wall behind them had been decorated for Christmas with silver tinsel garland. The cursive words spelled out *Silent Night*. They both laughed but it was short-lived.

"Is it over yet?" Noah entered the room and dropped onto a chair.

Seth frowned. "I talked with you about this before we left the house. Improve your attitude."

"I don't want to be here." The boy crossed his arms and glared back defiantly.

His dad huffed in frustration. "This isn't about you or what you want right now. We're joining in with the community. Besides, your grandma wanted you in town to make new friends."

"Not likely." He stomped from the room.

"I'm sorry about that," Seth apologized.

Despite the concern that settled on her forehead, Mira shrugged it off. "Don't worry. The holidays aren't everyone's favorite time of year."

"It's been the most difficult for him but that's no excuse for his behavior."

"Sometimes—" Mira began. She considered sharing her own struggles with Christmas this year. Her loss and grief shadowed all the regular traditions with loneliness. From the music book in her hand to the faces of people she recognized in the senior center, she thought about her mother, grandmother, and great-grandmother.

Her eyes trailed over to the struggling boy. Maybe Noah's way of mourning was different.

But she didn't have the opportunity to talk to Seth because Beverly returned to the room. "They finally caught the bunnies and will put them back in the barn. They'll make sure to give them a place to run and jump and hide, instead of those small cages they were in before."

Mira smiled.

Seth stood up beside her and asked, "Where to next?"

⁙⁙⁙

Mira had been hoping her group wouldn't end up here. But the hospital was large enough that it needed two to three caroling groups every year. Sliding doors gaped open as they walked in. Mira hadn't been back since...

Sterile air hit her lungs like breathing in bleach. It turned her stomach, trailing queasy tremors from her ribs down to her fingertips. The grip lodged in her throat as she sucked in another gulp. It stung the corners of her eyes. Her spirit sank and her feet slowed until she trailed behind the others.

She'd walked through these same doors when her mother's breathing became more difficult. They took tests, paced these halls, and waited for the worst news of their life. She avoided looking in the direction of the cancer ward. The place her mom entered alive. But left in a casket.

A small hand gripped hers, tearing her away from bleak thoughts. She glanced down at Liam.

"I don't like hospitals." The expression on his face mirrored hers.

She pulled to a stop and kneeled down, blinking back her own tears. "Me neither," Mira said. "But sometimes hospitals are good places." Her eyes trailed after Charles and Beverly. "Sometimes they catch the sickness before it spreads. Sometimes they can help people who have been hurt."

"But not all the time."

She wrapped him in a hug and held back her own tears. "No, not all the time."

As they followed the others and stopped occasionally to sing Christmas Carols to small groups of people, Mira couldn't get back in the spirit. A heavy cloud settled on her shoulders and dampened her mood. She watched Liam's face while he sang words he didn't feel, Mason's slouch as he stared at every beeping machine, and Noah who disappeared further within himself. His scowl deepened and his body grew tense. They were the wrong group to sing in this place.

Even Seth's demeanor changed. He didn't share jokes with Charles or pull his boys closer. At one point, after singing a particularly mournful rendition of *Joy to the World*, Mira couldn't even find him. She pointed it out to Charles who went off to look for Seth.

Mira sank into a chair across from the vending machines and pulled out some change from her pocket. Most people used debit or credit cards, but she preferred the feel of actual cash in her hand. It meant more when she made her purchases. She handed each boy a $5 bill and some of their energy returned while they debated which snack to buy.

Beverly sat beside Mira. "Back in my day, when dinosaurs roamed the earth, those treats were only several cents."

Mira attempted to laugh but the sound choked up her throat and came out a dry, wheezing sound. Beverly reached over and took the younger woman's hand in hers. "How are you holding up?"

She shrugged. It was easier than speaking out loud. All her emotions were trapped in her chest, feeling like she'd choke if she tried to make a sound.

"I can't imagine how difficult it is to come back here—"

"It's the first time," Mira stuttered.

"But your mother isn't here." Beverly squeezed her grip. "Her memory is alive in you and you honor her by living each day." Mira fought back the tears as the older woman continued, "There's a secret us *old folks* should probably share with younger generations. We know our time on earth is limited but we hope—truly believe—the thing that makes the most difference is what we impart to others. Charles and I can make lots of money, travel the world, and enjoy everything the earth has to offer. But none of those matter. What *does* make our lives meaningful, is the change we leave behind. I hope to influence others for good. It's essential through every relationship I am a part of. This is how I can help you."

"Even if we're not family?"

Beverly surprised Mira by laughing. "Oh, yes you are! Some families are born together, and others are made through this wild adventure we call life."

Mira smiled through her tears. "Are you sure you want to deal with me and all my drama?" There were other friendships Mira had through the years, but as things grew tough or they became distracted with their own changing lives, those had sputtered out or completely vanished.

When Seth and Charles rejoined them, Beverly hugged Mira tightly and answered, "I'm here for every bit of it."

Seth wasn't sure who scheduled the caroling and locations but why did their group have to be at the hospital? Each breath he sang grew more labored till he felt he was yanking every little note straight from his lungs.

He could see the others were struggling too. Liam's smile had faded and the bounce in Mason's steps became sluggish. It was worse for Noah who glared under his eyebrows at everyone and everything, as if this place was responsible for his mom's death.

Seth tried walking beside him. Maybe the proximity would help him open up to his dad or release some of the tension between them. Except it only made him worse. Noah crossed his arms and huffed each time Seth tried to encourage or reminisce with him. When he'd seen the glassy look in Noah's eyes earlier, he'd stood behind his son and placed an arm around his shoulders. He'd hoped the comfort would draw him closer, help his son share the ache they both felt. But Noah had shoved him off and grumbled, "Leave me alone."

Each word cut Seth deeper. To the point his own wounds couldn't heal.

Ana was much better with these things.

After Noah stomped away, putting as much distance between him and his dad, Seth studied the others in the group. Charles and Beverly looked somber. How many of their friends or family had passed and how did they cope with the grief? Maybe he could speak with Charles and get some advice before the emotions he shoved away came back full force.

His eyes trailed to Mira. Her eyes gleamed with unshed tears and her shoulders stooped forward. She blinked erratically, keeping her gaze from focusing on anyone. Who had she lost to reflect such heavy hurt?

Everyone's misery weighed on him. He wanted to be strong for them, but he didn't have the energy or the willpower. The more he considered ways to comfort them, the more his own sorrow reared up inside his chest. He tried pushing it away, but at their last song, *Joy to the World,* he almost lost his grip on the wave of grief washing over him. Before the last note ended, he slipped from the room and down an empty hallway until he found an exit. He burst through the doors before the despair came crashing down.

This time he couldn't hold back the sobs. He leaned against the shadowed wall of the hospital and let it all out. His shoulders shook from the aching he was finally letting himself feel. It wasn't the first time he cried after losing his wife and he was sure it wouldn't be the last. But this time felt different. It was bitter and perhaps selfish. Ana had died and left him to raise three boys alone. After she passed, they lost much more than a wife and mother. Their joy, amusement, and stability vanished along with her. Seth couldn't balance all of it on his shoulders while holding back his own pain.

He slumped on a bench and pulled up a picture of Ana he had saved on his phone. When struggling through parenting and hanging on to his career became more and more difficult, he'd stare at her picture and talk to her, as if she were still here to listen and give him advice. Except this time, he couldn't form the words. He knew what the struggle was deep within himself and how she would answer, but he was too proud to admit it. Even beyond the grave, she knew better than he did.

A sarcastic grunt escaped his lips, recalling conversations they had when she was still alive. Ana always did what was best for her family, even before considering herself. Seth had to encourage her to take occasional breaks and spend time with her friends. In fact, he'd taught himself how to cook so she wouldn't complain about them only eating mac and cheese when she went on longer outings or trips with her sisters. But since she died, he had to learn to fill that empty space. And it was stretching him too thin.

Ana's green eyes lit with a playful smirk as Seth stared at her picture. She would turn those words back at him: *You're doing too much. You need a break. You can't handle this all alone. Give yourself grace.* He sighed and clicked the screen off. She was right. Seth and his boys needed a change, but he wasn't sure what it was. Yet.

CHAPTER SEVEN

WEDNESDAY, DECEMBER 19

A fresh dusting of snow covered the sidewalks and left prints of Mira's footsteps when she arrived at City Hall. The building was one of the newest in town showcasing a modern sleekness with its large windows and silver trim. The bushes on the premises were brightened with Christmas lights outlining the silhouettes of animals native to the area. Lights on the elk flickered out as Mira passed, and morning air grew warmer with the rising sun.

Business at City Hall was completed the week before and all the employees were enjoying their Christmas break. Everyone except Jenni, Mayor Chavez' assistant. She swung open the door and waved to Mira with too much cheer for this early in the morning. "Come in! Come in!"

As Mira stepped in with a haze of chilly air, Jenni grinned. "The cold outside is invigorating, isn't it? I love it!"

Mira nodded through chattering teeth. She didn't have time to settle into the warmth of the building before Jenni was off again, prattling a mile a minute.

"We have all these hallways for the Silent Auction tonight." She pointed toward the three main arteries that led to the different departments, town council rooms, and mayor's office. Instead of going through the straight hallway, Jenni veered them right, through a plain door and into the kitchens. "Here's where Betty can set up for the finger foods and then through here..." Jenni swung open a set of double doors to reveal a large, carpeted room with a stage at one side and chairs along the other. "...Is the meeting hall for the main event."

Mira stared at the large space in front of them, trying to push aside memories. While this City Hall was new, she had entered the old building quite frequently with her grandmother. Mary had been very interested in the town's politics and made sure to share her opinion at any opportunity. It was because of her grandmother the interstate hadn't been built to go through town. Sure, it would have boomed all the local businesses, but *"some things are more important than money,"* Grandma Mary had said. She wanted the town to remain small and family friendly. *"Children should be able to ride their bikes to their friends' house without worries. Parents could feel comfortable raising their children and trusting the school teachers. Grandparents would have a peaceful place to take slow walks and connect with old friends."*

Grandma Mary had been able to enjoy all of that until her last days and many people in town were thankful for it. Some weren't. Mira had never doubted her grandmother's plan...until recently.

No one knew Mira's antique shop wouldn't last another year. Not even Beverly. Mira didn't make enough sales to cover expenses and had defaulted on utility payments. Although she always supported her family and their decisions, she was beginning to consider they didn't plan far enough in the future. Neither did she.

Mira gnawed on her lip, pushing away her worries until she had enough time to focus on them. If she was ever ready to face her failure in the financial aspects of her shop. She didn't want to admit her own shortcomings or be a burden to anyone else. But this wasn't the place to let her feelings of being lost or scared overtake her. Mira ducked her head and followed the other woman.

Jenni continued walking, leading her to the back warehouse. The dull room with cement floors and dim lighting was stacked with cardboard boxes and old grocery bags.

"This is where we stored all the donations." Jenni twirled a hand at the mess. "And this year the whole town has really stepped up! You won't believe some of the gifts that were given to raise money for the local hospital and senior center. It's going to be the best!"

As Jenni returned to her desk, Mira hoped she was right. None of the other residents in Cedar Springs knew why Mira went all out for this year's 12 Days of Christmas. Only Mira knew...it'd be the last one. It was the only reason Mira went through with all the chaos of organizing the events and smiling with her friends even with the grief of the past year weighing down her shoulders. She wasn't ready to think about the challenges the next year would hold: of finding a new place to live, a new job when she wasn't qualified for anything, and doing it all on her own. Her greatest fear was leaving Cedar Springs. But she pushed those thoughts aside and focused on the present.

She began with the shoes, unboxing them and setting them on tables that lined the hallways. There were tennis shoes, boots, and even several sandals. They were all new and served a purpose.

Next, she gathered a box of items and placed one in every other shoe. There were gift cards, expensive jewelry, and household items. Several caught her attention: a liberty gold coin from 1893, a diamond ring with a stone larger than her thumbnail, a jar of red saffron, and a small leather wallet with a brand name logo. These items were valued at over $1,500. Each. If all the items at the auction sold, the hospital would have enough to cover the costs of low-income patients who couldn't afford their bills, and the senior center could give discounted rates to newcomers.

As she unloaded item after item, she was in awe with how giving her small community was. She was thankful to live in such a wonderful town with kind-hearted people. It was a place she wanted to stay connected. This was her home. Except without finances or her shop, would she have to leave it all behind? That was a decision for another day. She turned her mind from those gloomy thoughts and focused on the work.

Later that afternoon, Beverly joined with several other women, including Luella and Evelyn. They set out more items, but it took five times longer because each woman stopped to rave about the different donations they found.

While they gushed over a jewelry set, Luella pulled Mira to the side. "I apologize," she said. "I must get something off my chest. It's been bothering me for days."

Mira set down the Christmas decorations she was setting around the tables and gave the older woman her full attention. "Are you okay? What is it?"

"No, no, I'm not alright." Luella shook her head and stared around them, lowering her voice so no one would overhear. "I've been the worst friend, and I want to say I'm sorry."

The apology surprised Mira.

"Your conversations with men as a single woman aren't any of my business and I put my nose where it didn't belong the other day. Could you find it in your heart to forgive me? I promise to do better."

Mira blinked at Luella's self-awareness and apology. Although the way she'd wrinkled her nose at *"single woman"* was comical. It was a kind gesture to admit her meddling and showed growth in her character. Mira nodded and opened her mouth to thank and encourage her.

Except Luella interrupted any response. "You see, I'm just trying to help. I want what's best for you. Mira, do you like being alone? I don't think it's right for any girl."

Mira sighed. Luella continued prattling on about her rights to meddle in the affairs of others, but Mira tuned her out. The apology wasn't true if there were caveats attached. The longer Luella talked, the more it frustrated Mira.

"How uncomfortable it must be for a single woman home alone at night. What would you do if someone broke into your shop?"

Mira *would* have replied she had a fine collection of vintage weapons that would do in a pinch, but Luella didn't wait for an answer. She talked and talked, not even noticing Mira slip away.

Mira hid in the kitchen where she left a box of her own donations. To calm herself, she rifled through the items and consoled her soul with their history. An old tea set from her grandmother's China cabinet. It was too beautiful to use so Mira only had memories of staring at the floral design from afar. Now it would bring beauty into someone else's life and money for an important cause. Beside it was a vibrant dragon statue from her great grandmother's trip to China. Mira loved hearing the English translations her mother had read from The Art of War and Journey to the West. The Monkey King and his tales always intrigued a young Mira, and she would pretend to share his mystical powers while she ran around the shop. Next, she lifted the old pocket watch with gold plating and a cover that popped open when she pressed the top button. She'd seen her grandfather with it a handful of times. She also looked through a brass pill box filled with miniature trinkets, from hand carved buttons to loose jewels.

Mira had debated donating these items. They were sentimental but also held monetary value, an important aspect currently. If she could sell the entire shop and have enough money for a smaller apartment, she could make do for a while. But she'd tossed that idea away after she considered being the host of an event where she gathered all the proceeds for personal use. It rankled her as being selfish, despite all the time and effort she was already investing. She turned away and went back to work with items that weren't hers.

She was draping an exquisite quilt on the stage when Evelyn approached. "That is fine work!"

Mira nearly lost her balance and tripped into a heap on the floor. She barely managed to keep her feet under her. "Thanks." She dusted off her skirt and settled back on even ground. "It was donated by the Cedar Springs quilting society."

Evelyn clucked her tongue. "I bet most of the work was completed by Sharon. She's a master of the art."

Mira stood back and admired the work. It was a kaleido-scope of colors making a stunning coral reef. "Most likely." Somewhere at home, she still had the baby quilt Sharon made for her. Most of the town residents her age and younger owned one of those precious masterpieces. "We have several special items that won't be part of the regular silent auction."

"Why not?" Evelyn asked.

Beverly's voice broke into the conversation when she entered the room. "Because some items don't fit inside a shoe." The women laughed.

"What is the point of all the shoes?" Evelyn asked.

Mira answered, "Tonight we remember gift-giving tradi-tions, started by none other than St. Nicholas himself."

"There were the wise men before that."

Mira nodded, "And they will get their celebration. But tonight is about gifts inside shoes. Many cultures still cel-ebrate this way, from Holland to Romania." She thought fondly of the games she would play when she was younger. Her mother and grandmother would place wonderful goodies, from newly minted coins to an orange and candy, in each of their shoes and then hide it somewhere in the house. It was always a highlight for Mira to wake up on

December 6th and search every room until she found her treats.

"So, the larger items will be a regular auction?" Evelyn confirmed.

"Exactly."

"What about all the shoes?"

Mira reached out and picked up a child-sized pair of sneakers. "These are also donations and will be given to people in need. It's all in the brochure." She grabbed a stack of print-outs showcasing the hospital, senior center, and a nonprofit partner from the city.

"This is wonderful," Evelyn smiled. "Of all the places in the world, I'm glad I live in Cedar Springs."

Beverly agreed. "It's been my favorite for the past fifty years."

As they moved on to the next hallway to decorate, Mira heard Evelyn confide in Beverly. "If only I could convince my son and his boys to move here too, I'd be the happiest woman in the world!"

Mira startled from her work and considered the possibility. Was Evelyn going to persuade Seth to move to Cedar Springs?

***

Seth stopped at the mercantile and bought his boys dry gloves and then let them play in the park with a group of other children.

"Noah, keep an eye on them," he instructed. "I'll be right back." He turned toward *Vintage Treasures,* noticing the closed sign wasn't at the window and the lights were on. A bell chimed as he entered but Mira didn't come from the hidden staircase in the back.

As Seth waited, he browsed through the antiques. Some were stunning, like the complete uniform of a World War II veteran and an ammo can full of military pins. He rifled through them, studying a silver eagle lapel pin. He wandered between furniture and stared at black and white photographs and paintings on the walls. It was fascinating as he strolled through each section, organized not only by decade but even broken down by year, theme, and continent.

It wasn't until he was in the far back corner examining an Indian miniature painting of a Maharaja riding horseback and embellished with gold leaf, that he considered Mira wasn't at home to tend the shop. People in a small town must be more trusting than he was used to in the big city.

He'd never leave anything unlocked, not even his car when he sat inside it. But, since he was already trapped by history, he stayed several more minutes and traced the hardwood carving of a lotus throne and appreciated a silk brocade saree.

He was alone and could soak up the stories still alive in these items, without the worry his sons would break something again. Mira's shop was a trove of wonders as he ventured deeper and discovered more.

Seth knew he should leave but he took his time walking back toward the exit. Except more antiques snagged his attention time and again. From images of rock paintings in Algeria taken with an Argus 35mm camera on original film to a poetry book by Nobel Prize winner Gabriela Mistral in original Spanish with English translations. His feet stalled at golden replicas of Kazakh deer inlaid with turquoise and imitation bronze Mongolian coins with striking script. He couldn't pass the Scandinavian sun clock without tracing his finger over the copper numeric banding along the metal sphere or holding up the carved shell and amber bead necklace from Mauritania. This small shop was a treasure trove of remarkable pieces from all around the globe. No wonder Mira loved history. It wasn't an old-fashioned idea on the page of a book, but real life items linking her to the past.

Seth finally had to peel himself away from reading about Samurai in a translation from Hagakure. Later, he would revisit when Mira was here so he could purchase several artifacts. Before he stepped out of the shop, his eyes caught another photograph. It was signed with immaculate penmanship at the bottom, listing the names of each person. An elderly couple, Gheorghe and Margareta Ion, held hands beside Stefan and Mary Johnston, while a young woman named Michelle Turner held a little child in braided pigtails. The young Mira's smile was bright and happy, surrounded by a family of multiple generations full of life and lived history. It brought a grin to his face when he left the shop and rejoined his boys.

Seth found them trying to build a snowman, but it fell apart. The dry snow was like powder and worked better to toss into the air and watch it glitter down. Liam entertained himself for several minutes doing that until it melted into his jacket, and he cried from the cold.

To comfort his boys, he led them into the bakery and bought them all hot chocolate and donuts. As they ate and giggled over Liam's misfortune, Seth's eyes trailed back to the old newspapers on the wall. This time he recognized several faces. They were the ones from Mira's photograph but in this picture, they stood in front of an old mansion. A young version of Mira stood proudly, hand in hand with her grandmother and mom.

It suddenly made sense to Seth. It wasn't that Mira was awkwardly obsessed with history. It was her *life*. She grew up immersed in different time periods, cultures, and world-views, all snug inside a small antique shop in the mountains of Colorado. Her world was a mosaic of countless stories. When she shared through oral tradition at the 12 Days to Christmas events, she wasn't merely recounting something she'd read or heard. She was *living* it.

❧

People poured into City Hall. They filled the hallways, and stopped to stare at the silent auction items, at treasures tucked in brand-new shoes. Tables lined the walls, covered with every size shoe, and holding intriguing objects for auction. Papers tracked amounts and bidder numbers as values went up.

Mira hurried around the crowd occasionally glancing at their bids or advertising different pieces to gather in more offers. Dollar amounts moved up as the totals ticked higher and higher. It should have thrilled her but stress set in. She had so many depending on her to get this right and, where money was concerned, people became sensitive.

That's when she noticed Noah sitting in the corner playing on his phone and ignoring the crowd. In between describing a vintage doily and passing out desserts, she snuck over to the boy.

"Hey, Noah. I could really use your help. Do you mind?"

His eyes flicked in her direction indifferently. "With what?"

Mira was surprised he hadn't outright dismissed her. "We need more water in the coffee machines and extra cups."

Noah pulled himself to his feet and stuffed his phone in his pocket. "I guess."

As he walked away, Mira wondered what the best way to connect with the sad boy would be. He wasn't interested in talking about his loss like Liam or distracting himself like Mason. He held tightly to his pain and built walls to keep everyone else out. Or to protect himself. It was something Mira understood.

As the night became busier and the bid sheets filled, Noah helped swap the pages out with new ones. She showed him how to write the last bidder number and their amount on the top of the page so it could continue where it left off. After they ran out of seats in the main gym, he helped carry in folding chairs while Mira set them up. The older guests were thankful for a place to sit and rest between scavenging through auction items.

Occasionally she'd try to talk with him, but his answers were usually *humph* or shoulder shrugs. At one point, he met her eyes when she said, "There are more people than I was expecting." He replied with a nod.

Noah finally spoke, following Mira into the kitchen and balancing a tray of treats from Betty's Bakery. They had been passing out sweets to guests. "Someone was looking for you."

"Who?" Mira asked.

He lifted his hands in a shrug. "Don't know. Some old—older lady. Said you needed to make your speech."

Mira gasped, almost dropping the tray, but Noah reached up and took it. She ran back to the meeting hall before missing her cue. "Thank you!" she called back to Noah. He didn't smile exactly, but some of his grumpiness faded. It was enough to put a bounce in Mira's step as she took the stairs to the stage.

The hospital CEO finished speaking and handed the microphone over to Shawna, the Senior Center director. She talked about providing for the well-being and long-term care of residents and how they could give back to the community, but Mira's mind wandered to her own speech. She practiced it earlier that day during a spare moment in the restroom in front of the mirror. When she dressed in her red and white A-line peppermint dress and matching kitten heels, she'd run over her lines, except she still felt unprepared. The day had been too busy to let her mind focus.

Even now, before she formulated the exact words she wanted to say, Shawna handed her the mic. She'd hoped the confidence recently fueling her at these events would spark, but she stared at the audience, empty. Until her eyes met Seth's. He encouraged her with a nod and smile as he helped Noah with a tray.

She smiled at the audience, trying to hide the nerves that exploded beneath her ribs. She still wasn't sure she could do this, but she refused to fail, especially when Seth was watching. "Thank you so much to everyone who joined us tonight."

Her eyes glanced over the audience, trying to find Seth again. He'd stepped in to help Noah but was out of sight now. Most of the crowd was focused on her but she noticed Charles sneaking around the tables and changing several bids. She turned her attention back to her speech.

"Your support for these important organizations is truly uplifting and encouraging. I am so thankful to live—" her voice cracked, and she fought to regain control. "I'm so thankful for our community in Cedar Springs." She knew all the faces watching her, from her elementary school teacher, Mr. Rodriguez, to her piano instructor, Mrs. Stone. These were people she'd known since childhood. Some knew her even longer than that, since they were friends with her grandmother and great-grandmother.

All the fears she pushed away earlier were bubbling up. She had to spill out her speech before emotions clouded her vision. "You are all so giving...just like St. Nicholas! Many know him from European tales celebrated by the Dutch, but he was born in Turkey in 280 A.D."

It was a rare cool evening walking from Myra to Patara. The lighthouse gleamed in the distance along the rocky shore. Mira walked beneath the stone arch gateway and down the main street, between tall columns. Many people were gathered in the amphitheater cheering their fortune and laughing at a comedy. It left most of the city empty, but for the poor and beggars who couldn't afford entertainment.

"Nicholas of Bari was a very generous man, using his own wealth to feed the hungry, clothe the poor, and help the sick. But he never sought credit for his good deeds."

Mira slowed her steps, seeing a lame man leaning against one of the pillars before struggling back to his feet. He moved forward, tugging his right leg behind him. His bare foot curled under and scraped against his walking staff. It caused him to lose balance and fall to the dusty cobblestone. Mira rushed to him and gave him her shoulder to lean on. In this way she helped him return to his home to rest for the night. Maybe in the morning he would find the two gold pieces she had slipped into his pocket.

"Saint Nicholas was known to leave gifts in homes at night, a bag of money for three poor sisters' dowries, or a gold coin tossed through the window, landing in a shoe."

As she left the lame man, she continued her steps to a small shack. Inside, three sisters cried while hugging each other before they curled up on sleeping mats on the floor. Their father put out his pipe as he glared hopelessly out the window toward the sea before he too settled on his cot. When she was sure they were all asleep, Mira snuck in and placed a bag of coins on their rickety table. This would provide a good dowry for the girls, protecting them from immoral work on the streets.

"From a saint, he became a legend. In a poem from 1820, his story grew into the fat, jolly man we all know and love today." Mira blinked back to reality.

"We're all busy with our lives, especially during the holiday season, but this year I urge you to remember: it's not the amount of money you spend but the spreading of kindness and generosity, pouring into someone else's life. As I was recently reminded: *be an influence for good.*"

When Mira stepped down from the stage, the crowd was silent considering her words but she was thinking about something else. Her daydream into history was beautiful and lifelike as always. She could feel the warm sunshine on her skin, taste the salty sea air on her tongue, and even see the Patara Lighthouse shining across the beach. It was considered to be the oldest lighthouse in the world. Except something had been off and she couldn't put her finger on it.

She shrugged the feeling away and hurried back to the kitchen to help with all the work, but Mayor Chavez stopped her. "What a wonderful speech!"

"And what a crowd!" Tina added. "This is probably the biggest silent auction in Cedar Springs!"

"We are so thankful for you, Mira," Mayor Chavez said. "You bring the community together in a way no one else can. It unites us all despite politics, past grievances, and generational divides."

Mira stumbled over her reply, unsure how to brush away the compliments, but Tina swatted away the excuses. "*You* are a treasure! And if you ever decide to take a break from your antique shop, know you will always have a place at City Hall."

This time Mira couldn't fight the color filling her cheeks. Several others around gushed in agreement, including Jenni who regaled everyone with everything Mira had completed that day. The attention burned Mira's face into embarrassment, and she snuck away at the first opportunity. Other work called her.

But she was distracted again. Charles, hand in hand with Liam and Mason, walked around staring at all the items...or more accurately, their bid sheets.

"Someone wrote $1,000 on this!" Mason gasped.

Liam's eyes were wide with wonder. "That's a lot of money."

Charles chuckled. "What else do you think us old folks should do with all the wealth we've stocked up?"

"You can give it to me!" Mason offered.

The old man threw his head back and laughed. "You'd love that, wouldn't you?"

"Me too!" Liam shouted, not wanting to be left out.

Charles took the pen and added a bid while explaining to the boys, "You see, this offer is from my friend Jesse, and I know he *really* wants this first edition of The Fellowship of the Ring, so I'm going to bid him up. You think he'll fight me for it?" He scribbled his auction number on the page and raised the price to $1,500.

Mira stepped in. "Charles." Her voice was scolding. "You know that's against the rules."

Charles pretended not to hear her and whispered to the boys, "If we run fast, she can't catch us!" They clasped hands and ran in the opposite direction.

Mira couldn't help but laugh.

"He's incorrigible." Beverly stepped up to the bid sheet and crossed out her husband's bid. "One would think after five decades of marriage I could change the man, but it's impossible! I'd warn any girl looking to marry a man she wants to make different...don't bother."

"Then what advice would you give?"

The older woman raised her eyebrows. "Is there a specific reason you're asking?"

"No!" Mira stumbled over her words again as her face reddened for the second time that night. She continued scanning the crowd but wasn't sure why. "I was only looking forward to the wisdom you'd impart."

Beverly smiled. "Don't worry about it, dear. You know I'm only teasing. But my advice is: if he's good enough to fall in love with, he's good enough to live with."

Mira grew thoughtful. "Once again, you inspire me."

"Inspire you sufficiently to find you a husband?"

"Oh goodness, no!" She then shared about her earlier conversation with Luella.

"Sometimes that woman doesn't know when to stuff a cork in it."

Mira stifled a giggle.

"But don't take it to heart darling. We love you exactly the way you are." They walked down the hallway glancing at items. "But if you *do* choose to marry, know that I will support you in any way you need." Before Mira could feel awkward again, they stopped at a babushka nesting doll. It was hand painted and donated from a local Ukrainian family. "Oh, look! It's the old woman in the shoe!" Beverly reached out for the rest of the dolls, stacking them all around and on top of the shoes. "So many kids, she didn't know what to do!"

They laughed and continued on.

Eventually, Mira made it back to the kitchen and glanced around for what needed to be done. Evelyn leaned against the counter having a conversation with Carly but there were no more trays of bakery treats.

Evelyn waved her away. "Don't you worry about a thing! My boys have it covered."

Mira looked around to see Seth refilling the coffee machines and Noah walking around with the trays. "Oh." Once again, that strange warmth bubbled inside her. She attributed it to seeing people living out the advice of her speeches, to not feeling alone in this event and having someone supporting what she was doing, and, although her mother wasn't here to work alongside her, there were others who stepped in to fill that gap.

When Seth returned, holding the empty pitchers of water, Mira shuffled out of the tangle of thoughts in her mind—or heart—and thanked him.

"It's nothing," he said. "I'm channeling the inner St. Nicholas you claimed we all have."

Mira tipped her head to the side, puzzled. "I didn't say that."

"Ah, but you said we are like him, right?"

"I suppose so."

"I thought it'd be fitting to share this *special* water—"

Mira's face broke into a grin. Very few people would understand his reference to St. Nicholas' history. "You mean *manna*? The liquid that comes from his bones?"

Seth smiled. "If it heals everyone, we wouldn't need to raise money for the hospital."

"Except we're not in Italy and I hope you used filtered water instead of a dead saint."

"You'll never know." Seth winked.

"Did you know...St. Nicholas was imprisoned?"

"I did. But I bet you didn't know he was at the Council of Nicaea."

"How *nice*. But that's common knowledge. What about the sailors who stole his bones?"

"Ah, yes, and brought them to Italy? Also, he was said to ride a white horse."

"Or donkey."

"Not reindeer."

"Most definitely not." A giggle escaped Mira. If Luella appeared, what would she say they were talking about? Donkeys or bones?

Seth changed the conversation when he pointed out an auction item. "Is that from your shop?"

Mira looked at the gold pocket watch and nodded.

"It's fine work. Does it have a history lesson to go with it?"

"It was my grandfather's." Mira chewed on her bottom lip.

Seth's eyes grew wide. "Then why are you donating it?"

"Well..." Mira didn't know how to answer without going through her entire life story, one that began before she was even born.

Seth pulled out a chair and sat across from her. "So?"

She took a deep breath and began. "Most of the items in my shop are actually connected to my family history in some way. Those Christmas ornaments you saw? My grandmother hoarded them. Her attic was full of knick-knacks and decorations from the 40s. But my great-grandmother was worse. She had money to devote to her collection and didn't settle with her generation of heirlooms. Grandma Margaret gathered artifacts from multiple time periods, cultures, and countries all around the world. Her adventures took her to Europe on ocean liners and across Asia by train, even a stint on the Orient Express. She rode camels in Egypt and swam in the Nile."

"Your great-grandmother sounds like an amazing woman."

"They all were, and it's the reason I keep that shop, because it's a living memory of everyone I've lost." The worries threatened her again and she frowned at the thought. Maybe sharing with someone who wasn't at all connected and didn't live in town would help. "Actually...I have to sell it."

"What? Why?" Seth looked horrified.

Mira answered with a dry laugh. "Bills. Inflation. It's not a financially stable business. The list goes on." She fell quiet and was thankful Seth didn't interrupt her scrambling thoughts. He sat beside her, staring at his shoes.

Before the silent auction tables closed, Seth stood abruptly. "Then there's only one thing to do."

Mira stared after him, confused when he took a pen and wrote a bid. She wanted to glance at the paper, but Luella rushed by at that moment, collecting them all. The older woman waved the stack in the air. "We'll announce the winners of the auction now!"

Mira followed her back to the main hall as Seth gathered his boys. Her heart thumped in anticipation of all the items being sold while the local rancher, Mark, ran a quick bid for the items that were too large to place in shoes. Sharon's quilt went for nearly three thousand dollars and two businessmen fought over a prized prime rib gift card. Someone won an all-expense paid cruise and Charles was called out for overbidding on a weekend stay at a mountain lodge.

Beverly pointed a finger at him across the room and announced he better take her on vacation. Everyone laughed.

Jesse received his book, Elizabeth bought the tea set, and Luella got the pill box.

The auctioneer cleared his throat. "And the last item on the list...the one that goes for the most money...at $5,000...is this gold pocket watch!"

The crowd gasped and Mira's heart dropped into her shoes before she remembered how to breathe again. It finally occurred to her what had been strange about St. Nicholas' story. Since he came to town, Seth had ambushed every historical daydream she'd envisioned. Except this one.

Her eyes searched the main hall until they snagged on Seth. He met her gaze and smiled back. Maybe he wasn't in her imagination this time because reality was better than dreams. Someone saw her clearly and made her feel less alone.

Chapter Eight

THURSDAY, DECEMBER 20

Mira bit down on the bobby pin as she studied her face in the mirror and braided her hair in a crown around her head. After tucking in the loose end and clipping it in, she applied powder to her face but a ringing phone interrupted her. She dropped the brush and hurried to where the phone shrilled on the wall.

"Hello?" It was always a surprise to hear the voice on the other side. She refused to get a cell phone because it ruined the mystery.

Beverly coughed on the other end of the line. "Mira? I hope you're doing well, but...we're not. Charles has come down with a terrible cold. You should see him! I almost mistook him for Rudolph the red-nosed reindeer this morning. The worst part is he's trying to share it with me." She sneezed.

Mira glanced at the grandfather clock ticking in the corner and gnawed on her lip. They were supposed to pick out the town Christmas tree today and Charles had offered to drive his truck with the other volunteers trekking up the mountain in their own cars.

Before her worries gave way to panic, Bev added, "But don't you fret now. I've arranged everything. You'll have the truck at the house soon and helpful hands to assist!"

"What?" Mira was confused. "Who?"

The doorbell rang from downstairs, and Mira jumped.

"Oh, it sounds like he's there." Bev's voice smiled across the phone. "I hope everything goes smoothly. Have a wonderful day!"

Mira was left standing with the disconnected tone ringing in her ear. "Who could she have possibly sent?"

She took the stairs two at a time and almost landed in a heap, but managed to collect herself before unlocking the shop door. "Thank you for—" Her words stalled on her lips as she glanced up at Seth. He wore a red plaid flannel shirt with the sleeves partially rolled up past his forearms.

He grinned. "Good morning. Bev said you need help today." Charles' old truck honked behind him and Liam waved from the front seat. "They gave me the truck and told me to stop here."

Mira glanced back with wide eyes. "I...suppose...this works. Uh...thank you."

"Are you ready?"

Mira glanced down at her slippers and remembered her half-powdered face. She fought the dread of embarrassment. "Oh, no. I suppose you can come inside and wait." She scrambled back but paused halfway. "Please...um...don't break anything."

Seth winced.

Mira hurried back upstairs and scowled at her face in the mirror. Her pale skin had a rosy blush that wasn't there before. She stuck her tongue out at her reflection, trying not to recall the bubbly feeling in her stomach at last night's auction.

When she felt presentable enough, she stepped out to find Noah, Mason, and Liam sitting around her table.

"Um?" she hesitated. The boys played with knickknacks, knocked over a stack of unpaid bills, and glanced at her Christmas cards.

Noah rolled his eyes. "Our dad made us sit here so we don't break anything." He shot a pointed look toward Liam who dropped a roll of stamps and stared back with innocent brown eyes.

"I already said sorry!"

Mira's eyes trailed up behind them to Seth's form beside the fireplace mantle. His hands were stuffed in his pockets as he stared at the photographs, a crease forming between his eyebrows. Her breath caught in her throat.

"Is this...?" He reached toward the shattered teapot and picked up a broken piece.

Mira blinked several times and pushed away the emotions threatening to drown her. "Let's go," she blurted. Taking Liam's hand, she led him downstairs and safely around the fragile objects without looking back to see if the others followed.

The day was crisp and cold when she stepped outside. A puff of breath lingered while Mira spoke to Liam, zipping up his winter jacket. She was glad she dressed warmly, with a scarf and hood that hid half her face, which was very helpful after she turned to see Seth and the other two boys passing her and climbing into the truck. She avoided making eye contact with Seth again, confused about the nervous energy making her heart twitch. Mira scrambled to lock the shop and then settled in the passenger seat.

It took Seth two tries before the truck started. Mira glanced over with the corner of her vision and prayed their trip would be uneventful. The boys laughed at something Noah said but Mira was focused on Seth turning the key in the ignition again.

When the engine roared to life, he turned to Mira. "Where we headed?"

She unfolded the paper map she used every year to navigate the mountain roads and pointed forward.

"Woah! What's that?" Mason leaned forward and stared at the map. "You can see the whole mountain on that thing."

"Cause it's almost as big as the mountain," Noah snorted. "Why don't you just use your phone?"

Mira turned to him and raised an eyebrow comically. "Because my phone only has numbers and is stuck to the wall."

Noah made a face. "Why?"

"Do you have a telegraph?" Mason bounced forward. "I heard about them at school."

"Mason, sit down and buckle up," Seth said.

Mira smiled back at the boy. "Actually, yes, I do. Want to see it after we get back? I might even have a letter my great-grandfather sent to my great-grandmother when he was fighting in World War 1."

"Woah!"

"So, which way, boss lady?"

Mira turned back to Seth. This time she couldn't avoid eye contact, so she diverted attention with facts about the highway. "There's only one main road through Cedar Springs. One side leads up Cedar Mountain and the other leads out of town."

Behind her, Noah mumbled under his breath. "We should take that one."

Seth bit his lip. "I apologize for him."

Mira folded the map, pressing tightly on the creases. "You shouldn't have to."

"The kids have been through a lot this past year."

"I understand." She met his eyes, and this time didn't turn away. He needed to know that she identified more than most people. "The holidays are tough, especially after losing someone important." She took a deep breath. "They say it gets easier, but it doesn't."

Heavy rock music erupted from Noah's phone and Seth spun around. "Use headphones."

Noah frowned and stuck buds in his ears. "Happy?"

Mason bounced in his seat. "Can we listen to music? Where do I plug in the cord?"

Mira smiled back at him. "This is called a radio." She pointed to the black box sitting in the center console.

"Can you play *The Gummy Bear Song*?"

Seth and Mira exchanged glances with a laugh.

"That's not how it works," he responded. "You listen to whatever is playing, whether you like it or not. We didn't get to be as picky as you when we were kids."

Mira turned it on, and *Santa Claus is Coming to Town* filled the truck. Liam started singing along before he yelled, "I need to pee!"

Seth shrugged at Mira. "I'm sorry, but I think this is going to be a long ride."

———

"She's here!" Kids cheered seeing the truck pull into the trailhead. Several families waited, bundled up in winter gear, building snowmen or making snow angels. Charles' truck pulled into the plowed parking lot with a lurch and the boys jumped out. Mason and Liam had already connected with several of the children in town during events the past several days and rushed off to join them.

Mira pulled her scarf around her face after she stepped from the truck. The awkwardness of arriving late was embarrassing, but to show up with Seth and his sons might cause uncomfortable gossip. She avoided meeting Luella's gaze, but she could see her eyebrows lift before she scampered to a group of women. Mira was sure she knew what they were discussing. She tugged the scarf tighter around her face, to cover the blush growing in her cheeks. Maybe she could excuse it on the cold weather.

She'd never been the center of their gossip until now. And she didn't like it one bit. So, when Seth came around asking how he could help, she dismissed him with a quick shake of her head.

"No, thanks. I got this." She hurried away with another glance at the chatting women.

Mira started the group down the trail. Several of the men carried chainsaws, kids tried to lasso their friends with ropes, and women pulled their coats tighter and held their warm travel mugs close.

As she stomped forward through a foot of snow, Elizabeth left her son with her husband and joined Mira.

"So, Luella—"

Mira shook her head. "Luella doesn't know anything."

Elizabeth fought back a smirk. "I was going to say Luella came with Mark but...now I'm wondering what you *thought* I was going to say."

Mira bit her lip. "Nothing."

"Mirabel Nora Turner. Now I know you're lying."

She flushed. Elizabeth and Mira had been acquaintances all her life, but she'd never really considered the other girl a close friend. They were too different. Usually, Mira joined her when she didn't know who else to talk to and they could discuss old books. But in the last couple days, something had changed. Sure, they still weren't connected by similar interests. Elizabeth preferred modern tech, media, and fashion but she'd reached out to Mira, understanding their differences and accepting her regardless. It was a strange concept to Mira, to relate to someone because she cared about her.

"How would you know if I'm not telling the truth?" Mira tried to fend away her curiosity, but Elizabeth rolled her eyes.

"We've known each other practically our entire lives. Even though you usually keep to yourself, Mira, others see you and know you. Like your favorite decade is the 1950s, you'd rather read a book—a classic—than hold a conversation, and you've glanced at a certain stranger five times during our conversation."

Mira's cheeks burned.

"I know you're a private person, but this is a small town and you know we don't do that," Elizabeth laughed. "And with Luella on the prowl, you need to make sure she doesn't get the wrong idea...or she'll share it all over town."

"I think she already has."

They turned to look at Luella behind them. A gaggle of women followed her while the gossip spoke in an animated way and pointed to the gang of boys having a snowball fight.

"Then you need to take your narrative back." Elizabeth smirked.

"How?" Mira could explain the exact details of the Industrial Revolution in the Western world and share the history of Wu Zetian, the only female emperor in Chinese history during the Tang dynasty, but she was at a loss of how to speak and convince living people.

"You need a distraction, something to make the day memorable for other reasons, something to bring Christmas cheer to everyone, including yourself." Elizabeth winked and started singing, "Frosty the Snowman..."

Mira smiled and joined. Soon most of the group sang along as snow crunched under their boots and breath frosted around their faces. They passed pines too skinny or tall for the perfect Christmas tree and hiked down a cleared trail farther up the mountain. When the ladies pointed out the trees they approved of for their homes, the men cut the down and left them by the path to drag back after the town Christmas tree was chosen.

Walking beside Elizabeth and several others who joined them, Mira didn't feel awkward or alone. Luella moved on to different topics of conversation, like how to make the best meal or the only way to raise children correctly. Some women nodded in agreement but most cast each other side eyes and didn't comment.

As they sang together, Mira smiled at the look of joy on others' faces, but her own sadness returned. She watched couples walk hand in hand, daughters laugh with their mothers, women share stories about their families.

It was like a lump of coal sitting heavy in her heart. The bright colors and lights, ornaments and holiday joy were a stark reminder during the busy days and longer lonely nights. She didn't have someone to walk hand in hand with, she couldn't laugh with her mother, she had no stories or family to share.

This year, she didn't care if the tree was tall enough, the branches full or symmetrical. It didn't matter to her if it was decorated or left bare. She hadn't even bothered to decorate her home. It was something she'd done with her mother. Somehow it seemed wrong to put up twinkling lights, hang ornaments full of family stories, or fill the house with delicious holiday smells alone. It renewed her heartbreak and reminded her with sharp clarity of all she'd lost. All she was going to lose. There was no merriment in that.

She lifted her hand to point to the first tree on the next rise of the trail with a resigned apathy but was interrupted by Liam running past. He screeched and ducked.

Mira spun around to see Mason throwing a snowball. The little boy tripped and fell in a cloud of snow. She hurried over to him, but his head popped back up in a flurry of snowflakes, with his red cheeks gleaming. A laugh exploded from him.

"This is the best Christmas!" he giggled. "We need to find the most *ginormous* tree ever!"

Mira smiled back, a bit of Christmas cheer breaking down her barriers. "Will you help me find it?"

He grinned. "Can we beat Mason first?"

They looked back at his brother winding up for another throw.

"Of course."

A full-on snowball fight launched in earnest. Mira formed one and passed it to Liam. The ball sailed in the air and splattered across Mason's coat. Elizabeth and Jesse joined in, with Elizabeth tossing them at her husband but not hitting her two-year old son sitting on his shoulders. The boy squealed in excitement as Jesse swerved to avoid getting hit. Luella ran off while the other kids jumped in. Soon snowballs whizzed past with no aim and in every direction. Liam was pegged in the face and laughed it off. Mira shook down her cloak and dusted her gloves while she continued passing the young boy snowballs.

When she looked up, she noticed Noah had joined Mason. The brothers ducked behind a ridge.

"They're making a plan," Liam muttered. "We have to get them first."

Mira wasn't used to snowball fights or war strategy, but she was having too much fun to worry about it. She joined in his scheming. "We need a shield and a lot of ammo."

Liam nodded with a serious expression, like it was a life or death situation. Mira rolled more snowballs, stacking them in a pile at their backs, and handed them to him one at a time.

"I know what to do!" He jumped to his feet and dashed off.

Confused, Mira continued making snowballs until a moment later when Liam returned.

"I got help!"

Seth joined them. "What are we doing?" He glanced between Mira and Liam.

"We're beating the big boys!" Liam stood up and pointed in his brothers' direction. At that moment, they popped up from their hiding place and pelted him with snowballs. He fell in a heap of flurries between Mira and Seth. With a dramatic gasp, he said, "They won."

Seth chuckled, "Not yet, they didn't." Mira handed him a snowball and he tossed it back at the boys. It fell between them, and they threw themselves back into hiding.

"Maybe you'll have better luck next time," Mira shrugged.

"That was just a warmup." He winked. "Let's see if the years I spent playing baseball pay off."

She grinned back. They had a decent pile of snowballs when Liam spied his brothers reemerge. "They're out!" he shouted.

Seth didn't miss a beat. He took two snowballs and tossed them, his arms moving quickly. His aim was true. A snowball knocked Mason off his feet into a snowbank, another whizzed over his head and smacked into Noah's chest. But Seth wasn't done. He continued to throw snow at his boys and at other kids joining in on the fun. He pegged Jesse, who had passed his son off to Elizabeth, and even threw some far enough that snow splattered at Luella's feet. She shrieked.

Liam fell over laughing. Even Mira couldn't stop a giggle. When she glanced back up, Noah had managed to get back to his feet and throw another snowball. Aimed right at her.

Before she could react, Seth pulled her aside. The snow sloshed across his jacket and splattered them both. He lost his footing and fell in a heap, taking her down with him.

They collapsed in the snow, side by side. Mira giggled.

"You alright?" Seth asked.

She brushed powder from her face. "I don't mind a bit of snow."

He chuckled but made no move to get up. Neither did she. Seth grinned back and Mira felt a flurry of emotions. Perhaps the Christmas spirit was reviving. She wasn't sure what else it could be. Even as she returned a smile of her own.

"There it is!" Liam squealed.

Seth and Mira spun around to look. He was pointing over the snowy ridge. The little boy's mouth hung open and he had stars in his eyes.

Seth helped Mira up. Together, they waded through the snow until they reached Liam's side and saw the pine tree he was staring at.

"No way," Seth chuckled.

Mira's eyebrows shot up. "Wow."

It was easily the tallest tree in the area, with green boughs stretched out to greet the cold winter sun. It was beautiful.

For a short moment, Mira stared up at the grand tree, forgetting her worries and sadness, melting in the joy and cheer. The perfect tree rose from the crystal sparkles of snow, strong against winter storms, and blooming with emerald needles. She could envision how majestic it would look with bright red ribbons, glittering gold bells, and shimmering silver tinsel. Liam was right. This was the perfect tree.

When the rest of the group joined, Mira called them together and had the kids sit in the snow while she shared a story.

"The Christmas tree tradition originated in Germany and became popular around the world after Queen Victoria and Prince Albert published a picture celebrating the holiday around a decorated pine tree."

She wore a pink silk gown and a sapphire tiara as she stood in the grand room of a castle. Not a stuffy, dark one made of cold stones, but a warm place with a crackling fire and thick rugs. It was her favorite place away from home: Windsor Castle. She stood beside a tree decorated with a string of garland and the scent of dried orange slices and cinnamon twigs.

"Most decorations were edible..."

Mason bounced into her daydream, stuffing an iced cookie into his mouth that he'd plucked from the tree. Liam followed behind him balancing a tray of mini cakes. The plate tipped and Mira was worried they would fall but Seth stepped beside them and caught the edge, righting it. He glanced up at Mira and when their gaze met, he smiled. She blushed and reached for her gold heart locket hanging around her neck.

A child in the front raised her hand and shouted out, pulling Mira from her daydream. "Sometimes I wake up before my mom and lick all the candy canes on our tree!" The others laughed.

Mira pulled her smile back on, glancing at the beaming faces while kids shuffled in the snow and adults whispered to each other. Noah stood at the back of the group but appeared to be listening. Seth moved to stand by him. Noah immediately crossed his arms. Mira watched as she unfolded the paper from her pocket.

She turned back to the children. "So many Christmas traditions come from different places all around the world, joining together to fill this wonderful time with cheer and memories. We learned yesterday, St. Nick originated in Turkey but became a Christmas custom in Holland as Santa Claus. Hanging stockings by the fire came from France or Belgium, hot chocolate was from Mexico, and gingerbread houses and decorating Christmas trees started in Germany. When Prince Albert brought this tradition to Windsor Castle to share with Queen Victoria and their children...to use today's terms...went viral. But, as you can imagine, candles on a drying tree can be very dangerous. So, in 1882, a friend of Thomas Edison—yes, the inventor of the light bulb—decided to hang a string of red, white and blue electric lights on his Christmas Tree.

"What is something you decorate your Christmas tree with?" Mira asked the kids.

Hands shot up and children answered. They loved to place homemade crafts with their pictures, garlands of dried macaroni, or glittery stars that sparkled when the lights brightened their tree. One sad child said his mom decorated the tree and didn't let him touch it. The mom glanced away embarrassed.

Mira scrambled to change the subject. "How should we decorate the town Christmas tree?"

The children shouted out ideas and grew more excited by the moment. Mira realized she lost their attention, but at least they connected with history on a personal level. Several talked about making popcorn or candy garlands. Mason said he'd probably eat those.

She wound her way through the group considering who to ask to cut down the tree. Jesse was distracted in a debate with Elizabeth over which tree they should choose for their home. Luella kept Mark, an older man, busy in conversation and the other men were discussing a "football in the snow" match for later in the evening. She didn't even realize until she stopped that her feet led her to Seth. She hoped the cold was a sufficient explanation for the red coloring her cheeks.

"Would you mind doing the honors by cutting it down?" she asked him.

Seth glanced between her and the pine tree. "Are you sure? I don't think Charles' old Ford will be able to haul that down the mountain."

"It did last year," Mira offered.

Even Noah offered his two cents. "It's the coolest tree so far."

"See? Even Noah agrees with me," Mira said. She lifted her hand for a high-five, and he obliged.

Seth looked at both of them before finally giving in. "Okay, if you can get those kids to stand back."

Mira pretended to salute. "Yes, sir."

He broke into a grin which set butterflies loose in her stomach. As he hurried over to borrow Jesse's chainsaw, Mira's eyes trailed him. He had a confident walk and held his shoulders firm, but she was mostly thankful for his considerate attitude and easy-going nature. He was someone she would like to get to know better. With him around, the holiday didn't seem quite so lonely, the cold wasn't quite so chilly.

Before Seth revved up the chainsaw, Mira gathered the children and moved back down the trail. They could still watch while the men cut the base. And she could continue her musing.

"You should probably wipe that smile off your face before Luella notices." Elizabeth snuck up beside her. "Or nothing I try will distract her from your new interest."

"I'm only thinking about the Christmas tree...and how we should decorate it."

Elizabeth smirked. "Of course. Well, then, plaid flannel is good, but a dress shirt with a tie—"

"Oh my, you're ridiculous!"

"Am I?"

Mira couldn't meet her friend's glance. She fought to regain her composure. It wasn't that Elizabeth was wrong about Mira's thoughts, but she wasn't ready to acknowledge it. This Christmas was supposed to be about missing her mom, not finding someone else to love. "How about the gold and red decorations this year?"

"What?" Elizabeth raised an eyebrow. "That's so boring. I'd prefer bells. You know, the wedding ones."

Mira spun on her with a laugh. "You're worse than Luella!"

Elizabeth put her hands up in surrender. "Fine. I'll stop. But it's good to see you getting into the Christmas spirit."

"What do you mean?"

"Well, your shop is rather dark without the traditional Christmas lights on the doorway and the garlands in the window. Your house always had the brightest colors for the season. I love walking by every day on my way to the library, but this year…"

Mira sighed. She'd noticed the rest of the town decorating for the holidays at the beginning of winter but never had the energy or desire to put anything up. Her grief affected others, even from a distance. She knew it was depression, but she hadn't been able to shake it off. Until now.

"You know, Elizabeth?" she smiled. "You're right. I need to pull those out."

"I'm glad I could help. And…if you need any advice on anything else…" She winked.

Mira rolled her eyes. "No, thanks. I'm sure I can always rely on Luella for that."

Both women laughed.

When Mira rejoined the children, they yelled, "Timber!" Mira cheered along and watched the tree fall. Snow powder billowed up, bringing back memories of climbing the mountain every year with her grandmother and mother to pick a tree for their home and shop. She would always treasure those days. Today, though, she would make room for new memories.

With Liam's shining eyes staring in wonder, she treasured this precious moment. Even Mason stopped running for a minute and Noah stood alongside them to watch. Mira felt the need to say something, to make this memory special for them too but could think of nothing. Instead, they appreciated it in silence.

⁂

Seth finished strapping the tree onto the trailer with Jesse and helped him load another one in the back of his truck. Everyone had returned to the parking lot, bright with the prospect of bringing a fresh tree home to decorate.

"You sure you didn't want a bigger tree?" he asked.

Jesse shook his head. "We prefer a smaller tree we can set up on a table, away from the little guy and our cats. Easier clean up, too."

"That makes sense," Seth said, tightening the ratchet straps.

"Plus," Jesse added. "It means we don't overspend on ornaments, but don't tell her that." He nodded his head in Elizabeth's direction as she finished buckling their son in his car seat.

She leaned out and called back, "I heard that. But jokes on you! I'll still buy extra."

Jesse chuckled. "I love you, honey."

"I love you more." She smirked as she joined them. "Maybe I should go to Mira's shop tomorrow and ask her what her most expensive ornament is?"

"Except I spent all our holiday savings on that book yesterday."

Elizabeth shook her head and nudged Jesse playfully. "You know, if you wanted that book, you could have checked it out at the library."

"But it was a first-edition!" Jesse wrapped his arm around her waist and kissed the top of her head.

Seth turned away from their conversation and focused his attention on the ratchet straps, making sure everything was secure. "It's good to go." He interrupted their whispering. "Besides, Mira's shop is closed, so you couldn't get an ornament there."

He noticed Elizabeth's eyes narrow in interest and Jesse shrug. "Looks like you can't spend more money."

"I spend money?" Elizabeth rolled her eyes. "I don't want to hear another man talk about women's spending after you two paid thousands of dollars yesterday for things you could buy cheaper."

"It was for charity!"

"And who's going to show me charity when you go broke?" she laughed and waved to the leaving families. "We should actually head out now if we want the little guy to nap before dinner."

Jesse nodded and shook Seth's hand. They hopped in their truck and turned on the gravel road back to Cedar Springs.

Seth turned to survey who was still on the mountain, but it was just him and his boys. And Mira.

His eyes settled on her as she kneeled beside Liam with a laugh. The little boy was making snow angels. Mira leaned forward and drew in details along the edges; a halo above his head, clouds beneath his feet, and even a harp beside his arm.

"Make it a guitar!" Liam squealed.

Seth couldn't fight the grin. Mason and Liam's smiles reappeared after a long year of grief and behavior problems. They giggled freely again and chatted away with their grandma and him, something that'd been few and far between since last January. Their improvement began after the gingerbread decorating, when they'd connected with Mira. Both boys talked about her occasionally, always with a smile and exclaiming what a nice person she was.

As he watched the smile light up her face, he couldn't help but think how she had befriended him as well. Her support is what his family needed during the holiday, maybe even going forward. Some of the tense worry weighing on his shoulders loosened whenever she came around now. She was someone he enjoyed spending time with, who understood him. There was something about her that related to what they were going through. After he had seen the photographs on her fireplace mantle, it finally clicked.

Her family's history was written all over Cedar Springs. But they were no longer there. She was alone; her first Christmas alone, like him and his boys. She didn't just recognize their grief but was living through her own. And, based on her confession to him last night, she was losing everything that connected her to the past. Her shop was a treasure trove of personal history, family stories, and a generational investment.

Now he finally grasped why she'd been so tense with him after the accident in the store. It wasn't broken items, but a shattered family history.

This morning, when he saw the damaged teapot, it finally dawned on him. It wasn't an old relic, but a living embodiment of the people Mira knew and loved. It was even on the signage of the shop, between the words Vintage Treasures.

One small mistake led to a loss too intimate for him to fully understand.

He ran a hand through his hair in frustration at himself and turned away from Liam and Mira's merry moment. He wouldn't interject himself and interrupt their joy. Noah was already waiting in the truck, grumpy like usual. He glanced around to find his middle boy.

"Mason, where are you?" Seth called from the edge of the parking lot. He spotted the mischievous child climbing a tree. "Come down. It's time to go."

Mira and Liam heard him and dusted the snow off before racing back to the truck. She let the little boy win but ducked her head when Seth glanced their way.

"You ready?" he asked.

Mira nodded. "Thanks for...driving and loading up the tree." She nibbled her lip awkwardly and Seth wondered if it was because of something he did or said but he'd been very careful not to give the wrong impression. He knew what gossip in a small town was like. He'd also seen how that annoying woman Luella glanced at him every several minutes and whispered to anyone within hearing distance. All day, he'd made it a point to avoid her. But little communities, in a group like this, after seeing two single people arrive together, would speculate.

He wanted more time with Mira. After singing Christmas songs in the car, they'd talked about random holiday traditions around the world. Her eyes had lit up with an inner fire when he shared some of his adventures, domestic and abroad. It renewed his own wanderlust: the early morning run to catch a flight, the first scents of a country stepping off a plane on a foreign airstrip, and the whistle of a train before steaming the station with smoke. Even now, his fingers fidgeted with the truck keys. What journeys awaited him and his boys? She wanted to learn about all these places, and he wanted to share them with her.

But once she'd stepped out of the truck, she'd shut him out. The gleam faded from her eyes and her eager interest dulled into a mask of responsibility as she led the group on the tree hunt. He only saw the glimmer return in the occasional moments where they crossed paths again, during the snowball fight and when she glanced his way during her history lesson.

He held the truck door open for his boys to scramble up. Mira followed, her auburn eyes snagging on his.

Seth's pulse quickened. He closed her door once she was inside, then walked around to the driver's side, taking deep breaths. Before opening his door, he shook his head trying to loosen wayward thoughts that clung to him like sap from the pine tree. He couldn't allow any romantic feelings in his heart. This wasn't the reason he came to Cedar Springs, and he wouldn't let it yank him off track. He needed to remain focused and secure connections that encouraged his boys' and their healing. Mason and Liam were finally on the right track. If only he could find some way to plug in Noah.

He finally clambered into the driver's seat and stuck the key into the ignition. Hopefully they'd make it back soon so he could have some quiet time alone to process his concerns. Being around a group of people all day while keeping an eye on his boys, especially the wandering Noah, frazzled his nerves.

The truck sputtered and jolted.

"Uh-oh."

He turned the key again but with the same result. It sounded like it had run out of gas but the gauge had been over halfway when they'd left town. He frowned.

"What's wrong?" Mira asked.

Seth clenched his jaw. "Not sure." He climbed out and lifted the hood. Maybe he'd gain a better idea of the problem if he had a moment alone to collect his thoughts. He leaned forward and studied the radiator. It was old but well-maintained.

The car door shut and he glanced up to see Mira join him.

Seth ran a hand through his hair, worry beginning to settle in his temples with a throbbing headache. "Is everyone gone already?"

Mira nodded.

"Of course." He clenched his fists and unclenched them several times, trying to even out his breathing. Sometimes that helped ease his migraines, but more often than not, it made him more tense. He sucked in a long breath and held it. "Can you call Jesse and Elizabeth to come back?"

Mira bit her lip. "Um...I don't have a phone."

"What?" His mind buzzed at the irony of the situation. Of course, of all the people to be stuck on a mountain with, it had to be a girl who was so obsessed with history she refused modern conveniences such as a cell phone. He sucked in another breath and tried to focus his thoughts. He had his phone but no one's number. Beside his mom's. But by the time she could get help, they'd be out here for a couple more hours.

"I suppose in a moment like this, one would come in handy," Mira rambled. "But I've never needed one..."

She glanced up cautiously as he raised an eyebrow.

"Until now?" Seth wanted to be annoyed. He wanted to complain and, at least once, leave the burden on someone else. But she stared up at him with wide eyes, the color of dark honey. Even though it didn't resolve the situation, and they were still stuck, most of his anger melted away.

Just like he trained his boys, when emotions crowded in on him, he turned his mind to making the situation humorous. It had been Ana's specialty. From the time she started a fried chicken fire to the trip they forgot to get off the bus and ended up paying $30 in taxi fare to get back, she'd learn to spin situations into comedy. Before Seth could grow overwhelmed, Ana would find some way to make him laugh. After she was gone, he'd tried to do the same with his boys.

A smile quirked Seth's lips so Mira would understand his teasing. "You probably can't take your rotary phone on trips out of the house."

She breathed in relief and chuckled. "Actually, it's a touch-tone. The rotary phone no longer works." She stood next to him and glanced down at the truck's engine. "What's wrong with it?"

He shook his head. "I don't know." At her worried look, he reassured her. "We'll figure it out. And this will give the boys more time to play in the snow."

Seth wasn't sure if she recognized the doubt in his voice, but she gave an encouraging smile.

"I'll watch the boys."

He turned his attention to his phone for solutions, but the service was ridiculously slow. He leaned his head against the hood and groaned.

Finally, he decided to tinker around and see if he could cold start it. These older models were tricky, or so he remembered from his dad, a car fanatic. He'd never taken after him, preferring sleek newer drives, mostly because he didn't want to fix an old automobile all the time.

He turned the key and pumped the gas pedal slowly a couple of times, careful not to flood the carburetor, but it spurted and went out again. The more he tried, the more frustrated he grew. He grumbled under his breath, ignoring the boys building a snowman, as he stared under the hood again. Now he wished he'd helped his dad more often when he'd spruced up the old classics.

Remembering his bratty attitude, he glanced over to his boys. Only Mason and Liam played at rolling snow and stuffing sticks in its sides to make a snow monster with Mira. His eyes trailed back to the car, but Noah wasn't inside. He grumbled, wiping greasy hands on his jeans and walked over to them.

"Have you seen Noah?"

A frown crossed Mira's face. "No. I thought he was in the truck."

Seth shook his head. This kid would be the one who broke him. He tried not to show his frustration. "I'll check down the road if you can look back on the trail."

Mira nodded, taking Mason and Liam's hands. "I'll keep them with me."

"Thanks."

They set off back the way they'd hiked earlier, and Seth let his shoulders slump. He finally had a moment alone, but it was under a cloud of worry and irritation. He was reaching his wit's end with Noah after trying everything.

Ever since Ana died, there had been a disconnect between him and his oldest son. With each passing month, that gap grew wider. It worried him more than he let on but it was chipping away at him in bigger and bigger chunks until he wouldn't be able to hold it together anymore. Eventually, Seth would crumble.

The stillness of the snow settled over him as he slowed his steps between giant pine trees. He let that calm wash through him and tug the throbbing headache away until it was only a hum in the back of his mind. But as it did, it magnified the loneliness he tried to drown out.

At home in the city, it was easy to hide from the gnawing feeling deep inside. He couldn't focus on it long enough to pin down and identify because he was scrambling to catch up with industry tasks, the boys' homework, and keeping them alive. The daily things he needed to complete were a continual dripping: feed them, school, work, business meetings, screens, after-school program, dinner, homework, showers, bed. Repeat. Repeat. Repeat. It grated on him like sandpaper. And, after nearly a year since Ana passed, none of them had woken up from their grief.

Until Mason and Liam came to Cedar Springs. But he knew Noah was still lost somewhere in that nightmare alone.

Seth didn't have time to consider his own healing journey. He was too busy taking care of everyone else and keeping that train moving on those rickety tracks. Even now, he wouldn't have a moment to spare since he caught sight of Noah around the bend.

"Where do you think you're going?" he called out.

Noah glanced back and trudged to a stop. "Nowhere. Obviously."

"What's with you?" Seth finally caught up with the boy. "We're all trying to get everything working and you're fighting against us. Can't you be—I don't know—something other than this...grumpiness?"

"What? What do you want from me?" Noah glared between furrowed eyebrows.

"Just try to be helpful. Be a part of the family."

"What family? Can't you see we're broken, dad?"

Seth's headache returned with a vengeance. "Who isn't? The world is full of broken people but we have to keep living and doing all the things—"

"Why?" Noah crossed his arms. "What's the point?"

"The point?" he frowned. "Does that really matter right now? Get back to the truck."

They turned back the way they came but this time Noah walked quicker. His steps moved past his dad, bumping his elbow as he went by.

"What's the hurry?" Seth asked.

Noah didn't bother looking back. "To get away from you."

Breathe in. Breathe out. Seth tried to calm his thoughts, but they spiraled with anger, grief, frustration. All of it was lost and spinning inside him, confused. He clenched his fists and gritted his teeth, but it made the rest of his body tense. It only hammered home his concerns with certainty. He'd reached the end of his frayed rope. There was no way he could continue or reach out to his son alone. They needed help.

❧

Mira walked with Mason and Liam. She could see Seth had been growing frustrated and needed some time alone. Besides, taking the boys meant more eyes looking with her and it'd be easier to spot Noah if he'd gone this way. They followed the trail all the way back to where they had cut down the Christmas tree but there were still no signs of the oldest boy.

"He probably wandered off cause he's a big grump," Liam said.

"He's been a jerk since Mom died," Mason added.

Mira clasped the boys' hands in her own as they turned back. "We all deal with losing someone differently."

"I cried for a long time."

"I still cry every night," Liam confessed.

"Me too," Mira whispered. "But sometimes people grow angry. They don't understand why things happen the way they do, which I don't think we ever will, but it makes them mad."

"It's not our fault," Liam gripped her hand tighter.

Mason agreed. "Or Dad's fault. And Noah has been the meanest to him."

"That isn't right," Mira said. "But when someone is hurting, they aren't thinking about others' feelings. Only that their own are shattered."

"It's still not okay."

"No, it's not but maybe we can help him." Mira swung the boys' arms as they walked and their smiles came back. "Maybe we can do something Noah enjoys to help him remember how to be happy."

The younger boys perked up at this. "Noah likes Legos."

"And candy."

"Maybe we can get him a puppy!"

"Or a new video game?"

"What about hugs?"

"Nah, candy is better."

Mira chuckled at their ideas, but it sparked some of her own. She remembered how Noah had a better time yesterday helping at the silent auction. He needed something to keep him busy, redirect his mind to a different path, like she did.

They returned to the truck to find Seth and Noah already back. But they were locked in a fierce argument. Noah finally huffed and climbed back into the truck, slamming the door as loud as he could. Seth gave an exasperated groan and turned back to the open hood. He stared at the machinery inside, but his look was focused far away on problems he couldn't see a way out of.

Mira bent down to Mason and Liam, pointing to their snow monster. "How about you two build another snowman? We don't want to leave this one all alone out here."

They nodded and Mason added, "He needs a brother!" Both boys ran off to roll more snow.

Mira approached Seth and announced herself with a cough. When he glanced up, she noticed his eyes were rimmed in red. He rubbed a hand over his face and took a deep breath.

Before he could say anything, Mira shared her own story. "My mom died this year, too."

His glance snagged on hers and a wrinkle formed between his eyebrows.

"I'm not going to say I know exactly what Noah is going through because I wasn't a kid when I lost one of the most important people in my life, but I do understand." She moved closer and leaned against the front of the truck. Her eyes focused on a patch of snow several feet away. It was easier for her to talk this way, without making eye contact and worrying about her facial expressions giving too much of herself away.

This was the first time she'd finally opened up to someone who didn't know what had happened. Beverly listened often, but she didn't want to burden the older woman. It was cathartic to tell her own story. "My mom was everything to me. We did everything together. This whole 12 Days to Christmas festival was her idea several years ago.

"I wasn't going to do it this year but...it felt worse not to, like I wasn't honoring her memory. At first, I was confused and avoided everyone—which isn't easy in a small town," she added with a laugh. "And then I got angry. Why did other people my age still have their parents? One terrible thought was: why did Charles beat cancer, but my mom didn't. I know, it isn't fair, and I can't compare the two. But I was lost in my grief."

"I'm sorry," Seth whispered.

Mira looked up and met his gaze. This time she wanted him to see the reflection in her eyes, the understanding and concern it held. "I think Noah is lost, too. He needs to find his way back. To remember he still has the rest of his family and that you love him. He might run off to be alone, but it's probably the last thing he wants or needs."

At her words, Seth crumpled. He reached out and held the edge of the truck, his muscles tensing as he clenched the metal and released. He drew in a shaky breath. "How?" Seth asked. "How do I do that? Especially when I feel the same way."

Mira stared back down at her feet. Seeing the raw truth etched on Seth's face was too personal and intimate. Whatever he'd been through with Noah must've been rough. She wanted to help and give him advice, but she hadn't figured out this part either. Every day was still a struggle, when she'd wake up and the reality crashed down on her again or those moments where she was lost in a task and—for just a second—forgot, but she hoped she was getting better. She hadn't dissolved into tears today yet.

"I don't know," she finally admitted. "Because this grief will never go away. Sometimes it feels like a shadow lingering in the corner of my heart, but other days it flares up and reminds me of every little thing I lost." Her words felt heavy speaking them, but once they were out, her heart immediately lightened. A burden lifted.

Seth reached across the space dividing them and took her hand. The warmth of his grip radiated through her mittens and settled in her heart. In that moment, she did not feel alone. She clung to the sensation and let it comfort her. When she met his gaze, his steady eyes settled her worries.

Seth spoke, "I was hoping this trip to Cedar Springs would help and it has. Mason and Liam are happier here than they've been all year. And it's all because of you. Thank you for reaching out to them—to us."

Mira held his look but didn't know what to say. She wasn't sure if there was anything to say. Barely knowing him a week, and she'd already confessed heart topics she couldn't share with anyone else. In that short time, she had grown to understand Seth more than she knew people she'd grown up alongside. It was an invisible bond connecting them that pulled her from her misery. Her hand grew warmer in his grip, and she squeezed back. "I—"

"I found it!" Mason's voice echoed from the back of the truck, breaking the moment. Seth stepped away and hurried around to Mason standing in the truck bed. "Is this what we need?" He held up a red gas can.

Seth broke into a laugh that shattered the awkwardness. Mira couldn't tell if it was forced but it relieved the pressure and sensation building up around her rib cage.

"Could it really have been that easy?" Seth said. He took the can and filled the tank. When he tried to start the truck again, the engine roared to life.

As they scrambled back into the truck, Seth caught Mira's glance again and smiled.

She returned it. "Sometimes our most complicated problems have the simplest solutions."

❦

Seth gripped the steering wheel the entire drive down the mountain. He could feel the truck's engine rumbling with age and hoped it wouldn't give out again. Today had been awkward enough but now something strange was stirring inside him. Something he hadn't felt for a year.

He shouldn't have reached out for Mira's hand but he saw the same pain in her eyes that reflected back at him every morning in the mirror. He wasn't sure what would ease her grief. He'd only reacted the way he wished someone would for him. Since his wife's death he'd felt incredibly lonely. No matter how many hugs his mother or sons gave him, something was still missing. Was it wrong for him to feel that relief after he came in contact with Mira? It was as if the worries pressing down on his shoulders lifted for a moment.

Seth tried to push those thoughts away. He sang along to Christmas carols with the kids and was even surprised to hear Noah's voice join in.

Except whenever he glanced in her direction, Mira's smile glittered with life.

It was captivating to watch her eyes light up when she spoke with his boys or looked at him. At their first meeting, she'd been closed off, her loss a curtain she hid behind. The broken teapot, added to that grief. He didn't know how he could make it up to her, but he had to try. She'd already done so much for him, he considered as he listened to the boys singing. Even Noah responded to her despite being closed off to everyone else. If they enjoyed Cedar Springs and regained their old behaviors, with joking and laughter like they were before Ana's accident, it would change everything for him.

He pushed those thoughts from his mind, listening to Mira's voice rise over the commotion. The boys tried singing a round but kept losing their spot, so they sang along with Mira. She laughed and caught his glance. He wasn't sure if she was still cold from the hike in the snow, but her cheeks were flushed red. He grinned back and sang along, this time helping the boys keep to their chorus when they began the round again.

Chapter Nine

Friday, December 21

Mira took her time getting ready the next morning. Donning an 1840s-themed gown was difficult hooking the corset on her own. So was loosened the curlers from her hair, one at a time to preserve the perfect ringlets, while she stared in the distance. From her bedroom window, she had a clear view of Cedar Springs.

The town glistened under a fresh blanket of snow. The only place it was disturbed was where several volunteers set up the Christmas tree they brought back yesterday.

Her face flushed when she thought about the drive back home. Seth asked each boy to pick Christmas songs and had Noah play it from an app on his phone. They even sang along to the song Mira chose. Their voices blended differently than at caroling. It was still a beautiful sound and left Mira feeling happy and light-hearted after Seth dropped her off.

Liam and Mason had nodded off to sleep so Mira whispered her good-bye. "It was a wonderful time. Thank you for the ride."

Seth grinned. "What's the theme for tomorrow?" He pointed to her Victorian-style gloves and braided hair. "So we can dress appropriately."

"The Christmas Carol." Mira smiled back. "Are you going to be Scrooge?"

With a laugh, Seth answered, "Now there's an idea. Thank you again for all you do. Have a good night, Mira."

Mira yanked herself back to the present after she accidentally tugged too quickly on a curl. The strange bubbly feeling in her chest, after hearing Seth say her name, remained. Even her hand felt warmer, where he had held it. For once, she didn't feel completely alone while sharing about her mother's death. Except, it was more than that...and this new sensation had nothing to do with grief.

It fluttered through her like spring butterflies. She hummed and swayed in place; a giddy smile reflected from the mirror.

For the first time preparing the 12 Days festival this year, she honestly looked forward to the day. Spending time with Liam and Mason, and Seth too, brought some of the cheer back to the holiday. Hopefully a Christmas miracle was in the works to bring joy to Noah as well. To distract her from thoughts of Seth, she brainstormed ideas of things Noah would like to do, something that would bring a smile to his face. She didn't have much interaction with pre-teen boys except when she volunteered at the school. Perhaps he'd be interested in the vintage weapons and armor she had in her antique collection.

She pulled the blue and purple silk dress over her hoop skirt and buttoned her waistcoat over the top. Last of all, she twirled her hair in a messy bun on her head with the curls brushing the sides of her forehead and placed her red and purple ruffled bonnet over the top. She figured this would become one of her favorite outfits because the skirts were full of volume, and she could add warm leggings underneath. It felt like a cozy blanket, but fashionable. Obviously in a different era, not that it altered her opinion.

When she was finally ready, she grabbed her cloak from the stand by the door and headed out. She tried not to focus on her shop as she hurried through, ignoring all the items she'd have to sell come the new year. Today, she would focus on enjoying the present and living through Christmas traditions.

She arrived at Cedar Springs Community Library when Elizabeth was unlocking the building. "Wow, I haven't seen that fancy dress before. Did you make it?"

"You know the local market doesn't sell vintage fashions. I've checked," Mira laughed.

"How are you so talented?"

Mira's eyebrows furrowed at this. Sewing hadn't been something she considered herself especially talented at, more of a hobby she enjoyed, but perhaps putting together an entire dress made her useful at something. She'd need to inventory all her abilities and see which of her *talents* could land her a job in the future.

Elizabeth continued chatting away. "I have an assortment of Christmas books set aside if you want to read any of them aloud or kids can go through and choose their own."

When they entered, she pointed to the comfortable seating in the main area of the library. There was also an electric fireplace and Christmas tree surrounded by sitting pillows. It was a perfect space.

"Sounds wonderful! Thank you!"

It wasn't long before town residents joined. The fire crackled warmly at their backs while the Christmas tree flickered with red and green lights and soft instrumental carols poured from the speakers. Grandparents cuddled with their grandchildren in their lap, reading *The Night Before Christmas* and *The Polar Express*. Mira had a group of children sitting around her as she reenacted *The Mitten*, using plastic animal figures and stuffing them into a child-sized mitten. They thought it was the silliest thing and laughed with every animal she added. She faked a sneeze and all the animals fell out. The children roared. Mira couldn't help but giggle at their joy.

"Again! Again!" a four-year old girl, Elsie, clapped and shouted.

Mira showed the children both mittens, one the original size and the other stretched out. "I'll read it again later," she said. "How about you pick one of the other books to read?" Several of the children hurried off to choose a book. Mira's attention was pulled by another family entering the library.

She looked up to see Liam, draped in shimmery costume fabric with a craft paper top hat. Mira burst into laughter. "Who are you supposed to be?"

Liam grinned in his silly way. "I'm the ghost of Christmas past!"

Mason appeared behind him and Mira's laugh grew louder. He was dressed in all red with a baby's bib around his neck that read, "Let's eat!" and a flashlight in his left hand. "Guess who I am?" Mason asked.

"The ghost of Christmas present?" Mira said.

"Yup!" Mason grinned and stuck his right hand in his pocket. "Want a snack?" When he pulled his hand from his pocket, he opened grubby fingers to reveal half-melted chocolate candies.

"No thanks. I'm good."

Last of all, Seth and Noah walked in together. Noah's costume was startling compared to his brothers. He was draped in a long black trench coat, *Matrix* style, and said nothing. Mira was at a loss for words.

Until she saw Seth. He wore a fancy tuxedo with a bright green vest and shiny top hat. He rapped his cane on the floor when their eyes met and spoke in a poor rendition of a British accent. "Hello there! Young lady!"

Mira covered her mouth to hide her amusement.

"Ah, yes, you." Seth approached her. "Are you the head-mistress of this establishment?"

Playing along, Mira dropped in a short curtsy. "How may I help you, fine gentleman?"

"You call me fine?" He raised an eyebrow and a blush bloomed on Mira's cheeks. Before she could stammer a reply, Seth continued, "My name is Ebenezer. Ebenezer Scrooge, that is."

The four-year old girl who wanted to hear *The Mitten* story again pointed a finger at Seth. "I know you! You're the bad guy!"

Mira kneeled next to her. "Have you heard *The Christmas Carol*?"

She shook her head. "But I watched the movie."

"Maybe this kind gentleman would be willing to read the book to us. An abridged version, of course." Mira glanced up at Seth with a question in her eyes.

"As I said before, my name is not *"Kind"* either. It's Ebenezer Scrooge." He took his top hat off and bowed. "But I would be honored to share my tale to you all and perhaps you may learn a lesson from it."

All the children hurried over and plopped themselves on the floor or on the pillows. Even adults gathered around and listened while Seth retold the story of *The Christmas Carol*.

As his voice rose in the introduction, Mira was mesmerized by his acting skills. He spoke to other adults standing in the library as if they were part of the production, calling out Jesse as Bob Cratchit. Elizabeth sat next to Mira with her son on her lap and giggled at her husband's stage fright. Jesse stuffed his hands in his pockets and replied in a monotone voice. The children found it hysterical.

When Seth pretended to fall asleep, he pushed a group of boys from one of the library couches and laid down. A fake snore rippled from him. That's when Evelyn walked in, draped in a nightgown and holding an oil lamp she bought from Mira's shop. "Scro*ooo*ge," she cackled. She played the part of Marley's ghost so well that Mira didn't mind the lamp was from the wrong era.

Most people laughed but Elsie moved closer to Mira, frightened. Mira put an arm around her and whispered it was only a show but they both jumped after Liam dashed past them, careening to the front.

"I'm the ghost of Christmas past!" he shouted.

Seth followed Liam around the library. They greeted individuals in the audience like they'd just arrived at a wonderful party. He tipped his hat at Elizabeth and stopped in front of Mira. She blinked. What came next in the story?

"My dearest Belle," Seth stretched his hand out toward her.

Mira's face burned bright red. Luella, sitting in the far back, snickered loud enough for all to hear. Mira hesitated, unsure what to do. Should she play along with his performance? Elizabeth elbowed her in the side, pushing her forward. Finally, Mira reached up and took Seth's hand. He pulled her to her feet with an apology.

They stood in a small cottage with warm candles lit in the windows and snow along the sills. Some of the cold seeped in but she was happy since he held her hand as the lilting melody of a harpsichord echoed faintly from the other room. She'd dressed in her finest gown, although it wasn't much since the fabric was repurposed and the slippers were wearing thin, but she wanted to look beautiful tonight...just in case. She looked from their clasped hands up to his face and the black hat he purchased for the special occasion. He worked hard and she was grateful but she wanted him to understand that riches weren't the most important thing in his life. Maybe she could show him. But before she had a chance, he spoke.

"I'm sorry I have spent all my time at work. But I must make money. I must make more money!" Seth spoke in a theatrical voice. It spilled from reality and seeped into Mira's dream to the point where she wasn't entirely sure where she was in that moment.

She read *The Christmas Carol* every year and knew how to play her part to perfection.

She yanked her hand away dramatically and frowned at him.

"Money! That's all you think about!"

Was it wrong that she had hoped he would forgo buying the hat of his dreams and instead buy the ring of hers? Any ring would do, because it wasn't the material possession she cared about. She wanted to spend the rest of her life with him because she loved him...

That thought shook Mira from the daydream and back to reality. Yet Seth still stood right beside her, looking smug in his top hat. He turned toward the audience and raised his hands in a shrug. "What else is there?"

The adults in the audience chuckled and the little girls gasped. One little boy shouted something about food being the most important. It may have been Mason, but Mira wasn't sure because the daydream was sucking her back in.

"What else?" Mira said.

She placed her hand against her chest acting affronted and then waved it around. Although they were alone in the sitting room, their friends and family were waiting in the parlor. They were all hoping for a proposal.

"What about your friends? What about your family?" Mira paused.

Something about her daydream wasn't right.

Something was spinning out of control.

It was growing more difficult to distinguish the emotions from her imagination and reality.

Where there once had been a line differentiating between the two, it grew blurry.

She stared back at Seth in confusion.

"What about *me?*"

The crowd *ooh*-ed.

She fought back the blush burning her cheeks again when Seth looked at her with concern framed in his furrowed brows...

...this time in front of the whole town. They leaned closer, watching with interest. She finished her lines before she lost the nerve.

"Do you even love me as much as you love money?"

Their gaze held each other a moment too long.

Even though they were in a crowded library, all Mira could hear was her own heartbeat while she stared into Seth's eyes. She was aware how he moved toward her, tilted his head lower, opened his mouth to speak...

Mira almost forgot the role she was playing, the reality, or the dream. She wasn't sure which. She blinked rapidly and yanked away. "No, it's impossible." She dropped back down next to Elizabeth.

As the retelling continued, all the children were enraptured with the story. They cried for Tiny Tim and scowled at Scrooge. They cheered on all three of Seth's boys playing the ghosts, even for Noah who they regarded with a nervous respect. When Scrooge finally changed at the end, everyone stood and clapped. The kids cheered.

The little girl from earlier, Elsie, approached Seth and took his hand. "I'm glad you're nice now."

He grinned. "Me too. It's always better to give than receive," he answered, remaining in character with his ridiculous accent. "Christmas is a time to care about others—" As he spoke, she pulled him in Mira's direction.

"Are you going to marry Belle now?" she asked.

It was Seth who turned red this time. He glanced at Mira and Elizabeth who turned from their conversation at that moment. "Uh...well." He coughed and dropped the accent, using his real voice. "Scrooge didn't learn his lesson until he was too old."

"But what happened to Belle?"

Seth looked back at Elsie. "She married someone else who knew what the most important thing is."

Elsie whispered, like it was a big secret. "What is it?"

"What's what?"

"What's the most important thing?" she asked again.

"Lov—" he cleared his throat again. "Family. Loving your family is the most important. And that's what Christmas reminds us. To care about others and help them when we can."

"But Scrooge didn't have any family." She tilted her head to the side. "Oh! I know! He made a new family because he was kind to Tiny Tim!"

Seth chuckled when Elsie ran back to her mom.

"You have a way with kids," Elizabeth remarked.

Seth shrugged. "Not always." They followed his glance to Noah who had found a corner seat once the story was over. He was slumped on the chair, scrolling through his phone again. It was an odd sight, since he was still dressed as a holiday version of the Grim Reaper. "But at least they all wanted to wear costumes with me today."

They chuckled at Liam who was spinning around in front of Luella and some of her friends. He waved his hands up and down making the fabric glitter between colors. "I'm a dragon!" Liam ran in circles around the fireplace.

"Where's Mason?" Mira asked. They looked around but couldn't find the middle boy. She stood and helped Seth look for him in the aisles.

"He's probably climbing one of these bookshelves somewhere," Seth commented.

Mira smiled. "I wouldn't be surprised. But he's the cutest tornado I've ever met."

He laughed.

"Thank you." Mira paused between stacks of young adult fiction books. "Your storytelling was amazing and perfect for today's theme."

"My pleasure," Seth bowed dramatically again. "It's been a lot of fun. I see why you plan these events."

"Oh!" Mira's eyes widened. "I was supposed to plan a speech about the history and theme of *The Christmas Carol*."

"Do we need to go back?"

Before she could answer, they heard a giggle on the other side of the shelf. Seth peered over but since Mira wasn't tall enough, she pushed aside some books and peered through. Two brown eyes stared back at her. "Found you," she said.

Mason was sitting against the bookshelf, eating all the candy in his pockets. His mouth was smeared with chocolate and candy wrappers littered the carpet around him.

"Oh no," Seth grimaced. "You were supposed to share those with all the kids."

Mason attempted a weak smile. "I forgot."

Seth shook his head and stepped back where Mason couldn't see him, but Mira could. A wide grin broke across his face, and he covered his mouth to keep from laughing too loud. "Some days I have no clue what I'm doing, but at least we have fun with it."

"Dad?" Mason's voice echoed from the other aisle. "My tummy hurts."

Seth's shoulders drooped. "And other times, I can't keep up." The humor faded from his face, and he looked defeated.

Mira stepped nearer. "You're doing everything you can." She considered reaching out like he did the other day, but her hands remained stiff at her sides. "Kids will be kids. They make life an adventure."

"It's been a wild adventure," Seth said.

"But it's worth it." Before he could make an excuse, Mira pointed to his top hat. "Right, Scrooge? You said this was the most important part of life."

"I suppose..." He met her eyes and nodded. "If I get myself quoted back to me, I must give wise advice."

She chuckled. Until they heard Mason make a gagging sound. They rushed to the other aisle and Seth took Mason to the bathroom. Mira rejoined the group and continued reading stories to the other kids while Liam sat in her lap.

Elizabeth and her son sat beside Mira, but Liam grew distracted and made up his own stories, acting them out for the two-year-old. Elizabeth took the interruption as a time to nudge Mira.

"So, what was that?"

Mira frowned. "What was what?"

"You know exactly what I'm talking about." Elizabeth winked. "And the whole town was watching. I can't save you from Luella now."

"Maybe I don't need saving."

"Oh! You admit it!"

"I won't admit to anything." Mira pressed her lips together.

"That's fine. You don't need to share your secrets. Besides, we all saw the two of you flirting."

"I did not!"

Elizabeth smirked. "Then what happened between you and Mr. *Scrooge*?"

"We were reenacting the story. That's it!"

"Really? Is that what you were doing when the two of you snuck off a couple minutes ago?"

Mira's face burned red, especially after Luella caught her glance and pursed her lips. "What do you mean? I was helping him look for Mason."

"Sure, girl." Elizabeth waggled her eyebrows.

They turned their attention back to the kids before the boys started break dancing or showing off their wrestling moves. Elizabeth gathered them together and read *How the Grinch Stole Christmas* in an animated way, even imitating Jim Carey's voice.

After Seth and Mason finished, they came back to the group. The middle boy was clean of all melted chocolate, but his face was pale. He slumped on a seat, holding his belly.

"Sorry," Seth apologized. "But we have to go. I need to get some real food in this guy."

"I'm hungry for French fries!" Mason simpered as if he didn't throw up two pockets worth of candy.

"Connie's Diner has the best fries and burgers in town," Mira offered.

"Sounds good," Seth said. He waved Noah over and Liam pulled himself away from Mira. "Hey," he glanced down at his watch absentmindedly. "You've been here all day, right?"

Mira nodded.

"Then you should join us."

Mira stuttered for an excuse, but Elizabeth jumped in quickly. "That's a good idea. Mira, go to lunch. I'll keep an eye on everything here until you get back."

Without a reason to avoid time alone with Seth and his boys, Mira finally nodded.

✦

The diner was quiet when they entered but the waitress, Joy, broke the silence with her laugh on seeing their costumes. "Ya'll look like you walked right out of a book!"

Seth nodded. "It's something like that."

She sat them at a corner booth. "So, what's the occasion?"

"I'm a ghost!" Liam said.

"Oh, wow," Joy side-eyed him. "I guess that means you're scary."

"No!" Liam laughed. "I'm the nice one. Noah's the scary one." He pointed across the table at his older brother.

Noah's eyes flicked up from his phone. "Boo."

Joy raised her eyebrows. "Well, now I'm scared. Frightened." She pulled out a small notebook from her pocket and snapped it open to an empty page. "So, what you ghosts eating today?"

"French fries!" Mason cheered.

Seth opened the menu. He'd been in a hurry to get himself and the boys ready this morning and forgot to eat breakfast, even though his mom made her banana buttermilk waffles, fried eggs, and breakfast sausage. When he was younger, he'd pile all the food on top of the waffles, drizzle the whole thing with syrup, and eat three of them before his mom slowed him down. It was a special moment stepping into the kitchen to see his boys around the table with her, eating his favorite meal from childhood. Only Mason ate it the way Seth did. The food on Noah's plate was separated so nothing would touch each other, and Liam ate with his hands, even his eggs. Seth had basically given up trying to make the boy eat with silverware. It was a battle he was okay to lose. Someday, utensils would finally make sense and he'd use them. Until then, Liam would continue pretending to be a wild animal, complete with a T-rex roar that startled Grandma.

Now, thinking about food, Seth's stomach growled. "What's good?" he asked.

Joy's eyebrows rose even higher, if such a thing was possible. "Everything. Obviously."

Mira nodded. "She's right. Connie makes the best food." She ordered her food on a split check, ignoring his glance in her direction. He'd invited her for lunch, mostly to give his boys more time with her, no other reasons of his own, but he planned to pay for her meal, even if it wasn't a date. He knew Mira was in a tight spot financially.

"I'll take the same," he said. "A grilled Reuben sandwich sounds like the perfect comfort food for a winter day. Extra sauerkraut, please."

Joy nodded and took the boys orders: grilled cheese, tomato soup, mac 'n cheese, and French fries. "Calories at Christmas don't count." Joy winked.

When she left, Seth followed Mira's gaze out the window at the Christmas Tree in the center of Main Street Park. "Tomorrow several friends will decorate your tree, Liam," she said. "Then on Monday night, we'll have the lighting ceremony after the Christmas Eve service at church."

Liam stared at the tree with a grin. "I'm glad I picked that one. It's the best."

Mason snorted. "The only thing you pick, Liam, is your boogers."

Seth had just taken a gulp of water and nearly spit it out. "Boys! You can't talk like that at the table!"

But Mira surprised him by giggling. "It's still better than picking the wrong fork in the Donner Party."

His eyes grew wide, and he snorted a laugh. "Whoa. I didn't expect that." His boys stared between him and Mira.

"What's the Donner Party?" Mason asked.

Liam answered, "It's one of Santa's reindeer."

Seth chuckled again and shook his head. "Oh, no. This is something else." He raised an eyebrow at Mira. "A little dark?"

She shrugged. "We're hungry. They were hungry."

This time he couldn't contain himself. He broke down laughing, a deep sound full of levity he hadn't felt for months. "I—can't—believe—" he stuttered. How did she catch him off guard so easily?

The boys still looked confused.

"Some things are worse than picking your nose," Mira explained. "Like a group of people who were trapped on a mountain and ran out of food."

Mason frowned. "That's sad."

"It was very..." Seth said, "...distasteful."

This time he caught Mira by surprise, but she collected herself quickly. "I'm sure it was very hard to *chew*-se—" She couldn't finish her sentence.

"That's cold." Noah stared over the top of his phone at them.

Seth tried to compose himself. "Did you Google it?"

"Yeah."

"I mean, there was a blizzard. They were freezing," Mira nodded.

Seth wheezed. "I get the cold shoulder." Their laughter began again. "The rest of the party should *chill* a bit."

"Don't you mean *a bite?*" Mira asked. Between laughing at their puns, she saw Noah shake his head.

"You both are terrible."

Seth glanced at his oldest boy. Even though Noah was acting annoyed with him, he noticed the slightest upturn in his lips and caught interest in his eyes. He was still displaying attitude, but something changed. Maybe it was that Noah was participating in the conversation.

He knew he was forcing it and going overboard with his antics, but bad jokes were part of being a dad, and, if it brought Noah into the exchange, he'd continue. "Just the *wurst*," Seth pointed at the bright orange special listed on the lunch menu.

Mira tipped her head back, confused why he was pushing the jokes, but she continued, "Quite *egg*-scellent."

"Can we just eat?" Noah asked. He rolled his eyes at the adults but his grumpiness had fallen away. Now he was acting like a boy embarrassed of his dad's goofiness.

Seth shrugged. "It'd be a *piece of cake*."

Mason's eyes lit up at the mention of dessert.

"*Pie* agree with Noah." Mira grinned. "*Butter* late than never."

Seth watched as his oldest and Mira exchanged a look. Without a twitch of his lips, the barest of smiles reached Noah's eyes. Mira smirked and they both turned raised eyebrows and sarcastic glances at Seth. He wasn't sure what to make of the moment. It made him glad to see their connection, but he wasn't so sure about them teaming up against him. Still, a warm assurance replaced his worries. His boys would need to have a strong bond in the coming months. It was important for siblings to be able to depend on each other.

Joy interrupted their jokes by bringing the food. The smells of fresh French fries, warm Reubens, and coleslaw drowned out all other senses. She set the tray between them while she spoke to Mira. "How is the festival going?"

Mira smiled politely and shared about the day reading at the library and how many people showed up. They talked about a couple people Seth didn't know and Joy recommended a stop for Mira's sleigh tomorrow.

"They could use a bit of cheer this year," Joy said.

Mira nodded. "We all could. Thanks for letting me know. I'll make sure to swing by there when we deliver gifts and meals."

Joy grinned back. "Enjoy your food!" She ruffled Liam's messy hair before turning back to the kitchen. Seth made a mental note to ask his mom to give the boys a haircut. It was another thing he overlooked and often forgot to schedule.

Mason was the first to dive into his food. "I'm starved!"

The kids were silent while they ate, stuffing their faces with the best diner food dipped in globs of ketchup. The quiet unnerved Seth. Although he appreciated calm moments, it felt awkward in a group of people. So, as he ate, he asked Mira about Cedar Springs.

"Everyone knows each other and helps out when they can. Which can be great! Like with Joy recommending a family who needs some extra help this year. Our neighborhood loves to look out for each other," Mira said. "But that comes with a unique set of drawbacks."

"Such us?" Seth asked before taking a bite of his sandwich, one of the best Reubens he'd ever tasted.

"Well, if everyone knows everything...then everyone knows *everything*." Mira chuckled. "I can't buy groceries without making small talk with at least five different people. They always ask about the shop, or a random question about history, or—my favorite—" She rolled her eyes. "When I'm going to get married."

After the words left her mouth, she blinked and blushed awkwardly. It made her nose a bright shade of pink. She hurried to amend that statement, "I mean, they want to know all the details about every decision I make. It's like they don't understand personal space."

Seth shrugged. "I get it. I don't live in a small town but people at work are the same... family is even worse. I love them, don't get me wrong, but sometimes they need to understand some questions are too personal to speak about." He snorted. "Especially similar to that last one you mentioned."

Mira nodded in agreement as Seth continued.

"Because it makes a decent conversation uncomfortable, I turn it around on them."

"Really? How so?"

He chuckled. "Well, the last time an aunt asked me if I'd remarry—similar to Luella on the game night—I asked her if she had anyone in mind."

Mira quirked an eyebrow.

"But, before she could answer, I decided to share my requirements: a list of impossible demands. My aunt shook her head and said I was doomed."

Mira's giggle brought a grin to Seth's face until she asked, "And what was that list?"

"First, she must be great with kids, especially boys. They can be wild sometimes."

Liam decided to roar at that moment to prove his point. It startled them and they laughed.

"I can see that." Mira handed Liam a spoon when he reached for the mac n cheese. He took it and swallowed a giant bite. "After all, you're raising dinosaurs."

Seth continued, "Second, she would have to be hard working, maybe own her own business, or be an expert in her field of study. Someone who can teach what she knows. Also, helping others is something that's important to me." As he spoke, he loosened the collar of his shirt. His skin felt warm beneath it, but he wasn't sure why. Hopefully he wasn't catching the bug going around. "And, last, but most important, she needs to know the secrets of the Rosetta Stone."

Mira tilted her head and Seth was sure he stumped her this time. It'd be awkward if she knew the answer since he was trying to make a point.

Noah interrupted, "The language app?"

Seth shook his head. "No. That was named after an important artifact."

"It wasn't that important," Mira said. "It was a decree. The temple priests proclaiming their support for the king."

He stared at her, impressed that she checked off every item on his list. It shouldn't have surprised him, though. She'd caught him off guard multiple times already, but not in a worrisome way. It inspired and challenged him. He sensed his old self coming back to life, the man who could joke and be witty, smile without tears, and feel without aching.

"What was fascinating about it though, were the three languages inscribed," she explained to Noah. "From Egyptian hieroglyphs, demotic script, and ancient Greek, it made it possible to translate the ancient hieroglyphs and cartouche. It was found in 1799 when Napoleon was campaigning in Egypt but wasn't deciphered until Thomas Young read the name of the Ptolemy. Later, Jean-François

Champollion discovered it was the sound of the language—"

"I've seen the original," Seth interrupted.

Mira spun and stared at him with large auburn eyes. They sparked with a gleam Seth admired. "In the British Museum? Of course, you said you traveled there. What's it like? I mean, the Rosetta Stone in real life."

"It's a giant slab of stone in the center of a room usually crowded by people. They ruined the moment. But, in the Enlightenment Gallery, I was able to see and touch a copy."

Mira gasped. "I dream of going there someday. If I could ever leave this small town, I'd explore the world, from East to West."

"It's not all bad. You have friends, family history, connections here."

"I suppose."

"What about the schools?" Seth asked. His mother had been pressuring him about visiting Cedar Springs since she moved. Now that they were here, she was campaigning for them to stay. The main concerns she voiced were the boys having no family in the city, especially with Seth busy at his job. He wasn't interested in planting roots, but the change in his sons was unmistakable. If they returned home after

Christmas, would life go back to the discouragement it was before?

Mira shared about her times as a substitute, how she enjoyed talking with the students, and how wonderful teachers like Carly taught well. Then he shared about his difficulties in the city with his boys' school and the trouble finding an afterschool program for all three of them. He worked long hours, and it was difficult to make it on time for drop off and pick up. Next year would be more of a challenge when Noah moved up to middle school. Cedar Springs was a small enough town that all three schools, elementary, middle and high school were located on the same street and shared some of the same property.

"You know, if you finish up your degree," Seth said, "I'm sure Cedar Springs High School would love to hire you for a history teacher."

Mira frowned. "I'd have to go back to the university, and pay for tuition,...and my home is here."

"You mentioned a change in the future." He looked at her knowingly, referencing the confession she shared at the silent auction, about the possibility of losing her shop. "Wouldn't now be the best time? And you can take the classes online. No need to move to the city."

Liam decided to jump back into the conversation between bites of French fries. "You can visit us!"

Both Seth and Mira glanced away. From the corner of his eye, he could see a blush reddening her cheeks.

"Online might be a good option," Mira rushed to say.

"I mean, when you have all this, why move there?" Seth tried to save her from embarrassment. He waved a hand toward the window. *"Small town living is the life for me."* He sang his own version of an old TV show intro song. He knew she'd recognize it and feel comfortable again.

Mira reacted as he expected, with a light laugh. But her next words caught him by surprise. "Then why don't you and the boys move here?" Seth was taken aback, unsure how to respond. Joy came to the rescue, a distraction while she refilled their cups, but she had heard Mira's words. It made the waitress' eyebrows perk up again. Mira quickly added, "For the boys' school and to be close to their grandmother, of course."

Joy snorted. "Of course. And us folks who live in and around town ain't bad either. We have lots of small community events, fun activities, and loads of space to avoid each other when we want to."

Noah's eyes pulled away from his phone. "Do people fish around here?"

"Do people fish?" Joy laughed. "What type of question is that? Of course we do! We have lakes and rivers and streams for everybody. And some good hunting too if you're into that."

Noah nodded. Seth watched his son set the phone on the table and lean forward in interest. He studied the moment, putting his own arm around the back of the seat.

"Well, it don't get more free-range or organic than what's out there," Joy continued.

"What about sports?" Mason asked.

"What do you play?"

Mason tapped his chin. "Everything."

Joy smiled. "Then we have everything. All the sports!"

"Basketball?"

"Yup."

"Soccer?"

"Affirmative."

"Football?"

"What kind of American town do you think we are? Of course!"

Mason grinned at the possibilities.

Seth enjoyed watching his boys grow animated, interest sparking on their faces. They talked about all the camping trips they'd go on, games they'd win, and places they would explore. It made him happy to see their old enthusiasm returning. They were already sold on the idea.

Perhaps his mother had been right all along. Maybe this was what his sons needed. They hadn't been so open or engaging with each other since Ana died. Cedar Springs was a good place for them. But he wasn't sure it'd be the best for him. He stared down at his empty plate, trouble weaving through his thoughts.

His feeling pricked into concern, and hyper-awareness, as he noticed his boys had moved to one side of the booth to make future plans. Their heads bent together scribbling ideas on the paper placemats. Meaning Liam had slid out from between him and Mira. And his arm was still draped around the back of the seat. Around the spot where Mira was now sitting.

When Mira returned to the comfort of her home, she couldn't stop smiling. Each day with Seth was better than the last. Each day they grew closer, and she felt both of them healing. This was the magic of Christmas.

She sank in her favorite chair and glanced around at the plain walls and dark corners. The grandfather clock chimed and the sound echoed in the lonely house. Her mother would be appalled at the lack of holiday cheer.

With the giddy energy flurrying inside her, Mira climbed the ladder to the attic and brought down multiple totes, stuffed full of Christmas decorations. She started with garlands, hanging them around every doorway in the house on hooks that were already installed, draping them over the mantle around candlesticks and picture frames, and stuffing them in window ledges. Red lanterns with golden candles were placed snug between the green branches. Although these candles wouldn't be lit, the scent of cinnamon filled the room. Then she tied red velvet ribbons and swathed them across the room. The room was already more cheerful, but she wasn't done yet.

As she opened the box of twinkling lights, Mira thought it was too quiet. She turned on the radio to the local music station and danced as carols poured from the speakers. From old favorites to new pop songs, the music filled Mira with hope and happiness. She bounced from room to room, twirling lights around the garlands, lanterns, and ribbons.

The room was bright enough now that, after she turned out the main switch, the glow from Christmas lights illuminated the space. They flickered and danced along the walls and ceiling, like a holiday nightclub. Not that Mira had ever entered a club before, but she made the most of it while Angela Lansbury's *We Need A Little Christmas* played. She bounced from room to room, waving tinsel behind her and doing the jitterbug.

She stalled when she stepped back into the living room and stared at the dark corner where her mother's chair still occupied a spot near a table lamp and bookshelf. Usually, Mira and her mother would move the chair to the bedroom and set up a real tree they picked from the mountain in the corner. Nothing beat the smell of a Douglas Fir. But Mira hadn't cut one down this year.

The space needed something though. With a deep breath, she finally did what she didn't have the courage to do all year long. She moved her mother's chair and corner table. Mustering strength she wasn't sure she had, she dragged it across the old carpet and down the hallway. When she reached the closed door, she let out a ragged breath and steeled herself.

A small nudge was all it took to swing the door open and reveal the empty bedroom. Blankets laid neatly across the bed, pillows fluffed, and curtains drawn. Before she'd taken her mother to the hospital, Michelle insisted on making her bed one last time. It hadn't been touched since.

Mira focused her attention back to the chair. She tugged it inside and propped it next to the window where she threw open the flowery curtains and watched the sun pour across the room. Before the dust could irritate her eyes to the point of tears, she rushed back to the living room and popped open the box with a fake tree. The squashed branches were depressing but Mira fluffed them out and hung soft golden lights to spruce it up.

With the music on full blast and the lights brightening up the space, Mira finally opened a cardboard box of ornaments. These were the special ones, each with their own story her mother would share as they hung them on the tree. This time, she repeated the stories to herself.

She began with the cracked Shiny Bright from when she had been a baby. It was vivid blue and pink with a silvery star indented in the center like a flower. It caught and radiated the light in multiple directions. The day her mother and grandmother set up the tree, little Mira had crawled over and reached up with chubby baby fingers, knocking down this ornament. It suffered a crack but didn't shatter. Her mother had been overwhelmed. After all, it was the first year she was navigating Christmas with a child. But her grandmother brushed it off and said they'd always have this memory. *It might be cracked, but never broken*, she said.

Then Mira hung up the Santa ornament her great-grand-mother brought from a trip to England. She always thought he was creepy with his fuzzy white beard and beady black eyes, but it held a part of her history she never wanted to erase. She placed him on the far side, where Santa couldn't see her sleeping...or awake.

Next was a garland of dried orange and cinnamon sticks, now cracked and dusty with age. Most of the color had fad-ed but she draped it anyway. This was Mira's first memory of Christmas, stringing this garland with her. They used sewing thread and needles, and Mira had pricked her finger. *Don't cry*, her mother said. *Instead, think about how beautiful this will be if we don't give up*. Mira sometimes wondered if her mother was talking about the garland or something more personal. They'd replace any cracked or broken pieces over the past two decades and kept the memory alive.

Then there were the paper mâché mittens with pictures of the women in her family. One year, all four had gathered and made mittens, using their own designs and favorite colors and then posed for pictures. After printing them, they cut and glued them to the ornament. Mira stared at her great-grandmother Margaret's impossibly long braided hair, tucked in a bun at the nape of her neck. She was full of stories and more than willing to take Mira into her lap and share her adventures. Mira always wanted a life like hers, an explorer full of amazing tales from around the world.

Her grandmother Mary gained her poodle cut hairstyle from Lucille Ball, with curls pinned to the top of her head, even though her hair was thin and straight. Grandmother was always adamant her hair had to be perfect in public and would keep her curlers in whenever they were home or when she was working in her garden. Sometimes Mira would pause in the grocery store and smell the fresh sprigs of dill to remember her.

Her mom had a simple hairstyle, cut to her shoulders and always loose. Several times she had bangs but usually she grew them out because she preferred simplicity.

In contrast, Mira never settled on her own style. She flit from decade to decade, sometimes imitating Audrey Hepburn's pixie cut, other times a Diana Ross bob, but usually Grace Kelly's soft curls won out. In the past year, she'd let her hair grow and could pin or braid it. She appreciated having more options. But on her ornament, Mira had a simple ponytail, tied back with a big red bow. She wondered if that style would work now, maybe with a Christmas ribbon, or if she'd look like a child again.

She hung up more ornaments: triangle trees made from old Christmas cards, crocheted hearts, wooden carvings, painted gingerbread, a cross made from twigs, even a reindeer she made from her footprint when she was in preschool. She filled the remaining spots with other, less memorable glass ornaments, pried carefully from their boxes so they wouldn't shatter, until the tree was a gleaming space in the previously lonely corner.

The glow filled up her small apartment and brought her joy. Mira smiled as the warmth bloomed inside her, swelling with the spirit of Christmas. Not because her house was filled with red, green, and gold decorations, but her heart was finally open to receive it.

CHAPTER TEN

SATURDAY, DECEMBER 22

Sleigh bells tinkled when Mira rounded the corner to the veterinarian's office. Two horses, one dun with a white mane and the other a chestnut whisking his black tail in annoyance, were hitched to a sleigh in the center of town. The red sleigh was piled high with red bags full of toys. A tag listed family names and addresses. Several boxes stacked in the back with holiday meals for those in need.

"Here you go!" Stephanie, the town vet, walked up with a hand full of grain. "This is Kairos." She lowered her hand for the horses' snuffling noses to find the food and munch it down as she nodded at each in turn. "And she is Rocket."

Mira's eyebrows rose, unfamiliar with the chestnut horse, but Stephanie laughed.

"Don't let her name fool you. She's the slowest girl around." While she spoke, she held up a pail of water for the horses to take a long drink. "You have anyone helping?"

Mira nodded. Yesterday after lunch, Seth offered his support with the next event. It made her feel more confident about driving a sleigh through town. The past two years, she had Charles and Beverly helping her mother and her. Today had nothing to do with wanting to spend more time with Seth. Not at all. She fought back a smile, eager to share another day with him.

"Great!" Stephanie's voice yanked her back to the cold. "Because you might need someone to walk in front of Rocket with a carrot to bribe her to move."

Mira rubbed the offending horse between the ears when it snorted at her. "Sounds good. Thank you for this!"

"No problem. It's us that need to thank you, Mira. You're the one delivering all the donated toys and food right to people's doors." Stephanie handed her the leather reins after Mira climbed up.

She had driven a sleigh before, but never alone. With a quick intake of breath, she took the front seat and tucked a blanket over her dress. She'd worn her warmest vintage outfit, with a billowing quilted skirt, and it was doing a good job keeping her cozy. The goosebumps on her arms were most likely from nerves. Jitters about leading a team of horses around town. Not a flutter of emotions because the first house she was stopping at was Evelyn's, where she would pick up Seth and his boys.

When Mira clucked her tongue, Kairos chewed on his bit, but Rocket only flicked her tail. Mira jiggled the reins, bouncing them on the sides of both horses. Rocket lowered her head and sniffed at the dead leaves beneath layers of snow while pawing across the thin layer of ice.

Stephanie moved close and slapped a gentle hand on Rocket's shoulder. "Walk," she said with confidence Mira didn't feel.

Finally, the horse tipped a hoof forward. The sleigh lurched and they were off...at a very slow, meandering pace. They walked along the edge of the park until they reached Kohler Court. It took several tugs and clicks of her tongue for Mira to convince the horses to turn. They tossed their manes in disapproval.

Kairos had joined her on this activity for the past three years and did well responding to her voice, possibly because she'd taken him out trail riding during the summers. So, when she finally rounded the corner and tugged the reins, he stopped quickly. Rocket stomped her hooves in irritation but followed suit.

Seth and his boys were waiting outside. He was building a snow fort with Noah in Evelyn's front yard. Tunnels zigzagged around the yard like World War I trenches. Mason dared to run across the no-man's-land in the middle, dodging the snowballs Liam threw. When they saw her, the younger boys squealed with excitement and took off running toward the sleigh.

Rocket tossed her head, startled at the boys bouncing erratically in front of her but Seth jumped forward and slowed Mason and Liam with a quick lecture on how to behave around the large animals. Liam nodded in understanding, but his eyes didn't leave the horses as he grinned from ear to ear. With Seth holding their hands, they walked over and pet Kairos.

Noah bypassed them with a curious side-eye and sat on the front bench next to Mira. He stared at her and then back at the horses. "How do you make them listen?" he asked.

Mira shrugged. "I can't make them do anything. They're a lot bigger and stronger than me. I can only hope they follow their training. I reward them when they obey."

Seth joined them on the other side of Noah while the younger boys scrambled onto the back bench between the gifts and boxes of meals. "This is a great idea," Seth grinned at Mira. Her goose bumps returned with a flutter, and she blushed back. She didn't care anymore if he noticed, nor did she blame it on the cold, but she did redirect their attention to the sleigh.

She explained how the sleigh had been in the center of the town mall, or "*s-mall*" as the locals called it, the past several months. People had left donations in it since October, from canned food, box meals, gift certificates, and toys. The last day to add items had been the first day of the festival, when the sleigh decorated the town center stage. She waved a list from her pocket identifying the seventeen places they'd stop that day to drop off the items.

"Everyone deserves a merry Christmas!" Mira grinned before clicking her tongue at the horses.

Kairos turned an ear back to her but didn't move. She mustered the little confidence she had and spoke loudly, "Kairos, go!" Rocket snorted but neither horse took a step forward.

Mira tried not to let her frustration show. Instead, she applied one of Seth's tactics, joking about it with the boys. "And I thought donkeys were stubborn. Silly horses." She glanced over at Noah. "Why don't you try?"

His eyes lit up at the idea. "Kairos, Rocket, walk!"

Rocket shook her mane as both horses stepped forward. Noah's face broke into a grin.

"Great job!" Mira cheered.

The horses pulled them back around town, stopping at a local foster home down the road from Mira's shop. Liam and Mason grabbed the bag of presents and Seth carried a box to their front door. When seven kids came out, they brought over carrots and pet the horses. Rocket perked up at this, twitching her ears forward and snuffling the outstretched hands.

Mira stayed with the sleigh, holding the reins during the exchange, watching the horses' movements and studying their ears, while Seth stood beside the kids and explained how to hold out their hand and the best way to pet them. Everyone was in good spirits and enjoying the day. Mira smiled.

As they waited at the next stop, a low-income daycare that would pass the food and gifts to the families that came by,

Mira passed the reins to Noah. His eyes grew wide with immense responsibility.

"Keep a firm hold on the reins," she advised. "Nice and taut. They're doing great listening to your voice." Normally she wouldn't pass it off to a minor, but the horses were already following his directions better than hers. She also noticed his interest and wondered if this would be the best way to help him out of his grief, even if it was only temporary. Everyone needed a breath of fresh air once in a while.

Noah sat up straighter. His smile came easily, and he looked genuinely happy. "I think I can do this."

"You're a natural," Mira encouraged.

When Seth and the younger boys climbed back into the sleigh, Noah grinned and told the horses to walk again. Kairos and Rocket didn't give him any sass like they had to Mira, possibly because they knew each place they went would give them treats. At the daycare, they'd received a sugar cube each. Even Mason and Liam enjoyed a handful of the extra compacted sugar.

Seth gave Mira a worried glance when he saw the reins in Noah's hands, but she waved him off. A little responsibility went a long way towards encouraging the preteen and, for the first time since she'd met him, he was having a great time. She glanced past Noah and made eye contact with

Seth. Hopefully he understood what she couldn't say out loud, how his boy had to discover who he was and what he could do for himself.

Their next two stops led them farther out of town to a mobile home community where all the kids came running out to see the horses.

Mira had been anxious about all the responsibilities she'd need to take care of since she didn't have her mom, Beverly, and Charles to help with the sleigh. They had all taken on a role: one would stay in the sleigh and keep a tight hold on the reins; another would guide the children around the horses, letting them pet them one at a time and feed them snacks; and the other would speak with the parents and deliver the food and gifts.

Except Mira didn't need to worry. Seth quickly took charge and had the children wait in a patient line as he led each boy and girl forward to pet the horses and feed them a handful of hay. Noah, having the time of his life, but still apprehensive, held the reins with a skilled hand. His eyes never left them, studying each twitch and movement for signs of irritation or jerking at the bit. But the horses remained calm. They cocked their ears back at Noah whenever he encouraged or directed them and waited patiently.

Mira delivered the baskets and returned to the sleigh while Seth and the two younger boys were still helping children have a chance to pet Kairos and Rocket.

As Mira settled back on the front bench, she tucked the quilt around herself.

"I can't wait to tell my friends at school about this," Noah said.

Mira turned to him, still surprised but grateful for the smile on the boy's face. "I bet you're one of the few kids who's driven a sleigh."

"It's awesome! Someday I'd like to have my own farmhouse with dogs and horses."

Mira could finally see the real boy underneath the mask of grumpiness. "I always wanted both too. But I'm sure that'd be difficult while living in the city."

"What if he wants to move here?" Noah shrugged. "I'm confused since my dad asked about stuff in town yesterday."

Mira was also puzzled about this. "I don't know," she answered truthfully. "What do you think about it?"

"I don't want to leave my friends," he sighed. "But, it'd be cool to live somewhere I can ride my bike across town to make new friends and not stay in an after-school program every day."

"I'm sure you'd make new friends quickly."

"Yeah, kids who don't make fun of me."

Mira frowned. "What do you mean?"

His smile faded but the gloom from before didn't settle back in its place. It was more of a resigned sadness; one he didn't want to dwell on. "Some of the other kids say mean things. I hate when they make those mean *'your mom'* jokes but then look at me and laugh saying I don't have one."

Before she knew what she was doing, Mira reached out and gave Noah a side hug. "Don't listen to anything those kids say. People who only know how to tear others down aren't worth our time or effort."

Surprisingly Noah didn't pull away from her hold. Instead, he turned and hugged her back. "But they're such jerks."

"I know," Mira whispered. "But they're wrong. Your mom loved you and she would be so proud of you right now. She'd probably say that she can't believe you're old enough to drive a horse-drawn sleigh by yourself and that you're becoming a handsome young man. She would be glad you, your brothers, and dad are having a good time here."

A single tear dripped down Noah's cheek. "Wouldn't she be upset to see that we're happy without her?"

"No, no, no." Mira had to wipe some of her own tears away. "She would say the time for being heartbroken is over. You will always remember her but she wants you to live your life, to enjoy what the world has to offer, and to hold your family close."

"Liam said you lost your mom too?"

Mira nodded. "We'll always miss them and sometimes we'll be sad, but they will be a part of us forever. That's the wonderful thing about moms, their legacy will live on through us."

"But it hurts even more at Christmas." Noah loosened the reins as his dad and brothers walked back.

"That's why this time of the year is important for all of us, whether it makes us happy or sad or both. Christmas is about the traditions we have with our family and friends and the best ones take years to make. They're mixed with all kinds of emotions, so we don't forget what's important."

As Seth climbed back into the sleigh, he gave them both a quizzical look. Instead of snapping grumpily at his dad or hiding in his phone again, Noah smiled. "You ready to move on?"

"Wherever you lead, coachman," Seth replied.

Mira wasn't sure what shifted, but with that quick exchange between father and son, she knew walls were beginning to come down. Anger had dissipated and both were open to the other. Even though it didn't affect her personally, it renewed a sense of hope inside Mira and bubbled up holiday joy.

With one word, the horses followed Noah's direction, and they continued on their journey, delivering gifts and enjoying the ones they'd received along the way.

Mason and Liam lost interest about halfway through the ride. As the horses plodded down a winding pathway dusted in snowy trees between the church and school, they ignored the boys' complaints to go faster. At one point, Noah told his brothers they could pull the sleigh if they continued whining.

Seth laughed. "Now you know what dads have to deal with."

"My grandmother was even worse," Mira said. "As she got older, she forgot where we were going and why. We had to distract her with songs. Only then would she be happy and stop pestering us why she wasn't at home in her favorite rocking chair."

"What did you sing?" Mason asked.

"Anything and everything. Sometimes I would even make up songs," Mira answered. "But her favorites were Christmas carols. She never forgot those!"

Liam piped up. "I like *Jingle Bell Rock*!"

Seth began singing and they all joined in, their voices announcing their arrival to the next house.

This place was a small home with a dead tree in the front yard and broken toys sprawled in the snow. When they pulled up, the screen door slammed open and two little girls ran out. One was barefoot while the other had her hair in lopsided pigtails. They squealed seeing the horses.

Seth lifted one at a time to pet the "horsies" and then Liam and Mason gave them each a Christmas gift. The girls bounced in place while wrapping paper went flying in every direction. When they saw their gifts, a warrior princess and a glittery robot pony, they squealed again and hugged Liam and Mason. The boys rolled their eyes but grinned with holiday cheer.

Mira gave a basket of food to the mother and wished her a Merry Christmas. The woman broke down in tears and pulled Mira in a hug. "God bless you, Mira. You're always thinking of others." She set the basket down on her front porch, smiling at her girls running around with Liam and Mason. "It seems Christmas may bring us all what we need."

Mira smiled, unsure what she meant but feeling the joy of the season. Then she returned to the sleigh where Seth waited for her. He pointed at Noah who was occupied with watching the horses and running the leather reins through his hands.

"My boys are all making core memories this year."

Mira glanced at him with a confused look.

Seth explained, "Things they'll remember for the rest of their life." He reached out a hand to help Mira step back into the sleigh and she took it. "I'm glad this Christmas will bring them joy instead of loneliness. Watching them help others brings me happiness, too."

"That's what Christmas is about," Mira agreed. "It's better to give than receive, right?"

"Most of the time," Seth answered with a laugh.

As the two younger boys jumped back on the sleigh, Mira glanced down and noticed Seth was still holding her hand.

He realized it at the same time. He quickly pulled away and walked around the sleigh to the other side.

After delivering the last of the food and gifts, Liam sat in the front on Mira's lap, bundled under the warm quilt, and Mason sprawled along the back bench, his arms tucked under his head, staring up at the soft falling snow. Noah had grown comfortable driving the sleigh and did so with confidence, even singing along with Seth and Mira.

As they rounded the last bend back into town, with the words of *The First Noel* still fresh on their lips, Mira glanced at Seth while he stared thoughtfully in front of them. She wondered what he was thinking about but glad the frown he wore when he first arrived in Cedar Springs was now gone. Perhaps he was thankful his boys were doing better. Maybe he was healing, too. She also hoped, with a glimmer of interest, he thought about her.

⁘⁘⁘⁘

After dropping the horses off with Stephanie and giving Kairos and Rocket more pats, Mira returned home to prepare for the evening's event. Liam made her promise to meet them at the gazebo so they could walk over to the Apple Shed together.

Mira showered and put on a black polka dot swing dress, applied red lipstick, and curled her hair. As she coiled and pinned her bangs into a victory roll, she considered the next several days and how Christmas was coming up quicker than expected. She'd thought these twelve days would drag on with lots of tearful moments, but the days had rushed by. Although she'd shed tears, it was cathartic and healing. Instead of curling up deeper within herself, she felt like she was breathing fresh air for the first time in a long while. She carried this light-hearted feeling when she pulled on her white Converse shoes and walked to the gazebo.

Christmas lights twinkled from every shop and the lit garlands wrapped around the street lanterns. Snow was beginning to pile up along the edges of everything, softening the hard corners and concealing the dormant trees and bushes. She spun around, walking backwards to gain a better view of her shop. It had been a dark spot for so long she decided to outdo herself this year. C style bulbs flickered in patterns of green, blue, and orange around the window trees. The trim was spiraled in white and red lights, decked out with giant red bows fluttering in the cold breeze. A garland draped under the *Vintage Treasures* sign was weighed down with snow. Several icicles formed along the edges, right above the window where bubble lights flickered like candles.

The gazebo was empty when she arrived, so she stepped inside and sat on one of the benches. She wasn't dressed for the cold weather and tucked her feet close. The sheer pantyhose didn't hold in the warmth and soon she was shivering.

"Mira?" A voice interrupted her chattering teeth.

Mira turned to see Luella walking by. She was alone as well.

"Aren't you going to the rockabilly? Why are you out here in the cold?" the older woman asked.

Mira tugged on a smile. "I'm waiting for some friends."

"Oh, how could Beverly and Charles make you sit out here in the cold? Come with me, dear. You can meet them inside the Apple Shed."

Mira knew she was being considerate...but nosey at the same time, so she kept her answer vague. "Thank you for the offer but I'll wait a bit longer. I'll meet you there."

Luella shrugged. "Well, there's no point in both of us walking there alone. I can keep you company."

"Oh." Mira's heart fell when Luella sat beside her. "Thanks."

"How is this Christmas treating you?" Luella filled the silence. "If you ever feel lonely, dear, come to my house. We can enjoy each other's friendship."

Mira responded with a noncommittal head nod.

"After all, being alone at Christmas is just terrible. When my dear Marv passed, bless his soul, I didn't know what to do with myself. I was so lonely all the time," she said. "But I discovered that I have so many friends and I can help them. No one is alone if they're surrounded by friends."

Mira understood the truth in her words. But she also knew it depended on the company. The past several days had been pleasant. She'd had fun with Liam and Mason, saw Noah open up and smile for the first time, and laughed with Seth. Those were the friends she'd surrounded herself with.

As if her thoughts conjured him, Seth and his boys walked up. He stepped into the gazebo and smiled. It was a polite smile directed at Luella, forced and awkward. The two exchanged *hellos* as she stood.

Mira blinked, surprised at herself because she knew Seth's smile was fake; because she knew what he looked like when he was enjoying himself. Because the way he smiled at her was different. It was genuine. When she looked up and greeted him, she saw that smile beam back to life and a flutter went through her chest.

It didn't bother her that Luella pursed her lips with a knowing smirk or walked slower so she could follow behind them and listen in to everything they said. The moment Luella was out of her sight, Mira forgot about her and turned her attention back to Seth.

He'd slicked his hair back reminiscent of Elvis Presley. 50s fashion looked good on him. When Mira realized she was staring, she blushed. "Did your mom have hair gel and a leather jacket in her closet for you to borrow?"

Seth raised an eyebrow. "You underestimate my mom. She knows how to find anything. I think she's had everything planned out from the moment you announced the 12 Days to Christmas events."

"But that was back in November—" Realization dawned on Mira, and she thought back to the many times Evelyn visited her shop the past two months. She glanced back at Seth and recognized the biker jacket. "That was my grandfather's."

Seth's face stilled, unsure of what to say. Concern lined his eyebrows. "Do you—do you want it back?"

A laugh burst out of Mira. "It looks better on you than it would on me."

"I'm flattered," Seth grinned. "But doesn't this hold memories for you?"

Mira turned her gaze away so his eyes wouldn't be such a distraction. The things she loved about the past and what she enjoyed about the present finally clicked together in her mind in a way that finally made sense. "That's just it. Memories are better when they're shared with someone; otherwise, that jacket would be lost in a closet gathering dust. But if you—or someone else—enjoys it, it brings it back to life."

They shared a smile before Luella broke back into their conversation. "It looks like there's a crowd already waiting for us!"

Several people, dressed in poodle skirts and bandanas, waited for Mira to enter the Apple Shed first, where the live band was warming up. She stared at the many people who'd come together to set up and decorate, grateful for their help. All of Cedar Springs had stepped up and contributed in some way this year. Tonight's event was supported by the local mercantile. Danielle Chen was filling up the last of the candy jars with sweet treats for guests. Her son, Jordan, was on stage testing his guitar with the sound system and waved at them when they entered.

Yesterday, the fire and police departments teamed up to set up the Christmas tree and then the crafter's club brought the ornaments and directed where they should be placed. Mira thanked Luella for her assistance on that project before the older woman joined some of her friends. Tomorrow's events would be hosted by the movie theater, high school media class, and the historical society. Although Mira worked tirelessly to put the festival together, it wouldn't have been possible without the multitude of hands that helped along the way.

She was especially grateful to Seth, since he had stepped up, going above and beyond in helping since Charles and Beverly were sick. Hopefully they'd feel better by Christmas. If she had a spare moment in the next couple days, she'd bring them homemade chicken soup and check how they were doing.

As more guests arrived and poured into the Apple Shed, Mira found her attention diverted in multiple directions. She greeted as many people as she could, always placing extra consideration on speaking their names out loud. People would light up when their name was remembered, and they were personally acknowledged. Although it was mentally taxing for Mira, the rewards were worth it, like seeing little Abby's face fill with a glow on hearing her name.

"I read a book about space!" she announced to Mira. "There were aliens in it. Did Neil Armstrong meet any aliens on the moon?"

Mira suppressed a giggle. "You learned about the astronauts who walked on the moon?"

Abby nodded. "I'm still trying to learn the other guys' names."

"Buzz Aldrin and Michael Collins, although he had to stay and babysit Apollo 11 while the other two stepped on the moon."

"But they didn't meet aliens?"

Mira shook her head. "Not a single one."

Abby frowned in disappointment but it quickly bounced back to a laugh when she spied her friend Elsie. The two girls ran off together. Mira chuckled and greeted her parents.

As she circled the room and moved from group to group, making sure everyone was happy and enjoying the 12 Days to Christmas events, she was acutely aware of Seth, where he stood, who he spoke to, and how his boys gathered around him. But she was mostly attentive to how often he glanced her way. Each time his eyes met hers, she couldn't help her growing smile or jittery nerves. This time, it wasn't the speech that left her flustered.

At precisely 6pm, she stepped up to the stage and borrowed a microphone from the band. "Thank you everyone for joining us today!" There was scattered applause and one *hoot*. She looked over and saw Mason standing on a chair next to Seth. Her grin glimmered to life.

"Today Santa's sleigh went through town and delivered some amazing goodies to some wonderful families. Tonight, we are celebrating with a rockabilly as we track the sleigh flying around the world. How many of you check on Santa's sleigh every year?" Several hands went up.

This was a Christmas tradition Mira didn't know much about until she researched for this event. She didn't know NORAD, the North American Aerospace Defense Command, celebrated this way every year and she was eager to share this story with her town.

"It was 1955 at a top-secret operations center when a U.S. Air Force Colonel had to answer the dreaded red phone. In the heart of the Cold War, this was a terrifying prospect and Colonel Harry Shoup feared the worst."

Mira slouched at a desk, poring over papers with confidential information. She worried over each page, making sure every little mark was correct. Then, the moment she dreaded most, occurred.

The red phone rang.

She stared at it for a second, before it dawned on her what this meant. Her heart raced and her face paled. If this was the call she expected, the world she woke up in that morning would never exist again. She would be responsible for releasing nuclear warheads and the damage that transpired afterwards.

She shook the emotion from her face and adjusted her uniform before answering the red phone.

"It took the Colonel by surprise. Instead of the president of the United States of America calling the order to break the Cold War and initiate World War III, a little boy was on the other side of the line. He was looking for Santa Claus and wanted to share his Christmas wish list. Colonel Shoup played the part."

The boy's voice was quiet and nervous, not the serious command she'd expected when she lifted the receiver. She blinked rapidly, recalibrating her thoughts. A future of nuclear war and a destroyed world fell apart, making way for the hopes and dreams of a child on Christmas. Instead of guaranteeing the loss of millions of lives, Mira smiled and promised he would get the tinplate toy typewriter and scooter under his tree. It was a Christmas miracle.

"Later, he learned a local newspaper printed the Sears Roebuck phone number incorrectly, changing out one number and sending him all the local children's calls to Santa."

She stood in the call room of the Colorado command center and saw hardened soldiers answer children's phone calls while more came flooding in. For the first time in her military career, she watched as the active-duty forces broke into joyful grins and chuckled with each other. Some shared the funny things the children asked for and others considered how to provide these toys to the families. It brightened the mood and established camaraderie between them.

"This became a Christmas tradition through the decades. The Colorado command announced Santa Claus traveling at an altitude of 35,000 feet at 45 knots per hour to prerecorded records, TV commercials, and, currently, on Google Earth."

She stood in front of a map of North America while the lieutenant colonel reached forward and stuck a pin above it. He turned toward her with a grin instead of a salute, but she wouldn't be a stickler on protocol during the week of Christmas, especially since it was Seth. She smiled back and he...

...winked.

She fell like a star plummeting to earth, dropping back to reality where the real Seth actually winked at her when she was on stage. No one else noticed but they would begin to wonder if she continued to stare at him. He was trying to encourage her, she was sure, but it distracted her and made her thoughts spin wildly out of control. She had to tear her gaze away from him and focus on the end of her speech.

Mira turned to a table with a record player sitting on top. She moved the needle and it played static. "Today, before we begin dancing the night away, let's listen to one of these messages."

Everyone leaned in. It was an old-fashioned news report, speaking in a quick transatlantic accent about an unidentifiable object. With each new update, listeners discovered the object was moving South from Fairbanks, Alaska...appeared to be eight objects pulling something...a sleigh...it's Santa! At this revelation, the crowd clapped and cheered and the music began.

As Mira walked through the audience, people stepped into the dance. They twirled in wide skirts and tapped their toes, having a jolly time. Some paused long enough to thank her for the hard work planning the events and others told her what wonderful memories the recording brought back. Mark, an older man, looked at her through tears. "I forgot all about it, but when your record played, I was a child again, sitting on my papa's knee and hoping Santa would visit me."

She shook his hand and wished him the best Christmas season. He found Luella and they both began dancing the stroll.

In other corners of the room, friends danced together, and families gathered. Mira's favorite part about a rockabilly was the excitement people could enjoy together in a group. The songs didn't force romance or set up awkward moments.

Mira wasn't moving anywhere in particular. Or at least, that's what she thought, until she rejoined Seth. He pointed to the record table at the side of the stage. "With a news report like that, good thing it wasn't an H.G. Wells novel."

Mira laughed. Although they stood near the back of the room, they were surrounded by people dancing. It sparked something warm in Mira's chest, but she wasn't about to ask Seth to join her. She still felt jittery from the wink he'd offered so she turned her attention to his sons. "Are you going to dance?" she asked the boys.

Noah made a disgusted face and Mason stuck his tongue out.

"They don't know how much fun they'll be missing out," Seth laughed. "Is this a line dance?" He moved beside her and her face warmed.

Mira nodded. "It's super simple. Come on boys! You can join me." She took Liam's hand and stepped to the right. Then to the left. Then two steps to the right and two steps to the left. When she took two steps back, she bumped into Seth. "Sorry!"

"No, it's my fault." He placed a steadying hand on her back and heat rushed through her. "How do you do this?"

"Do you know how to dance?"

Seth shook his head. "I've only danced once and that was a long time ago."

She stared at him incredulously. "How?" He'd traveled the world, explored places she dreamed about but he didn't know this one simple thing?

"Will you teach us?" he motioned to Noah and Mason as well, making the moment less embarrassing. They groaned but soon all five of them stood in a line.

Mira gave them clear instructions, stepping and counting a rhythm but the boys had more fun falling over. Liam kept tripping and she had to catch him more than once. One of these times, she swung him around, spinning him to the other side. He cheered and asked to whirl around more.

"Only if you dance," Mira said. It filled her heart with happiness while she moved in time to the music with Seth and his boys, like she was part of a family, like she belonged somewhere.

Soon the boys got the hang of it and were moving as a group to the rhythm of the guitar, bass, and drums. Even Mason and Noah were enjoying themselves, so Mira added more of a challenge. With each step, she added a pulse, and the boys followed her movements, the music thrumming through them.

"Step, touch. Step, touch. Rock, step," she instructed. Her eyes darted between them.

The boys picked it up quickly. Even though Mason marched like a soldier, he kept time. Liam added a spin and giggled before he fell over.

"This way?" Noah asked. He moved through the steps with ease.

"Perfect!" Mira grinned. "Now try this with Mason." She took Noah's hands and showed him how to do a double overhead and then spin.

"I want to try!" Liam asked as his brothers laughed through the moves.

They twisted until they fell over, and Mason pinned Noah down. "It's kinda like wrestling," he said. When he looked up, Noah bucked, pushing Mason over and sitting on him.

"I guess I'm winning," he grinned.

Mira laughed, unsure she agreed with them, but helped Liam until he only wanted to spin at the end. Mira chuckled and looked back at Seth.

He was struggling, trying to keep in time with the music and remember each step. Mira moved next to him, feeling the static between them instantly. "Keep your center of balance," she advised.

He shook his head. "I have no idea why people do this for fun. It's a workout!"

"Here." She held out her hand and he took it. His grip was warm and rough. Mira forced her mind to focus on the dance. She reminded herself again, it was supposed to be a fun time for friends and families, not a place for romance. "Step out and then back in. Good. Again." His eyes focused on her face instead of his feet, whisking away all her thoughts. So, she turned her attention down at her Converse as if they were the most interesting pair of shoes in the world. "That's better," she coached. "Not on your toes because you need to step back on your heel."

Back and forth, they stepped out, to the side and back toward each other.

"This is called the jitterbug," she said. When they stepped in, she looked up at Seth's face, just inches from her own, and her heart skipped a beat. He was almost a head taller than her and had to tilt his head to look down. Her steps paused and she lost the rhythm, stumbling to the side. Seth lifted his left hand over Mira's head, spinning her, and pulling her beside him. They stood side by side, with one of his arms around her back.

Mira held her breath and met Seth's gaze. He smiled and stretched out his hand while she rolled out. Laughs broke from both of them, releasing the tension but their eyes kept catching and fingers entwining.

The beat swelled around the room, wrapping Mira in its magic. She bounced in time and reached for Seth. She could drown herself in finally living the life she wanted. The rhythmic noise of the music helped spin gloomy thoughts away as she swirled beneath Seth's arm. She could enjoy the truth of their relationship: two people who knew loss and were learning to love again. Someone like her who'd grown accustomed to an empty heart but was now ready to fill it.

The music thrummed between them as they fell back into the swing of the music, moving back and forth, reaching for each other and pulling closer each time around. Finally, Seth spun Mira under his arm and caught her when the band stopped playing. All she could hear was their heart-beats.

CHAPTER ELEVEN

SUNDAY, DECEMBER 23

Seth woke up groggy and a headache pounded in his temple. But it was his heart that ached most. Before his mom or boys were awake, he dragged himself to his feet and went out for a jog. He needed fresh air and a new perspective to understand what was happening.

This time, he avoided Main Street and the park altogether. He ran down empty, dirt roads and let his mind wander. It spun in two different directions, leaving him dizzy until he finally had to slow down and stop. He found himself on top of a hill, surrounded by oak trees with branches covered in snow. A Blue Jay glared down at him and honked in displeasure at being disturbed but he ignored it and stared out over the small town, stretched under a blanket of frost.

That's how he felt when he first arrived in Cedar Springs, cold, empty and lost. But in the past few days, he felt like he was finally waking up. It wasn't a good feeling. Because it meant he needed to acknowledge the emotions he'd struggled against for so long. He loved his wife Ana and was left heartbroken after she died in the car accident. He became a shattered man, barely surviving each day, barely keeping his family together, barely able to keep himself from falling apart. He hated the feeling.

But now, even while his heart was struggling to find the pieces, it was beginning to glue itself back together. He thought of Mira's face, her beautiful smile as she danced in his arms and it...

He threw his head back and groaned. He couldn't think like this. He couldn't let these thoughts enter his mind. His responsibility belonged with his boys first, except he was too broken to care for them. Most importantly, he wasn't sure he was ready to put the pieces back together. Wouldn't that be breaking his vows to Ana? How could he promise to love her and then find someone so soon after she died? He hated that his heart was already betraying him.

But he enjoyed Mira's company and the moments they spent together. He felt himself come back to life, breathe deeply again, and remember the joy of living when he was with her. Her conversations intrigued him, her stories enthralled him, and the way she viewed the world was a mystery he wanted to understand.

But it was too soon. He had too many worries to juggle and other challenges he needed to resolve before he could consider a relationship. If only he could remind himself of this as he was staring down into her amber eyes.

⟡⟡⟡

Mira wanted to sleep in since the rockabilly went late and she didn't get home until midnight but she woke up early with a smile on her face. As she followed her normal morning routine, making tea and sipping it by the window, the happy and content mood continued. She didn't focus on the broken teapot still shattered on the silver tray or the photograph of her mother smiling at her.

When her eyes snagged on her Converse tossed by the door, her giddiness grew. She set her cup of tea down and danced the jive alone in her living room until she collapsed on the couch laughing. She tried reading a book but couldn't focus long enough. Then she dug out some of her old music and sat at the piano, but her fingers moved too quickly over the keys, matching her heartbeat from last night's dance.

She was still trying to distract herself when her doorbell chimed. Her heart rate spiked, wondering who would visit. She ran down the stairs, two at a time, and spun around the corner.

Evelyn waited on the other side of the door, snug in her winter coat, her red curls stuffed under a Christmas beanie. She hurried inside, out of the cold wind when Mira opened the shop.

"Thank you dear," she said and dusted snow off her shoulders.

"Evelyn, the shop isn't open today." Mira knew the woman enjoyed coming by, sometimes to buy items and other times to walk around and browse while chatting. Something about the old items brought the woman comfort when she was alone. There were times she would buy them both tea and sit in the shop to keep Mira company.

"I know, I know." Evelyn smiled. "I'm here to see you."

"Oh." Mira led her upstairs to the apartment and set the tea kettle on the stove. "Would you like Earl Grey or Chamomile?"

"Anything is fine, dear." Evelyn answered as she sat at the table. "What happened here?"

Mira glanced over to see Evelyn pick up a piece of her shattered teapot and tried not to cringe. "It was an accident." She walked over with two teacups and set them down, moving the tray with her broken teapot to the fireplace mantle where she wouldn't see it every time she sat down. "I'll try to glue it back together after the holidays."

"Is this—?" Evelyn shook her head. "I'm so sorry. Seth told me Liam broke something. I should pay you for the damage. How much?"

Mira shook her head. "Please, don't worry about it." Her eyes snagged on the sharp pieces of her beloved teapot, and she tried to forget the loss. Instead, it reminded her of the day Seth came into town, and she had poorly misjudged him. New memories already replaced her first impression.

Her mind grew distracted thinking about the past several days and looking forward to the evening. She tried not to consider what Seth would think about her dress, a gorgeous red gown with white lining, similar to the dresses in *White Christmas*, but she pushed it from her thoughts while she was with his *mom*.

Mira changed the subject, pointing to her Christmas decorations. "I finally put them up. I wasn't sure if I would this year."

Evelyn glanced around the room, at the garlands, twinkling lights, and bright Christmas tree. "It looks so beautiful, as do you, Mira. When you smile, it lights up the room. And, recently, you've been smiling more."

Mira blushed, wondering how much Evelyn was watching and if Seth had talked with her about their growing friendship, or possibly something more. "It's Christmas. It's a time to be joyful." She tried to pass off her giddiness on the season, but Evelyn wasn't fooled. She could tell by the way the older woman's lips quirked in a grin and how she watched her through narrowed eyes.

"It's good to see you happy. And I've been so glad to see the joy you share with others, especially with Liam, Mason, and Noah. I've seen a difference in them this past week."

"They're good boys," Mira said. She always had a wonderful time with them. The way they interacted or things they came up with caught her by surprise and made her laugh. She wasn't on guard or worried about what she'd say like she was around many other people. It was with a comforting thought she realized it was because she could be herself around them and they not only tolerated her quirks but appreciated her.

"Seth, too, has changed."

The tea kettle whistled, a perfect distraction, and Mira used it as her excuse to interrupt the conversation. Of course, his mom would notice how much time they had been spending together lately. Considering it now, maybe Evelyn had even skipped several of the activities so Seth would be alone, and someone would step up to help. She turned back with the tea kettle, still musing. "How would you like some orange cinnamon tea? It's perfect for the season."

Evelyn accepted but continued where she left off while Mira filled their cups. "I think I have you to thank for that. Seth is finally opening up to me and his boys. He's been through so much and has tried to be so strong. But everyone needs help once in a while."

Mira stumbled over her words and finally settled on an awkward, "You're welcome."

This past week had brightened her life as well and she caught herself smiling at random moments. She understood the struggle of trying to balance everything but knowing it would eventually tip and she'd crumble under the weight. She was sure it'd happen during the festival but, just when she'd felt herself slipping, she discovered she was no longer alone. The puzzle pieces fit together. With her loss, she could comfort others with an empathy she'd experienced.

"I remember buying ornaments like that when I was a little girl," Evelyn changed the subject and pointed at the Christmas tree. "It brings back so many wonderful memories. Do you have more for sale in your shop?"

Mira grinned, "Of course I do." She jumped to her feet and picked one off the tree. "But take this one instead, as a gift." She found an empty gift bag and placed it inside and they continued to chat over their warm cups of tea. The 12 Days to Christmas festival had gone smoother than she'd imagined. Everything was beautiful and perfect and full of holiday joy. Both women were smiling after counting their blessings and considering that night's event. Mira was giddy at the thought. She even spun from the room to bring out her dress and get Evelyn's advice on it.

"It's stunning, Mira! You'll be the spotlight of the night!"

Mira laughed. "Oh, I hope not. But this is the only dress I could wear for a *White Christmas* themed gathering."

"And you don't know what's planned? I heard there might be a surprise."

"It won't be, if Charles continues telling everyone about his singing quartet." They both laughed before Mira continued, "No, the historical society offered to organize tonight so I only need to show up and enjoy the party!"

"That's perfect! You deserve a break. I'm sure you must be exhausted."

Mira shook her head. She'd thought she'd be haggard after so many days of leading events but she felt energized. Each day brought new aspirations and dreams. She was growing and learning.

After finishing their tea, they returned downstairs, and Evelyn paused with her hand on the door. "Thank you," she said. "Mira, if you don't already have Christmas plans, you are invited to brunch at my house. There will be a handful of people there, including my boys and several friends. Will you join us?"

This reminded Mira of an inkling new worry. Once the events were over, she wouldn't have an excuse for bumping into Seth and his boys or a reason to spend time in their company. Especially if he decided to return to the city. Maybe Evelyn could convince them to move to Cedar Springs. Maybe Mira could help. Her heart fluttered like the snowflakes spinning in the wind outside.

Mira smiled. "I'd love to."

✻✤✤✤✤ ✤✤✤✤✤

While she prepared for the night's festival, she sang every Christmas song that came to her, from old carols to new hymns to modern radio hits. She loved every decade of Christmas, from ancient to contemporary.

At 4:30, she finally left the house. The people in town were bustling, gathering last minute gifts or bringing children to the movie theater. Mira had pre-set everything so she didn't *need* to go there and check in on things, but she went anyway. The local teenagers were working the counter and passing out free popcorn to all the children and giving them a choice to watch between two movies: *Home Alone* or *The Grinch*.

"Everything is going great, Ms. Mira," one of the girls from the game night saluted.

Mira laughed. "I'm glad! Have fun!"

"That's not something you should tell teenagers." The girl's friend laughed.

She stalled for a couple minutes, talking to a group of children and asking them what their favorite event had been so far. Most of them agreed watching movies and eating popcorn was the best and Mira had to appreciate how they lived in the present. She'd been acknowledging that recently and enjoying it. She was beginning to consider what her new year's resolution would be and she'd finally settled on discovering more modern inventions, even the possibility of finally upgrading to a cell phone. After being stuck on the mountain without a way to contact anyone, she could see the benefits of modern technology.

Her dawdling paid off when she met Seth at the double doors. He glanced at her plain clothes in surprise. "You're not at the mansion yet?"

Mira laughed. Everyone in town called the largest house a mansion. It was strange to her, because it was her great-grandmother's house. Or it had been. Now it was a local venue for weddings and fancy gatherings. "I'm going after I checked in on the kids' event here."

Seth nodded as his boys ran in and grabbed their popcorn. Only Liam stopped to wave good-bye to his dad and give Mira a hug.

As they stepped out of the theater, Seth said, "You shouldn't keep your date waiting."

Mira tipped her head confused while Seth stumbled over his words.

"I mean, because I'm sure you've already had someone ask you, of course."

Mira shook her head in answer. Words failed her, probably because her mouth went dry at his assumption. In fact, she'd never had a boyfriend or had anyone ask her on a date, even when she was at the university. Mostly because she avoided talking and ran at the first sign someone showed an interest. She hadn't had that opportunity here...and no longer wanted to run away.

A smile broke across Seth's face. "Really? Then, would you be my date?" He coughed and rubbed his short beard, coming up with an excuse. "I guess, because I don't know anyone else in town."

Mira's breathing staggered, and she bit her lip, hoping to hide her reaction. How could he offer such a compliment and then trivialize it? But she could play along. "Really? You know your mom." At the quirk in his eyebrows, she continued, "Isn't she coming tonight? You couldn't leave her all alone..."

"Are you saying I should bring my mom instead of you?" Seth shrugged. "I mean, I suppose she'd enjoy the evening but, sadly, she decided to stay home tonight, said something about needing a break from company or something like that."

"Oh, I understand. She went from living alone to having four other people in the house."

He shook his head. "I warned her. My boys are noisy and I'm not easy to care for either."

"Well, maybe as a kindness to your mom, I can give her a break and keep you company."

Seth took a deep breath. "I'd *like* to go with you. May I escort you tonight?"

Mira smiled. There was no use trying to hide her frequent blushes anymore. She'd have to accept having a red face all the time or hide it by adding makeup. "Yes," Mira answered. "It sounds perfect."

"I'll meet you there," Seth grinned.

⁂

Didn't Seth tell himself not to get lost in Mira's eyes? And now she was his date tonight. This was the first time he'd gone on a date with a woman he was interested in since...Well, he wouldn't let his mind dwell on that. Instead, he needed to focus on the surprise tonight and make sure he didn't give anything away.

He needed an excuse to distract Mira and this was the only option. Of course, it'd been with mom's encouragement, although the idea had been his. He'd hoped there would be a different approach, but at the same time, this was all he wanted: to spend a little more time with Mira before he returned home.

His time in Cedar Springs had been everything he'd hoped for: healing and promising for his boys. But he'd felt a shift inside himself, too. He'd fiercely held onto his grief for so long, and now it was slowly slipping away. It frightened him. He didn't love Ana any less. He still missed her and grieved, but somewhere deep inside his heart, he felt the wounds scabbing over. He no longer felt raw and bleeding every moment he remembered their wonderful memories together.

Tonight's event and surprise weren't romantic but instead, as Seth's way of expressing his gratefulness to Mira and all she'd done for him. At least, that's what he told himself.

But those concerns disintegrated from his mind, like snow melting on the heated sidewalk where he waited, when Mira appeared. All thoughts of his boys and other worries vanished as he became transfixed. Only she remained.

This was the first time Mira and Seth would spend time together without his boys around. She wondered if it would grow awkward or they would run out of things to say, but when she arrived at the mansion and saw Seth waiting for her near the front steps, all her fears vanished.

He held his arm out to her, and she took his elbow. "I hope I don't trip and make a fool of myself," Seth said as they walked up the wide staircase. The carved oak doors opened, and they stepped inside. Before the rush of memories in this home could drown Mira's emotions, Seth leaned closer and whispered in her ear. "By the way, you look beautiful."

A shiver tingled inside her, not from the cold. She met his eyes and let his smile warm her from the inside out.

It was a strange sensation being yanked from her sad past into a glittering present. Instead of the reminder of this front door shutting behind her for the last time, watching Grandma Mary sign paperwork to sell the home, or the rainy day funerals for her great-grandparents...Mira was transported to a new reality. Gleaming Christmas lights, gently falling snow, and her hand held warmly in another's. Her feelings fluttered like a cozy flame in a fireplace, making her feel pleasantly heated in her core. She couldn't stop smiling.

Her thoughts were still spinning with Seth's words as they walked into the main room where other couples tasted hors d'oeuvres and sipped champagne. Everything in the mansion was decorated in silvery snowflakes, white ornaments, and pearlescent garlands. It was a gorgeous sight, and made Mira stand out in her dress. Yet she was too focused on the spot where her and Seth's arms touched, radiating heat through her, to even notice the glances cast their way. Gathered in a group of other women, Luella whispered overzealously, and Evelyn smiled knowingly. Beverly tried to hush the former with no luck.

"I thought you said your mom wasn't coming?" Mira whispered to Seth.

"I suppose she changed her mind. No one wants to miss the surprise." He winked.

She rolled her eyes. "Charles has already told everyone. His quartet isn't a secret anymore. I hope he's recovered from his cold."

But Seth only smiled and pointed at the old man entertaining a group with the story of the bunny chase at the senior center.

As they walked farther into the room, Charles turned and greeted them. "I hope the kids are all settled at the movies?"

"I'm glad you're well," Mira said.

Charles frowned. "Yeah, never better. Why?"

"You were sick..." Mira said and then cast a glance in Beverly's direction. The older lady caught her eye but quickly spun to speak to a friend instead. "Were you...?"

"Ah, uh—yes." Charles faked a cough. "But I'm feeling all good now. Thanks for your concern." He hurried away.

As her friends evaded her, it dawned on Mira. Was it all an elaborate plot to give her time alone with Seth? He didn't seem to mind.

He raved over the delicious food: smoked salmon dip and almond crackers, pastrami bites with cheesy potato slices, bacon wrapped dates, and feta and olive bourekas. Once they'd filled their plates and sat on matching Savonarola armchairs, Seth glanced up and took in the room. He pointed out the chandeliers, wall of mirrors marbled in gold, and other architectural designs of the mansion, especially the spiral wood staircase.

"It was built to mimic the Neo-Renaissance period and Peleş Castle from Romania, where my ancestors are from," Mira said.

Seth paused, glancing between the mahogany staircase and back at her. "Is this—?"

"It was." Mira sighed. "My great-grandparents built it but we sold it to the town's historical society, to keep the place alive."

Before she knew what he was doing, Seth pulled her from the main room, leaving their empty plates behind, and into her grandfather's old office. "So, this was all yours?" he waved around them.

Mira nodded. It would take too long to show him where she took her first steps in the dining room, or said her first words in the kitchen, or read her first book in the window seat but she wanted to. She knew he'd appreciate the stories, her own growing up in this place and all the items that hid their own history.

But he frowned. "And now you can't keep your shop open? Why isn't anyone in town helping you?"

"They don't know. About the shop failing, I mean."

He studied her face for several moments and then shared a secret smile. "So, how about instead of standing around in there where everyone is awkwardly staring at us—"

Mira laughed nervously. "You noticed that too?"

"They're not even trying to hide it. Anyway, how about you give me a tour of your mansion and nerd out about the history?"

His idea sounded like the best type of party Mira ever attended.

She started by sharing her memories of her grandfather's study, brushing a hand over the leather armchair still in the same place and reading through the titles of his book collection.

Seth reached into his pocket and took out the watch he bought at the auction. He held it out to Mira, but she closed his fingers around it. "It belongs to you now. You get to make your own history."

"I'll cherish it. Thank you." Instead of pulling away from her touch, he hooked their fingers together, the watch trapped between them, and pulled her from the room. "What's upstairs?"

Mira laughed when they ran up the steps, two by two, remembering racing around the house as a child. It had bothered her great-grandmother, but Grandma Mary would always roll her eyes and state how she should enjoy being young while she still had the energy. This same excitement pulsed through her tonight. But it was fueled by her proximity to Seth.

He continued holding her hand while she pointed out paintings and named the dead relatives. They all had a story, and she shared them with him. He listened and offered the occasional joke or pun, and they laughed together. It was a relief for Mira because she'd been worried the ghosts of people she knew once walked these halls would crowd her mind the entire night. And, although she missed their memories, she didn't feel alone or sad.

Mira showed him inside each room, all themed with items from that continent or country, like Peleş Castle. Her favorite was the Moorish Hall with exquisite ottomans and replicas of weapons on the wall alongside Middle Eastern trays and ewers. A beautiful Moroccan tapestry hung from the opposite side, filling the room with a mosaic of colors. Behind it was a hidden passageway that led to another bedroom which Mira and her mother shared for the few years they lived here. Seth was impressed with the music room: the harp from Greece, a kettle drum from Ethiopia, shamisen from Japan, and reed pipes from her great-grandparents' home of Romania.

After exploring each room and sharing the history of many antiques, Seth led her to the window seat. A Christmas tree glowed under the lights outside as snow fell softly around it. "You told me several days ago how you wanted to travel the world," Seth said.

Mira nodded. Wanderlust had always itched her feet but she never had the opportunity. "Actually, the place I want to go most is Romania, where I can experience my family history." She shared one of her secrets. Many people didn't know about her ancestral home and the few that did only knew of the difficult times the country had faced. But she'd studied and learned so much of its history, of the beauty it hid within its borders, and the amazing people who'd lived there and what they'd faced. One of her greatest dreams was to walk the boulevards and stare at hundreds of years of history.

Seth waved at the photographs, antiques, and valuables around them. "I hope you do someday. But even though you haven't left Cedar Springs, the world has come to you. These rooms are filled with history and stories only you can share."

Mira smiled. She loved all these things and the warm feeling of seeing them again filled her, but it couldn't replace the experiences she wished she had. "My great grandmother traveled to six of the seven continents. My grandmother visited three. My mother went across the states but I've barely left my hometown for the city, except for a short stint in college." She held up a fragile hand-painted Emu egg from Australia. "I know their stories, but I want to *live* them. I want to *experience* the world for myself."

"Then go," Seth grinned. "I have no doubt you can explore the world and bring all those stories to life."

She shrugged. "It's not that simple. For starters, it costs money—"

Seth shook his head. "That shouldn't be a problem for you. I could see you giving tours, teaching classes, maybe even making videos of the places you visit and posting them online. People would listen to you."

A thoughtful look crossed Mira's face. "Do you really think so?"

"I know it." He squeezed her hand.

She blushed and glanced away, only to look up and see the twinkling garland around the frame of the window had several sprigs of mistletoe, hanging right above them. Seth followed her gaze. "Oh."

Mira chuckled nervously. "Some traditions are ridiculous."

"I'm sure many are, like putting gifts inside a sock or sitting on a fat man's lap," Seth agreed. "But I enjoy this tradition." He leaned in and Mira blinked.

She had many memories sitting in this same window seat. This is where she'd devoured some of her favorite books, had long talks with her mother, and wrote letters to her traveling relatives. A first kiss was another memory she could hold onto forever. She closed her eyes and moved closer.

"There you are!" Charles' voice interrupted Seth and Mira and they spun around. Mira bit her lip. "Everyone is ready for you."

Mira frowned. "I didn't plan a speech for tonight."

"No worries," Seth stood, as if nothing had almost happened. "I think they're waiting for us to start the rest of the festivities."

She had no idea what he meant. Tonight was an evening of dressing fancy and eating finger foods while spending time with friends, after the theme of the movie White Christmas. Perhaps Seth and Charles wanted to join the rest of the group and be together.

"There's the surprise concert." Charles winked and led the way downstairs.

As she followed, she was slightly disappointed. Seth had wanted to kiss her, and her heart was still in flutters. It was something she'd hoped for as well. But those feelings would be awkward to consider while rejoining the rest of the gathering.

Just before she took the last few steps, Seth turned around and held up a hand. "Wait there a moment." Mira glanced back, confused.

Applause erupted in front of them, and she glanced at the other guests. Most everyone she knew in town stood in the main room clapping and staring *at* her. She turned red and tried to take the rest of the steps down. The attention was awkward and filled her with nervous energy. But Seth took her hand and led her back up the stairs, where everyone could see her. Then his grip loosened, and he stepped away.

Beverly filled the space he left and smiled at the crowd. "As you know, our beloved Mira has worked tirelessly to put on this wonderful festival." Everyone clapped and cheered again making Mira want to hide behind the velvet drapes. "But not everyone knows how much this all cost her."

Her breathing stalled and she turned to Beverly. What did her friend know? And what was she going to reveal to literally *everyone* in town?

Beverly smiled and took Mira's hand in her own. It was still warm from Seth's grip but the older lady didn't react to that. Instead, Beverly shared Mira's deepest worries with the crowd. "This year has been difficult for her since she lost the most precious person in her life. Some of us know what that is like and have comforted her these past months.

But our sweet Mira has kept secrets and added anxieties on herself."

Mira's breathing grew rapid, and she tried to pull away from Beverly, but the woman wouldn't let go. She stared back at Mira with a kind smile. "We may not be your blood-family, Mira, but we love you and want to help."

A public intervention was the last thing Mira wanted. Her fingers trembled and she tried to whisper but no words came out.

Beverly continued, "Many of us are admirers of Mira's shop Vintage Treasures but it has become a financial liability. So," she turned toward Mira, "As your friends and neighbors, we want to come alongside you and provide the support you need."

"What do you mean?" Mira gasped.

"The Cedar Springs Historical Society would like to purchase the shop from you. They will cover all the expenses and compensate you for your work. You can continue living in the apartment above the shop at no cost and, if needed, members from the Senior Center would volunteer on days you can't work or are out of town."

Mira frowned. "Out of town?"

Charles stepped forward with a happy smirk. "We have gathered a stipend from the members of this neighborhood who have been blessed by your contribution and want to support you...in covering the entire cost to complete your degree at the university."

Mira's jaw dropped when she took the envelope Charles handed her. "But..."

Mayor Chavez approached. "You and your family have been a pillar in our community for decades and we want you to know how much we value you."

Mira was speechless. She tried to fight back tears unsuccessfully. Beverly pulled her into a hug so she could hide her face on the other woman's shoulder as the crowd applauded again. Someone in the back yelled out, "Thank you Mira!" and everyone cheered.

When Mira finally pulled away from Beverly's embrace, the gathering had returned to normal, and everyone was talking in small groups among themselves or listening to Charles and his quartet. Many shared their favorite moments of the traditional 12 Days to Christmas festivities throughout the years, from the first 12 Days where each day was themed on the gifts of the song to last year's event focused on different ways people celebrated the holidays, including Krampus.

Mira swiped happy tears from her face. "Why would you do this?"

Beverly smiled. "Why would you do any of *this*?" Her hand waved over the filled rooms of the mansion, at people laughing and talking together. "Because it brings others joy. This year, we wanted to return the favor."

Mira was overwhelmed with love. All her worries of the future were now gone: her shop was taken care of, her school was paid for, and she could pursue her dreams of *living* out the stories instead of learning about them from dusty old books or too-bright computer screens. But one part still didn't make sense. She'd never told Beverly about any of these worries. She turned to her and asked, "How? How did you know? How did you plan all this?"

The old woman smiled back. "Oh, it wasn't us, Mira." She pointed across the main room, over the heads of the crowd to one figure standing in the back, talking to her friends. "It was Seth."

Mira's feet led her forward before she could consider what she would say. She passed people she'd known her entire life and thanked them when they congratulated her. She gave Elizabeth a hug and nodded to Luella but didn't let anything or anyone slow her from making her way to the back of the room. To Seth.

When she finally reached him, he took her hand and stepped out the double doors. The soft snow drifted past them, landing on her hair and cheek. Seth brushed it away, but his hand lingered on her chin. "I hope you can make your own story now."

Mira blushed. She didn't know what to say or how to respond, so she leaned forward on her toes and kissed him.

Chapter Twelve

Monday, December 24

That wasn't supposed to happen. Seth wasn't sure what to do now.

Yesterday, when Mira kissed him, his heart and mind disconnected. His heart filled with happiness, understood by someone who intrigued him. He enjoyed every moment spent in Mira's company and it made him crave her proximity more. The kiss replayed in his mind while he jogged to the bakery causing him to sport a goofy grin.

People he'd met at the different festival events waved or greeted him while he passed, making him feel like a member of Cedar Springs. Even slowing to a stop in front of Mira's shop, the smile wouldn't fade. For the first time in a year, he felt *joy*.

But that was when his mind kicked into full gear and guilt tripped him. His lips drooped back into a frown and a wrinkle formed between his eyebrows. He cursed himself. How could he move on so soon? How could he allow himself to feel this way? Did it mean he didn't love Ana enough? He crumpled onto a park bench and rested his forehead against his hands, taking in a deep breath.

The past year he felt stuck in this one step. He *knew* Ana had passed away, that he was a widower, his sons lost their mother, but he'd been so preoccupied with helping his boys heal, he'd lost himself in the process. Seth had buried himself as well, in his work, in keeping busy, as if, at some point, he'd look up and Ana would be back and life would be as it once had been.

But he *knew*, he understood so deeply, that reality was different. Ana had given him the best years of her life, three amazing boys, and so many wonderful memories but...she was no longer here.

At some point, he'd accepted it. He had to. Perhaps it had been the night at the hospital when his reality came crashing down.

But since then, he'd moved too fast. He'd let someone else's eyes steal his attention, the smile on her lips, the way she'd fall into character regardless of the story she was telling. These past two weeks he'd met a woman who could be a soldier standing on a battlefield, an astronaut in space, a king receiving a crown, a general leading an army. He'd watched Mira, no, he felt as if he experienced history alongside her, in discovering the internet, enjoying a silent night in an ancient town, joining St. Nicholas in bringing comfort, and decorating a Christmas tree like a family. He'd professed his love, albeit while an actor, danced the night away, and made her dreams come true. And in the past eleven days, she'd given him the greatest gift of all: hope.

Despite that thought softening the hard edges of his soul, it came crashing back down again. Because he knew he wasn't ready. Not yet at least. He still had so much healing to focus on but never the time or silence to do it. Just as his boys recovered in different ways, he knew he had to take the time on his own.

When his dad died, he'd run away to find himself. Somewhere, lost on a truck in the desert or climbing the snowy peaks of a mountain, he'd finally discovered what he'd been searching for. It had been in the moments where he was alone that he could truly dive into himself and study all the inner workings that made up who he was. Maybe he needed something like that. Maybe he needed time away from everything. And everyone.

The thought dug claws into his mind until he couldn't shake it loose, even when he bought donuts and returned to the house. He knew he couldn't be an impetuous young man again. He had his sons and a career depending on him. There were bills to pay and mouths to feed. And now, because of his visit to Cedar Springs on Christmas, there was a young woman who he had fallen head over heels for.

⊱⊰

Mira walked to the church a block away from her house. She didn't feel the need to button her coat or tighten her scarf over her black A-line dress because the cold air didn't bother her. Warmth radiated from inside. Her smile didn't fade all day. After her kiss last night, she felt like a balloon, losing its string and flying into the sky, no longer tethered or held down to the worries of the world. It wasn't the covered cost of the shop or ability to pursue her history degree. Those were nice things, yes, but she barely spent a moment thinking about those past minuscule uncertainties.

No, her mind was wholly and completely preoccupied with another thought. And he was waiting for her in front of the church.

She smiled at Seth while Liam and Mason wrapped her in hugs and Noah gave her a fist bump. Her heart leapt in her chest when Seth grinned back.

Earlier, she worried that yesterday's kiss was a fluke. Maybe they had been caught up in the magic of Christmas. What if he changed his mind? Too many thoughts swirled within her but those doubts settled now that his eyes were on her. Mira's fears melted away.

They entered the church together. *Almost like a family,* Mira thought, and let it warm her heart even more. Other groups filed in: mothers with their sons, fathers with their daughters, grandparents with their kin. And Mira didn't feel alone in the center of it all, because she was with her own company. Her hand tightened around Liam's and she smiled down at the boy, stepping through the open doors.

Luella stood in the foyer passing out candles for the Christmas Eve service. When her focus turned to Seth and Mira, her eyebrows shot up. Mira could see the gears working in the older woman's mind. With a smirk, Luella handed Mira two candles and then stopped. "Oh, dear. I'm sorry. I should've only given you one." She reached forward to take a candle away.

Seth's hand stopped hers, settling over Mira's. The warmth of his hand and his voice calmed her nerves. "No worries. She can share with me."

"Oh?" Luella asked in a voice an octave higher than normal. "Are you two here together?"

Seth smiled back at her without blinking and answered, "Yes."

Luella pursed her lips like a steam train, ready to explode. Neither Seth nor Mira responded when they walked past and found a row to sit in, the children on either side of them. She felt connected and close like she hadn't in a long time. It encouraged her to finally understand she craved interaction with others, but in her grief, she'd pushed what she needed most away. Her method of avoiding people the past several months only made her heartache worse. Now, as with Noah, they could both smile and speak with confidence because they knew they were in a safe place where others cared and would look out for them. Because they were accepted, faults and all.

Mira didn't look back while she took her seat, but she could hear Luella abandoning her post and rushing off to gossip with anyone who would listen. For a moment, she wondered about the woman and if this was her way of dealing with whatever struggles she faced. Maybe she was avoiding her own obstacles by meddling in others'. When this festival was over, Mira determined to take the time to befriend her and let her know she wasn't alone.

Liam and Mason were preoccupied staring at the flickering candles on the stage and debating what they would do if the church caught fire. Seth whispered at them to settle down. Meanwhile, Noah pulled up several searches on his phone and gave Mira new ideas for next year's 12 Days to Christmas festival.

"Did you know that Christmas Island was discovered on Christmas Day? Maybe it can be beach themed. Isaac Newton was born December 25!" He scrolled across the screen. "Yikes! Romania's leaders were executed that day too."

Mira nodded. "They were communist dictators. Now, Romania is a free country, more or less, under a parliamentary republic."

Noah pulled up a map on his phone to find the country in Eastern Europe while Mira watched over his shoulder.

"Wow, you can learn anything on that thing," she commented. "What happened in 352 A.D.?"

Noah typed in the date and pulled up a quick search. "It says it was the first time Christmas was celebrated."

"Officially," Mira added. "I'm so thankful because it's my favorite holiday. There are so many reasons to celebrate Christmas! We can enjoy the traditions, gatherings, events, even the history...but none of it would be possible if we don't go to the heart of Christmas and why people around the world started celebrating it in the first place."

"Jesus?" Noah asked.

"Exactly." Mira pointed to the stage as Pastor Jack stepped up. He began the night with a prayer and then the choir director, Greta, led everyone in several Christmas hymns. The boys had a lot of fun singing *Joy to the World* and ringing bells they had received when entering, instead of the candles the adults were given.

This time, while singing that song, Mira and the boys were happy. Cheer bounced between them as they made a game of grinning back and forth during the repetition at the end of the verses. It made Liam giggle uncontrollably. But neither Seth nor Mira stopped him. The last time they sang that song together, their hearts were heavy while they paced the hallways in the hospital. But this time they radiated the joy they sang about. They embodied the words.

Afterwards, the church put on a short performance of the Nativity, with angels sharing the birth of Christ, a young Mary, portrayed a new mother with her tiny baby, and wise men who sang while marching down the aisle. It became chaotic when the Sunday school children entered, dressed as sheep and continually *bah*-ing, while the innkeeper tried to tell the story out loud.

When the performance was over, Pastor Jack returned to the pulpit and shared the importance of Christmas. "We've been celebrating this special season the past eleven days with wonderful traditions and celebrations. It's only fitting we end with the origin of the holiday.

"Matthew 1:21 says '*She will bear a son, and you shall call His name Jesus, for He will save His people from their sins.*'" He stood next to the Nativity set up, now empty except for hand-painted backgrounds of a starry night and a manger full of hay. "Many people celebrate in different ways, and that's okay, but tonight I want you to search your heart for the true spirit of Christmas. Yes, we love the songs, gift-giving, and family traditions. I especially enjoy the food!" A chuckle rippled through the audience. "But when we light these candles and have a quiet time for prayer, remember that *Christ*mas is about Jesus and how he was born in an old stable for one purpose: to give us hope, to save us, and bring us freedom. Tonight, I urge you to reach out and trust Him."

Peace settled over Mira's heart. The year had been a rough one but all along, even when she felt the most alone, she knew she could still hold on to hope. As the overhead lights dimmed and ushers walked down the center aisle of the church lighting the first candle in the row, Mira knew she'd be fine tomorrow. Christmas was here and her mother wasn't, but she knew they'd see each other again someday. For now, Mira looked around her at Seth and his boys, and was grateful for the opportunity to be in their life.

Seth lit his candle from the person next to him and leaned over to Mira. As she tipped her wick next to his candle, his hand steadied her arm, strong and warm, centering her focus to this small moment in time. Not history. Not something that was facts in a textbook or details from someone else's adventure. This was real life, right now, her story.

Both candles flared, entwined and flickering in one brighter flame, and Mira met Seth's gaze. There was no other place she wanted to be, no other time in history. She was in love with the present and in living her own life. She greeted his smile with her own.

⁂

Eventually the moment passed, like all things do. The congregation sang one more hymn and then filtered out of the church, walking to the center of town for the tree lighting ceremony.

Beverly and Charles joined them, not batting an eye at how close Seth and Mira stood. Charles distracted the boys with jokes. "Did you know some people don't want Christmas?"

Liam gasped. "No!"

"They keep telling me to stop saying *Merry Christmas* because not everyone believes in Jesus. Instead, they want me to say *Happy Holidays.*"

"That's what we say at school," Noah shrugged.

"Well, jokes on them, because it's still religious. It's right there in the name, *Holy*-days."

Beverly smacked Charles' arm and shook her head. "No, you don't listen to others because you're a smart aleck."

Charles waved her off. "Did you know Scrooge was actually celebrating Christmas every time he said '*Bah*-humbug'?"

Mira chuckled at Charles as he skipped ahead with Seth's boys. He told this joke every year, about Scrooge being one of the sheep on the hillside when the angels announced Jesus' birth.

Beverly turned to Seth and asked him how his stay in Cedar Springs was going. He answered how his boys had a wonderful time, and it brought back so much joy they'd lost the past year.

"I'm so glad." Beverly smiled and then walked ahead, leaving Mira and Seth alone.

Seth cleared his throat and Mira's heart skipped a beat. Was this the moment he would ask her if they wanted to pursue a relationship? Would he announce he was going to move to Cedar Springs? Mira glanced up at him, but a frown had settled between his eyebrows.

"Mira." He coughed again. "I wanted to talk to you about something important. Something I've been considering for a while."

She took a deep breath.

"I'm planning to leave the boys in Cedar Springs."

Mira's smile froze on her lips. "What do you mean?"

Seth pointed at Noah, Mason, and Liam chasing Charles off the path and joined him when the old man sat down in the snow and made a snow angel. "They love it here. I finally saw Noah smile and the other two are getting along again." He sighed. "After their mom died, it was constant arguing. Noah even got suspended from school. But here, they are themselves again. They can be kids."

Mira nodded. "I have noticed a difference but I thought you mentioned moving here?"

"They can stay with my mom. She already agreed to it." His lips set into a line, awkward and forced. "This would be a better place for them to grow up."

They walked along the path for a minute in silence while Mira processed what he was saying. "What about you?" she asked.

They stepped up to the dark Christmas tree as people milled around it. Mayor Chavez waited near the gazebo with a switch to the electric plug. The countdown would begin soon.

Seth took a long breath before answering. "I can't. I have my job."

"What?" Mira blinked. "Wait. Do you mean you're leaving your boys here? Alone?"

"They won't be alone. They'll live with my mom."

"Dad?"

Both Mira and Seth spun around to see Noah standing behind them. He stared up at Seth with wide eyes. Tears rimmed the edges of his lashes. "You're leaving us here?"

In the background, Mayor Chavez' voice began the countdown. "10...9...8..."

"Noah," Seth sputtered. "I was going to tell you tomorrow."

"7...6...5..."

"Tell me what?" The boy bit his lip. His tears hardened to anger. "You're going to leave us behind?"

"4...3..."

"It's not like that—"

"2...1..."

"I hate you." Noah spun around.

Behind them, the Christmas tree roared with light. It filled the entire park with sparkling lights in white, red, and green. Music blared from loudspeakers and people cheered.

But Noah ran off.

Seth shouted after him but received no response. He turned back to Mira, his shoulders sagging and his face looking as exhausted as the day he arrived in Cedar Springs. When his boys broke Mira's teapot.

"He wasn't supposed to know yet." Seth stared at the snow on his boot.

"You were going to tell him tomorrow?" Mira asked. "On Christmas?"

Seth wrinkled his eyebrows. "You don't understand. This last year has been terrible. Noah skipped school several times and I still have no idea where he went. I was hoping they'd all be safer here."

Mira stared at him. She couldn't comprehend how he could decide on something like this and it was too difficult to focus with all the Christmas cheer erupting around them. Some families had poppers, others kissed under the mistletoe in the gazebo, some children started another snowball fight.

But Seth's family had just shattered.

"Now, Noah's run off again." Seth shook his head. "I have to go find him." Neither noticed the bright lights of the Christmas tree or the other boys cheering with Charles. Or people smiling and laughing, hugging and wishing each other a Merry Christmas, holding hands and gathering in groups.

Mira had once belonged in one of those circles, but she'd lost that place when her mother died. She felt as lost as Noah. "I'll go with you."

Mira hurried after Seth, and they searched around the park together. People were leaving, going to their own homes to enjoy their family traditions, like opening stockings, eating a midnight snack, and sleeping under the Christmas tree. But Mira only thought about the wandering 10-year-old whose holiday was broken this year and the one person he counted on was leaving him.

As they walked, Seth explained himself. Mira wasn't sure if he was rationalizing his reasons to her or himself. "With my job and the boys' school, we're rarely at home together anyway. They're in after-school programs and always getting in trouble. Noah skips, Mason gets into fights, and Liam lies." They hurried across the street down a side road, toward Evelyn's house. "Maybe he went this way."

"The boys are mourning their mom," Mira explained.

"Don't you think I know that?" Seth answered with frustration. "I signed them up to meet with their school psychologist, but Noah refuses. One of the lies Liam told was during his counseling session and they had to speak to me about it after. He said I bought him a pet raccoon. He told them all kinds of stories about his raccoon, Cuckoo, and how it climbed through the air filters in the apartment complex and scared several people. Animal control showed up at our doorstep at 10pm with equipment to take the thing away. I had to let them inside the house to show them: there was *no* raccoon. It was all made up!"

Mira wanted to laugh at Liam's antics but she was worried: for Seth, the boys, and Noah, now missing for nearly 30 minutes.

"I can't handle it all by myself," Seth confessed. "Mason has been hurt in several fights, which is bad enough, but he was sent home for hitting a girl because she made fun of his shirt. His counselor says he's been acting out in anger because of his emotions, but I don't know what to do to help him. At least he hasn't shut me out like Noah."

Evelyn's house was empty and dark, since she was still at the Christmas tree lighting with the other boys. Mira had seen her talking with Beverly and knew they'd take care of the two younger ones. For once, she wished she had a cell phone to message them about the situation.

Seth continued, "Noah's been the worst. He's been closed off to everyone. His counselor says he won't speak to him. They sit and stare out the window for 30 minutes and then Noah takes off instead of returning to his class." Seth stopped walking abruptly. His arms fell limp at his sides. "What else can I do?" His eyes pleaded with Mira, hoping she would understand.

Her voice was barely a whisper as she thought of her own recovery. "Have you spoken to anyone about your feelings?"

"Like a psychologist? No. I'll deal with it my way."

"Maybe that's the problem," Mira said. "Maybe your way isn't working. It's not helping you or your boys. And being away from them won't heal you either."

"Constantly being bombarded by everyone else and their problems is the opposite of healing. Mira, I just need time."

She closed the space between them and rested her hand on his arm. "Believe me, I understand. Losing someone you love is heartbreaking. It takes time to find the pieces and put them back in a somewhat mended way. But pulling away from everyone who loves and cares about you is only going to make it worse." He returned her grip as she continued. "Yes, we need some time alone, but we can't isolate ourselves."

Seth pulled her into a hug. This was different than their kiss yesterday. This time a myriad of emotions swirled between them: love, loss, and a closeness she never felt with anyone before. It felt like they both were looking at each other with all their problems and weaknesses, losses and strengths and willing to acknowledge the benefit they gained being together. At least, it was until Seth answered, "Those are good ideas, and I'll look into it when I get back home. But for now, leaving the boys here is the only solution. Maybe I need help to fix myself first before I can be there for them."

His words struck, a new loss all over again for Mira. She'd opened her heart to Seth, but he was leaving. Soon, she'd be alone again.

"I wanted to tell you personally," he said. "Because you have been so considerate to them and they genuinely like you. I was hoping you'd continue to be there for them, even when I'm not around."

Mira's mouth dropped open. Did he seriously think she was only kind to his boys because she was trying to gain his attention?

"I like you, Mira, but it scares me. It isn't fair to you or my sons if I'm divided by grief and blinded by the past. Maybe someday—"

Before he could finish speaking and Mira lost her nerve, she yanked his hand back so he would face her. "I befriended your boys on their own merits and because we had a similarity. It wasn't with any ulterior motives. I just want to make that clear." Her glare was hard and determined. "And, yes, when your boys need me, I will be there for them. Because you won't."

She knew her words would sting. As Seth winced, she continued, "Maybe that's how you fix yourself...*by* being there for them."

Seth's cell phone blared between them, tearing his attention away and offering a distraction but Mira hurried to finish saying her piece before he answered.

"They already lost their mom. Don't let them lose their dad too."

<hr/>

Mira crossed her arms and seethed while Seth stepped several paces away and spoke to the person on the phone. She felt something more than anger. It was hurt, on her behalf, of course, but more for the boys. Now they'd have to navigate a new life, in a different town, without both parents. It wasn't fair to them.

But she understood Seth's predicament, too, at least as much as a single woman who didn't have children of her own demanding her attention every day could. He'd gone through incredible loss when his wife died and had been left to pick up the pieces. Not only did he need to manage his own grief but support his three boys dealing with it. None of it was fair. For anyone.

Mira tried not to consider her own emotions broiling under all the pressure. She'd finally found someone to love and who she hoped reciprocated her feelings, but he was leaving.

Now, to add to the anxiety, Noah was missing.

Seth hung up the phone and turned back to Mira. "They found him. Actually, it was Luella who called. She's with him at the horse stables."

They turned back toward town and hurried to the stables near the vet clinic. For once, Mira was thankful for Luella's meddling personality because she'd spotted Noah when no one else had.

When they arrived, Seth paused at seeing Noah. The boy leaned against a stall door, resting one hand on Kairos. The horse dipped his head closer. Luella stood beside them, eyeing the animal suspiciously but talking with Noah. He nodded an answer before they both looked up.

As Noah and Seth's eyes met, they mirrored each other's expression: downturned lips, sagging shoulders, and burnt-out emotions.

Mira didn't wait for Seth to speak first. She crossed the sidewalk and pulled Noah for a hug. It surprised her that he didn't resist at all, instead hiding his face in her shoulder and leaning against her. She held him tightly. He needed to know he was not alone, despite everything. She was happy they'd enjoyed the last several days, but she was heartbroken with what they'd face tomorrow. And on Christmas of all days. It would be a rough day for all of them.

As Evelyn drove up in her car with the other two boys, Seth turned to Mira. "I'm sorry," he apologized. "But I need to get him home and explain everything to them."

Mira could see Seth was determined to continue with his plan despite her advice. She stepped back and watched Noah slump into the car. They drove in a flurry of snowflakes, turning the corner to Evelyn's house, and out of sight.

Mira found herself alone again. Even Luella had slipped away.

The night was muffled by the snow as she walked back to her shop. Mira didn't glance at the glistening Christmas tree behind her or the ornaments swinging from the street lanterns. She didn't feel like singing carols or joining in on Christmas Eve traditions. Instead, she would go home and make herself a warm cup of tea. Eventually the tears would come.

CHAPTER THIRTEEN

TUESDAY, DECEMBER 25

Mira didn't bother setting an alarm clock for Christmas Day. She let herself sleep in but still woke up groggy. Her mood matched the cloudy weather outside, gray and miserable. She pulled herself from bed with the blanket still wrapped around her and sat in her mother's favorite chair, the one that looked out over the main street and town park.

The Christmas tree was still lit but the sidewalks were empty. Mira couldn't help but feel a tinge of jealousy for those who woke up in the morning to celebrate with their fami-

lies. They weren't alone. They wouldn't miss out on traditions of joy and holiday memories.

She finally tugged herself to the kitchen to make a pot of
tea and then returned to her blanket cocoon. Her thoughts
wandered to Seth's broken family. They would be missing
him today. How she had wished things went differently
but she'd thought that many times, in her own life and
throughout history. Her 12 Days to Christmas events had
been chosen specifically to bring hope to people, not to
make them despair over past mistakes. If only she could
focus on something that could bring her happiness in this
moment.

Mira was mulling over these thoughts when a bell at her
front door startled her. She glanced down at her pajamas,
not dressed properly to take visitors, so she hurried to her
closet and threw on the quickest clothes to dress into: a
plain pair of jeans and an oversized red sweater.

But by the time she ran down the stairs, two at a time, and
made it to the shop door, no one was there. Except for a box,
wrapped in plain brown butcher paper, her name scrawled
at the top. A quick glance around the shop revealed no one.
Maybe one of her friends dropped it off and then returned to
celebrate with their family. She picked up the box and went
back inside.

One tradition she avoided thinking about the most was gifts. Her mother had always been thoughtful in what she gave Mira for Christmas and there was purpose behind each item. When Mira had been little and asked for horse riding lessons, her mother presented her with boots for Christmas along with a handwritten note. It detailed Michelle's own experience of horse riding, in which she slid off the back of the animal because the saddle hadn't been tightened enough but wished Mira better luck in her endeavors. Before going to the university, her mother framed a picture of the two of them for Mira to keep on her desk. When money became tight, her mother told her to look inside the back of the frame. Several hundred-dollar bills were tucked behind the picture and covered the cost of Mira's textbooks.

This year Mira worried about this specific day because there was no event scheduled to distract her. She'd be surrounded by emptiness and loss. It was palpable as she glanced over her kitchen table at the photograph of her mother on the fireplace mantle. She set the box down on the table and returned to her chair. Maybe she would save the gift for tomorrow so she could forget what today's date was.

Mira turned on the television and flipped through the boring cable channels. They all blared about Christmas or showed families gathered around mounds of presents.

Eventually she shut it off. She tried the radio next, but all the stations whined Christmas carols, and she wasn't in the mood.

After leafing through her bookshelf, she pulled a familiar story and settled back down. Her eyes glanced through the black and white print, but she didn't focus on any word long enough to piece the plot together. Everything she tried was empty of life and draining.

With a huff, she pulled herself back to the kitchen table and looked at the box. It didn't say who it was from, but she suspected Beverly. The old couple would be enjoying time with their children and grandchildren right now.

Mira's finger slipped under the tape and popped it off. She moved slowly to the other side, not in a hurry to discover the contents.

When the tape was off, she pulled off the butcher paper to see a blank box underneath. No gift could compare to what her mother had given her. Every Christmas would only be a reminder of the loss she carried; of traditions that were now only memories. She lifted the lid and took a deep breath.

She peeked inside.

When Mira saw the teapot, she gasped. Its broken shards had been sitting on the silver tray days ago, but she never noticed it go missing. With trembling fingers, she lifted it up and stared. It had been shattered the day Seth came to town. Now, lifting it up, it was whole again.

Her teapot was patched with clear glue, visible along the cracks, but holding it all together. She cradled it in her hands while shedding a few tears. It was as if her mother was sending her one last Christmas gift, holding her heart with so many precious memories trapped inside.

Mira thought of when her mother served her tea from this pot and waited until they were both sitting down before she shared her cancer had come back. Or when her mother was feeling weak the day after treatments and Mira brought her tea in bed, using this pot. The most sorrowful memory was after Mira returned from the hospital. Her mother had just died and she'd felt like she was walking through a daze, watching someone else's life. She'd stumbled into the kitchen late at night and made tea. She sat at this table until the sun rose, sipping the flavored water while it cooled, never registering the change in temperature.

She held the teapot and cried herself out of tears. When she finally brushed them away, she found her mother staring at her from the photograph. She was smiling, without a worry in the world. In that moment, Mira knew what her mother would advise her, and she smiled back.

"This Christmas hasn't been the traditional one I was used to with you, mom." Mira carried the teapot to the fireplace mantle, a collection of things she'd lost, from her great-grandmother, grandmother, and mother. Now she added the teapot. It was also a gathering of things she treasured deeply. "But I made so many new memories this year."

When she returned to the table, she saw a card inside the box. She took it out and read the scribbled print: *There are lots of things in life that break us. It's how we put back the pieces that define who we are. I'm broken but I'm not giving up. Merry Christmas, Seth.* She held the note to her chest and stared back at her mother's picture.

"Mom, I'm not alone anymore. I have friends and a family that needs me."

Mira dropped the note and pulled on her brown boots. Before she could talk herself out of the wild idea, she ran downstairs and out of her shop. She needed to get to Evelyn's house before Seth left to thank him for fixing the teapot, and her heart.

⁂

Seth pulled from the driveway. He'd said his goodbyes and left before their tears came. Once he was in the SUV alone, he could think clearly again. As he drove down Main Street, past Betty's Bakery and Mira's shop, he considered how the past twelve days had changed him.

When he had driven into town, he'd been frustrated. He and Noah were arguing, Mason was grumbling, and Liam was crying. But the past two weeks had provided smiles, healed hearts, and fostered connection with his sons in ways he hadn't expected. Staying with his mom had also offered him a reprieve. She'd distracted the boys and given him time to step away and recalibrate his priorities. It now made him doubt his plan.

When he came to Cedar Springs, he was hoping his mom would be willing to take the boys for several months. So, why did he feel extremely lonely now that his plan was successful? Why was the silence so loud?

He picked up speed when he passed the last houses in town and the road dipped down, away from the mountains, crowned in winter glory and staring at him from the rearview mirror.

Memories came unbidden: driving an old truck up that mountain to find the perfect Christmas tree. He considered Liam's shining eyes after spotting the tree, Mason's laugh while they threw snowballs, and even Noah's attitude as he craved attention but pushed it away. He tried to harden his heart and pushed further on the gas pedal.

This is what he needed. A break from Noah's arguments, a reprieve from Mason's fights, and an out from Liam's whining. So why did his gut feel like a stone, heavy with guilt. Ana would have been so disappointed in him...but she wasn't here. He couldn't take care of everything himself.

He should have avoided glancing in the mirror again or looking at the snow-capped mountains because it brought another memory, still fresh, to his mind. When he reached out and comforted Mira after she shared about her loss. When she glanced up at him with amber eyes, full of grief and hope. When he'd felt connected to her in a way he'd never shared with anyone else.

That's why he had to leave earlier than he'd planned. He could no longer trust himself or his emotions, especially when she was around. And, if they spent Christmas day together, he probably wouldn't have the heart to leave at all.

His right foot pushed the gas. He couldn't let himself grow distracted with those thoughts. Twelve days couldn't change the entire course of someone's life.

But it could break in one phone call.

Maybe he was like the shattered teapot he'd left at Mira's front door. Maybe everyone was broken in some way and had to pull themselves back together... No. No one could do it alone. Just like the teapot needed him to stay up all night and painstakingly fit pieces, bit by bit, it needed someone else to glue it back into shape.

He slammed the brakes and slid the SUV into a pull out. He opened the door and stepped out, feeling the cold air against his face. Though it brought him chills, it made him alert. He could think clearly.

Just like the teapot, he couldn't put himself back together again, not alone. He needed support, from his mom, his boys, and hopefully, if she was willing, even Mira.

But he had responsibilities and difficult choices he needed to make. He paced through the snow, ignoring the steam from the back of the still-running SUV. His feet led him to the guard rail where he could stare down at other small towns dotting the meandering highway, down the mountain. His eyes trailed past them, where he couldn't see because of the heavy winter clouds, to a city hundreds of miles away.

In that moment, Seth needed to make a choice. He had to decide where his priorities were: with his career and personal responsibilities or with his family. Would he pick himself or them? Or was there a possibility he could choose both? The question raged in his mind as he turned back to the car. As he slammed the door behind him. As he shifted back into gear.

Either way, he was a broken man trying to put the pieces back together.

❦

A soft snow started falling when Mira ran down the sidewalk and turned at the corner. The cul-de-sac was quiet but that didn't stop her. She ran to Evelyn's front door and knocked.

Mason opened it to find her breathless.

"Merry Christmas! Is your dad still here?"

Noah stepped out from behind his brother and shook his head. "No, he's been gone awhile."

Mira's face fell. She wanted to speak to him at least once more before he went back to the city. Liam ran out past his brothers and wrapped Mira's knees in a hug. She bent and hugged him back. "How are you boys doing?"

Noah shrugged; his face unreadable. Mason held out a Lego car he built while Liam pulled her inside the house. The distraction of Christmas gifts seemed to mollify them for the time being. Wrapping paper littered the floor with toys scattered in between but Evelyn ignored the mess, sitting on the couch talking with Charles and Beverly. Mira glanced at them with confusion.

"Our children are on their way to Cedar Springs but won't arrive until dinner," Beverly explained. "We came by to wish Evelyn a Merry Christmas and were going to stop by your place next."

Charles laughed, "Looks like we don't have to since we're all together here."

"Well, not everyone." Evelyn shrugged. She glanced at Mira; a knowing look of heartache passed between them.

Mira looked down at her empty hands wondering why she'd run over here so quickly. She should have brought Evelyn a gift. Or something for the boys. Now she stood awkwardly in the center of the house. "I'm sorry—" she began.

"For what?" Seth's voice echoed behind her.

She spun around. Seth stood in the doorway, snow dusted across his shoulders and in his hair. His face was slightly red as if he'd been running outside. He grinned.

"They said you left."

Seth took a step toward Mira. "I had to pick up a couple things. And drop something off."

"Thank you for the teapot," she whispered. Why was her heart in a flurry again?

"Sorry for breaking it in the first place."

"It was an accident." Mira closed the space between them and glanced up.

"So was yesterday," Seth confessed. "I've taken the time to think about it. In my reflection, it was something you said that stood out and convinced me. I needed to find my way back. There are times when I want to be alone, and sometimes I need it, but what I want the most is to be connected, to know others understand me, and have my back." He glanced at Noah and pulled him close, draping his arm around the boy's shoulders. "Noah and I have a lot in common. We can't run away from our problems, can we?" His son shook his head and studied his dad's face as he continued speaking. "I should never have considered leaving my boys behind." Liam and Mason hugged their dad on either side and Noah grinned.

"We need each other." Seth reached up and tucked a loose hair behind Mira's ear. "And you. Merry Christmas, Mira."

Mira wasn't sure what to do. Seth was confessing his feelings for her in a crowded room with some of her closest friends and his sons looking on. She flashed a hesitant smile.

"Several people who care about me have told me to care for myself and seek help navigating my grief, but I wouldn't listen." Seth focused on her. "Until you, Mira. You're right. I need to take care of myself, and in that way, I can help my boys better, too. We're all broken somehow. It's how we heal that matters."

Mira tried to speak but all words fled her. The only thoughts she could focus on was her heart thumping loudly in her chest, blood pulsing through her, and the audience looking on. Her mind spiraled to history, of a mutual devotion: strong as Abigail and John Adams', countless as Elizabeth Barrett Browning and Robert's, and connected as June Carter and Johnny Cash. Happiness rippled through her heart when she dismissed those stories for her reality and closed the space between her and Seth.

His arm wrapped around her waist, and he grinned. "And I can't leave yet. You owe me a hot chocolate."

She giggled.

Charles' voice broke through the exchange. "Well, kiss her already! You're standing under the mistletoe!" The old man pointed above their head to a sprig of mistletoe that wasn't there earlier.

Seth's smile grew wider, and he raised an eyebrow in question. Mira answered by leaning forward and kissing him first.

EPILOGUE

Autumn leaves painted the mountains around Cedar Springs in orange and yellow. Everything was aflame in color. The morning was crisp but not cold as a single SUV trailed up the one road into town.

A single leaf unhooked itself from one of the trees lining the main street and dropped in front of Vintage Treasures.

At the sound of the bell, Mira descended the stairs, two by two. She wasn't in a hurry today because Evelyn and Luella were volunteering. They helped the customers while Mira finished up her online classes. School and research became super easy with the laptop Beverly and Charles had gifted her for Christmas ten months ago.

It also helped that she connected her store online to thousands more customers. Noah built her a website and showed her how to take pictures and upload them. Her antiques were viewed by people all over the country and beyond!

A favorite activity of hers had become checking the website's purchase logistics and pinning places her items shipped off to on a map above the register.

Mira was excited for this year's holiday season because everything would be different. Now that she had finished her last final exam and was waiting for her diploma to arrive in the mail, she could relax and help with the Christmas festivities...as a newlywed.

She paused on the last step and glanced down at the ring on her finger. A small green emerald was set in a filigree gold band. When Seth proposed over the summer and held out this ring, she knew it was a precious family heirloom. It had belonged to his grandmother. Obviously, she said yes. The ring was an added perk.

When Mira stepped between the 1920s flapper mannequin and samurai warrior, she saw three women whispering.

Beverly nudged Evelyn and Luella, and they all glanced up guiltily.

"What's the secret?" Mira asked.

"We'll have our Christmas festival like usual this year of course. The entire community is chipping in and helping." Beverly smiled. A glint in her eye warned Mira the older woman had something else up her sleeve.

"Yes. And what's the theme?"

"Oh, that's not important."

Mira crossed her arms and narrowed her eyes at the three women.

"If you don't tell her," Luella burst. "I will! It's a Christmas tree theme. Each day, people will choose an ornament of the big town tree and follow the instructions. Some will direct the community to gather canned food or gifts for those in need. Others will be activities to do around the community. It'll be swell!"

"That sounds wonderful!" Mira smiled. But the women still appeared suspicious. "So, what's the catch?"

They glanced toward Evelyn who beamed, red cheeks to match her fiery hair. "Now, this isn't our doing..."

Mira's nerves were already frazzled, finishing eighteen units of university level classes over the summer, while planning for a future with Seth and his boys. She didn't have time for guessing or games. She tapped her foot nervously.

"It was all Seth's plan, actually."

Mira's eyebrow quirked.

Beverly's smile spread across her face and her eyes crinkled at the corner. "You'd be proud to know we've kept it a secret this long."

"I didn't even give away a peep!" Luella giggled.

"What secret?" Mira asked.

The women stepped up, Beverly and Evelyn each taking one of Mira's hands.

"Since Seth will arrive any moment and we'll all be busy preparing the next two weeks, we decided to make it a c ountdown..."

Mira stared with wide eyes at the three women just as Seth's SUV pulled to a stop in front of the shop.

"12 Days to a Wedding."

12 DAYS TO CHRISTMAS

THURSDAY, DEC 13

Cookie Exchange & Soccer

FRIDAY, DEC 14

Vintage Game Night

SATURDAY, DEC 15

Rec Center Update & Gingerbread Houses

SUNDAY, DEC 16

Ice Skating & Sledding

MONDAY, DEC 17

Ugly Sweater Party & Firepit S'mores

TUESDAY, DEC 18

Christmas Caroling

WEDNESDAY, DEC 19

Silent Auction Charity

THURSDAY, DEC 20

Find A Christmas Tree

FRIDAY, DEC 21

Reading at the Library

SATURDAY, DEC 22

Sleigh Ride & Rockabilly

SUNDAY, DEC 23

Christmas Ball

MONDAY, DEC 24

Christmas Eve Service

TUESDAY, DEC 25

Christmas Day

12 DAYS TO CHRISTMAS

1914

WW1 Christmas Truce

1968

Apollo 8 Orbits the Moon

800

Charlemagne Crowned

1776

George Washington
Crosses the Delaware

1990

Internet's Test Run

1818

Silent Night Written

280

St. Nicholas

1848

Victorian Christmas

1843

The Christmas Carol

1955

NORAD Tracks Santa

1954

White Christmas

3-4 BC

Jesus' Birth

Acknowledgments

There's so much to celebrate with 12 Days to Christmas!

First and foremost, to my Savior Jesus Christ for giving Himself as a sacrifice to pay the penalty of my sin. The true reason I have joy at Christmas is because He came to Earth to save me! Otherwise, I'd be a furious wreck and angry at the world. Thankfully, I have a God who loves me and showed me grace and mercy when I deserved none. Then He blessed me with a wonderful family!

I'm thankful to my husband and boys who have supported and cheered me on. Your encouragement is what keeps me going when I'm ready to give up. I love you! To my sisters and brother, I hope you read this someday! And no, Elijah, you don't get a cut. To my dad and mom, although 12 Days to Christmas is fiction, I hope you love it and don't notice the dragon I snuck inside Mira's antique shop.

This book is dedicated to three wonderful women who made a significant impact in my life. For Eleanora for demonstrating the qualities mentioned in 1 Peter 3:2-4: "...Pure behavior...let your beauty be...in the hidden person of the heart, in the incorruptible adornment of a gentle and quiet spirit, which is in the sight of God very precious." Although our language barrier kept us from communicating the way I wished and the fact that you're in Heaven now, your example continues to encourage me. Your strength spoke through your caring blue eyes. For Rodica, you sacrificed so much for me. I am so thankful to have you for a mom! To Carol, the gift of your time in training me in CEF and taking me to so many Bible clubs will forever be imprinted in who I am. Your impact has gone far beyond the few precocious teens you mentored, and now influences people even in the wilds of Alaska! Thank you for not giving up on me!

Thank you to my most excellent first readers and for all your input: Sharon, the quilting queen, Shawna, the best friend, and Allison, my book buddy! We'll always be family even if we aren't related (even if your daughters don't marry my sons, haha! But if they do, we can celebrate all our holidays together!)

For my writing group girls: Brandi, Caitlyn, Matti, and Esther – I can't wait to read more of your stories and to see how you use the talents God gave you! May your work be a light!

To my critique partner, Candance Kade, thank you for catching so much I missed and making this book flow better! To Nova McBee: we've been on this writing journey together for almost ten years and you've never given up on me! Thanks for cheering me on when I was down, for encouraging me, and for going out of your way to help connect me and my writing with the right people. Your support and guidance has been one of the most significant in my writing endeavors. And, if anyone is reading this, go read her book Calculated!

This book wouldn't be in anyone's hands without the friendship, influence, and hard work of my dear sister in Christ, Callie McLay! Thank you! As I'm writing this, you're probably formatting my book and walking me through the entire process. Because of your beautiful book (Go read What if We Met in a Bookstore if you want more sweet and cozy vibes!) and your writing success, I was encouraged to take the leap too! I miss our writing parties and hanging out but hope we can have one soon. I'll fly 3,000 miles to hang out again.

Finally, to all my friends and family who have asked how my writing was going, here ya go! To my dear family in Kenai, Alaska: all our parties inspired this! And I still don't like the cold, but I miss you all so much. To my friends in California: I hope we can have a real Christmas sometime, but until then, enjoy all the vibes in book form. We can drive up to the mountains for the snow or pretend its winter by blasting Christmas carols and going overboard on decorations.

Love the book? Scan to connect and leave a review!

ABOUT THE AUTHOR

 Rebecca Alexandru is the daughter of Romanian immigrants and grew up in Southern California. Now she has three wild boys, two sassy pets, and one awesome husband. Rebecca taught elementary school in a small town in Colorado, which inspired the setting of Cedar Springs. Then, she started a family in the wilds of Alaska, which encouraged her to appreciate winter. (She loves Christmas but hates the cold!) In her spare time, she imagines and types up books and screenplays. Her favorite writing activity is hosting writing parties with teens and kids, listening to their exciting stories and encouraging their love of creativity.

Milton Keynes UK
Ingram Content Group UK Ltd.
UKHW031208111124
451035UK00006B/593

9 798991 389402